To Catch the Wind

Jen Caruso

Jen Caruso

Monee, ILLINOIS

Jen Caruso
P.O. Box 579
Monee, Illinois 60449
www.jencaruso.net

Publisher's Note: This is a work of fiction. Names, characters, places, and incidents are a product of the author's imagination. Locales and public names are sometimes used for atmospheric purposes. Any resemblance to actual people, living or dead, or to businesses, companies, events, institutions, or locales is completely coincidental.

Book Layout © 2017 BookDesignTemplates.com

To Catch the Wind/ Jen Caruso. -- 1st ed.
ISBN 978-1-7362168-5-9

For Alex and Jasmine

Frente al amor y la muerte no sirve de nada ser fuerte..

Spanish Proverb

Contents

The Middle Part First
1983 – 1986
Chapter One

January 23, 1983
Chicago, Illinois

"Push now, Marie! There you go… that's it, one more!"

Exhausted, Marie pushed. A rough growl, turned scream escaped her throat. A nurse held her hand, brushing damp strands of hair from her face with a cool cloth. Her parents were somewhere, in a waiting room, a hallway. Marie was uncertain of their whereabouts. Neither of them opted to join her in the delivery room. Her mother was in no hurry to meet an illegitimate grandchild.

She fell back upon the stiff pillow, panting. A newborn wailed. Tears welled in Marie's eyes. "My baby," she breathed.

"Congratulations! Welcome baby girl," a voice in the room, said.

Everything felt discombobulated. The doctor and two nurses chatted as they worked on Marie and the baby. Someone pushed down on her stomach.

"You're doing well, Marie."

The wails of a newborn filled the room. "My baby?" Marie managed.

"Being prepped and washed. Everything looks good." A female voice above Marie's head assured her.

"Do you have a name picked out?" Another nurse asked.

"Grace. Her name is Grace Rossi-Rivera," she said, her voice husky.

Marie was grateful the nurses didn't ask about the infant's father. It was all too complicated. She didn't understand it herself. She'd gone over it too many times in her head. He left her, ripped her heart to shreds and stomped on it, just before college graduation. Then he disappeared like dust on the wind. The thought of him made her heart twist painfully.

One half of her brain convinced her that he did love her. She knew he did. He couldn't have faked all their moments together; their entire relationship could not have been a sham. The other half of her brain persuaded her that his brutal words were true. He used her. He never cared for her. That's what he told her.

During her pregnancy there were good days and bad. Days she was determined to move on and create a new life. The bad days were empty, when the hole he left in her heart felt bigger than Texas. He didn't know she was pregnant, and her attempts to locate him were fruitless. Maybe it was better that way. She'd already spent too many days both crying for and cursing him. No more.

A nurse placed the tiny noisy bundle in her arms. Marie took time to touch and study her newborn. Her fuzzy hair was almost black, her skin a pink yet darker hue.

"Hello, Grace. Hi, shhhh. Welcome to the world, baby girl." She pressed soft lips to Grace's forehead. No more crying or cursing Santi. She was a mother now. Someone tiny and helpless needed her to be strong. She could do this without him. She had to.

Once Marie was settled in her hospital room, Tony was the first to visit her. He'd left the office early, still dressed in a light blue dress shirt and dark tie. Dark brown hair curled carelessly over his ears and the collar of his shirt. He had a face like a movie star and a smile that made women want to follow him anywhere. But there was no pretension. He was just a regular guy to her. She could always count on her older brother. Two years separated them, and though they had their differences, they supported one another, always had each other's backs.

Tony peeked at his new niece, brown eyes softening. "Why do newborns always look like old people?" he joked. "She wouldn't even make a good cabbage kid doll, or whatever they call 'em."

Marie sat up, adjusting the white sheet over her legs. "Hey, don't insult my baby. People collect those dolls, they're the newest rage. Would you like to hold her?"

Tony shrugged. "Sure, why not." He carefully accepted the sleeping infant, cradling her in the crook of his arm as though he'd been doing it all his life.

"Watch her neck and head. Where's mom and dad?" Marie asked hospital staff to notify her parents when she arrived at the hospital, but since giving birth two hours ago, Marie had not seen them.

Tony found a seat at the nearest bedside chair. "Arguing somewhere. I saw them in the hallway. I'm sure they'll be here in a few." Tony studied his niece for a moment, his expression thoughtful. "She looks like him."

Marie noted his uneasy expression. "What's wrong?"

Tony tore his gaze from little Grace, meeting his sister's eyes. He pasted a half-hearted smile for her. "Nothing. I'm happy for you." Tony was privy to his parent's arguments regarding Marie. If it were up to his mother, his sister would be out on the street with nothing.

"Why? I'm an unwed mother, who got used, knocked-up, and dumped. A disgrace to the family, a stain on the great Rossi name. Oh, and did I mention that my child's father doesn't want to be found? I'm quite the high-society scandal. Just ask our mother." Marie didn't tell him mother's exact, malicious words those many months ago.

"I don't see it that way."

"Mom does. She never liked Santi. She's more concerned about what the ladies auxiliary or her country club friends will say." Marie adjusted her pillows and sank into them. "Someone knows where to find Santi. He should know he has a daughter, even if he wants nothing to do with me anymore."

"Marie, you weren't used and dumped. Listen....," Tony halted when Mrs. Rossi swept into the room, her heels clicking against the hospital floor tile with each step. Marie sensed there was something more her brother wished to say.

"Why did you put his name on the birth certificate?" Carla Rossi demanded. In her fur coat, and jewelry she reminded Marie of a circus bear. Removing thin kidskin gloves, Carla shifted her Louis Vuitton handbag from one elbow to the other. Her mother's hair was recently done. Shoulder-length bleached lighter than usual, it was styled and straightened so that it swept over her forehead in a side-bang.

"I'm doing great mom," Marie responded, unable to keep the hint of sarcasm from her voice. "Would you like to meet your granddaughter?"

"Carla," Vincent Rossi appeared at his wife's side. The look of admonishment was brief. "We talked about this."

Carla Rossi's mouth clamped shut, but her rigid posture said more than words could.

Mr. Rossi turned to his daughter. Despite the cold outside, a warm glow washed over his features. "How you doing, Cookie? How's the baby?" He removed his gloves, hat, and heavy overcoat, folding it across the back of a chair. January in Chicago was not for the faint of heart.

She wasn't his little Cookie anymore. They both knew it. His dark hair was thinning, graying at the temples. He looked tired. Marie hadn't been Cookie in a long time. Not since high school.

She knew dad wasn't looking for a real answer. He wouldn't want to know what she was truly feeling, how her heart still cried out for a young man who probably never thought of her once. She gave him an answer they both could handle. "A little tired, but I'm okay. The baby is healthy."

"What are your plans, now?" Carla's voice cut in sharply. She had not yet acknowledged the sleeping infant in the room.

"My plans are the same. I plan to continue teaching. That's why I went to college to get my degree, remember?"

"How can you do that now, with a baby?"

Marie's agitation grew. "The same way millions of other women work and take care of their kids, ma. I'll find a way."

Before the whole scene could escalate into another argument, Tony rose from his chair and strode toward his mother, attempting to hand off little Grace. Carla hesitated. "This is Grace Rossi-Rivera, ma. Your granddaughter. She'd like to meet you."

Marie wouldn't say that she'd witnessed her mother's cold heart melting before her eyes, but something happened when Carla Rossi held Grace for the first time. Marie would call it a visible relaxing.

Carla peered down at her granddaughter, unaware that her body took up a slow sway, rocking. "I don't want to be called grandma, or grandmother. Mrs. Rossi or *Nonna* is fine." She lifted her gaze to meet Marie's, her expression masked, her voice clipped. "She's a beautiful baby." It was a concession of sorts. It would do for now.

October 22, 1983
Beirut, Lebanon

"Something ain't right. You feel it?"

They'd been taking small arms fire since Memorial Day. Ordered to clear mines from the beaches and keep a low profile. It was hoped that the American presence in Beirut would quell hostilities, but the insertion of the joint multi-national peace-keeping force had the opposite effect, causing tensions to rise. They all sensed it, but Mike was the first to voice his concern.

Marine private first-class Santiago Rivera raised his forearm, wiping sweat from his eyes. He continued to fill sandbags, glancing back at the BLT building. The four-story concrete structure was home for now. They spent the day delivering supplies, patrolling, and now filling what seemed to be an endless mound of sandbags. "Feels like we're sitting with our hands tied. It's fucked up." Marines were trained to fight. With a strong belief in protecting others, Marines ran toward danger. Many began to wonder about their purpose for being here, aside from working with, and helping innocent people caught in the middle.

"It's bullshit," PFC Paul Dugan chimed in, a cigarette dangled from his lips.

"Rules of engagement," Mike reminded them.

Santi tossed a heavy sandbag on the growing pile. "Only fire in self-defense, 'cept we have no idea who's shooting." The peacekeeping forces were ordered to maintain their weapons at condition four. No magazines inserted, no rounds in the chamber. It was frustrating for a Marine to feel so defenseless in a war zone.

"Shit's been going down here for over a thousand years. Think we're going to stop a civil war with our mere presence?" Mike ground out his cigarette, disliking the taste in his mouth. He wasn't a smoker, wondering why he borrowed one from Dugan in the first place. "What does that even mean?" He shook his head. "Presence."

Santi responded with a shrug. Mike had a valid point, for there seemed to be no coordinated objective or well-defined military task here. Various religious groups fighting in the area divided the country, and each had their own foreign sponsors providing military aid.

When U.S. forces first arrived, they were welcomed, but in April a car bomb exploded in front of the U.S. embassy in Beirut, killing sixty-three people. Calls to bring the Marines home grew louder, but President Reagan disagreed, citing vital interests in Lebanon and the importance of maintaining peace. They were here to support the Lebanese government. Because the Lebanese president was Christian, it appeared as though the U.S. forces supporting the Christian side, instead of remaining neutral. It was clear that the peace-keeping forces didn't fully comprehend the cultural and historical significance of the region. They ended up in a place they didn't know a lot about, with little cultural understanding. The U.S. Marine patrols contributed to hostilities, rather than quell them.

Mike tossed another sandbag on the pile. "Know what I'm thinking about?"

"Shaving your balls?" Dugan asked.

"No, dickhead."

"No idea," Santi responded.

"Thinking about my wife Bev, and my horse Blueberry. Riv, when are you going to send those letters to that girl of yours?"

"What letters? She's not my girl. Not anymore." Santi lied. Marie was always with him, somewhere in a hidden corner of his mind. He couldn't shake her, and for the umpteenth time that day he wondered what she was doing right now. Since they were in completely different times zones, she was probably sleeping. He wondered if she ever thought about him. She had no idea he was halfway across the globe. She had no idea he'd enlisted in the U.S. Marine Corps. He wanted it that way.

"I see you writing to somebody, but you never send the letters. I figured you gotta be writing to a sweetheart." Met with Santi's hard glare and long silence, Mike chuckled, raising his hands in a gesture of surrender.

"Maybe he's writing to his *madre*," Dugan joked.

"Maybe I'm writing to your *madre*. Heard she's real sweet." Santi countered, aware of the possibility that starting an entire competition of 'your mama' jokes would likely ensue. Instead, Dugan laughed and flipped him the bird.

Mike changed the subject. "Hey Rivera, think you'll ever rodeo again?" Mike was a rodeo participant himself, having competed in local Black rodeo circuits back home. Their mutual love of horses and rodeo made them fast friends in boot camp. Most people were ignorant about Black cowboys, because they were fed the old west Hollywood fantasies of John Wayne and Clint Eastwood. Not Santi. Santi knew about Nat Love and Bill Pickett and Marshall Bass Reeves. He knew that early cowboys were mestizos, Native American, black, and mixed race. Mike could appreciate that from a brown brother, especially when movie depictions of Mexicans in Western films were usually villains, bad hombres, and banditos.

Finishing the last sandbag, Santi picked up his M16 and took up a guard position. "Thinking about getting out of this place alive. You should do the same."

When the Israelis pulled out of Lebanon in September, various religious militias began in earnest to maneuver for ground. Fire fights increased. U.S. Naval gunfire in direct support of the Lebanese army crossed the line, and the U.S. was no longer considered a neutral player. In the past weeks Shiite and Druze militias fired sporadic artillery shells, mortar rounds and rockets at the Marine airport base.

Mike took up his position. He shivered. "Something ain't right. I feel it in my soul."

Dugan lit a cigarette. "You ladies and your feelings." A trail of smoke blew past his lips as he rolled his eyes.

Santi scanned the horizon around the Beirut airfield. South of the BLT building was a black-topped parking lot. Buffer zones were created, dividing the lot with barbed wire. "Yup, something ain't right," he agreed.

Later that night as they all bedded down, Santi pulled out the letters he'd written to Marie, he unfolded the thick packet of pages, skimming over what he'd written the day before with the aid of a flashlight. He knew he'd never send them. When he finished, he folded the letters with care, tucking them into his socks. That night he slept in full gear with his M16 strapped to his leg.

No reveille on Sunday morning, because Sundays at the Beirut Airport barracks were slow, and many used the time to catch up on sleep, write letters, or relax. There was nothing out of the ordinary that morning. Marine sentries paid little attention to the yellow Mercedes truck. They were expecting a water delivery. The truck circled the parking lot twice before picking up speed and bursting through the barricade. By the time the truck plowed through a five-foot barbed wire fence and past two sentry guards, it was too late for anyone to react. When a guard managed to slap a magazine into his M16 and chamber a round, the truck had roared through an open vehicle gate, and was closing on the BLT barracks.

Santi awoke to the sound of a thunderous crash below. The building shook, rumbling. He put on his flak jacket, then turned to whomever was within earshot, "It's go time!"

After a silent pause of a second or two came a concussion, a blast, a wave of heat. The truck erupted in a massive explosion so powerful that it sheared the bases of the concrete support columns, lifted the building in the air, then collapsed the structure, falling from all sides.

Why am I outside? How did I get here? Muffled voices spoke to him, but they didn't register in Santi's muddled brain. *Why can't I hear?* Distraught faces appeared above him, but he couldn't see them clearly. Fog, ash, and the scent of gas filled the air. He felt nothing, didn't know where he was, how long he'd been there or why.

"Riv, you with me, bro?" Mike was shouting but his voice sounded cottony and far away. He and several others were removing concrete and building debris from Santi's body. "We're gonna get you out of here. Hang tight. No slack till the horn smokes."

Despite his words of encouragement and play at cowboy vernacular, the expression on Mike's face was a mix of fear and determination. He had seen bodies and parts of bodies everywhere, heard the torturous screams of survivors. They all struggled to grapple with the reality before them. How Mike managed to come out unscathed was an inexplicable miracle. Dazed and with minor wounds, when he was able, he twisted and crawled from under a tilted slab of concrete that sheltered him. Had it landed inches one way or the other, it would have crushed him.

They'd been at recovery efforts for hours. Fueled by adrenaline and a desire to dig out and find survivors remained heightened, urging them onward. They struggled to attend to the wounded, wrapping wounds in shipping plastic, wet towels, and anything usable they could grasp. Rescue efforts were hindered by hostile sniper fire. Mike was relieved to find his friend, Santi - not well, but alive. So far, there was no sign of Dugan.

Santi's pain receptors kicked in when they dug him out, lifting him onto a stretcher. He may have screamed, but his own voice seemed so distant that he couldn't be sure. He lost consciousness.

When he came to, even the thumping of the helicopter rotors sounded spongy and faint. Someone must have cleaned up his face. His vision had cleared, and the brilliant blue sky above offered an odd comfort. He thought he heard radio voices but couldn't make out the words. They must have given him morphine. Santi blacked out again. Scenes continued to cut in and out, like a badly edited movie. He thought he heard something about a hospital in Wiesbaden, Germany. He wondered where Marie was, and what she was doing. Did she ever think of him?

Chapter Two

Fall/Winter 1983

“A pretty blonde nurse with green eyes took his vitals. He'd suffered a concussion, broken leg, fractured hip, and three broken ribs along with various burns and lacerations to his face and body. Metal pins protruded from his leg. The burns were the most painful, but any wound paled in comparison to the anguish of losing most everyone in his unit.

Santi didn't recall much, and perhaps that was a blessing. He remembered waking, thinking the barracks under attack. One minute he was inside, and the next he was being dug out from a pile of concrete and steel. His hearing gradually returned. When his condition was deemed improved, he'd be shipped stateside.

Mike felt something wasn't right the day before the bombing. Security may have been lax; the rules of engagement order handcuffed them. There were too many troops in one building. The bombers knew the daily habits of the barracks. Marines were sitting ducks. He'd heard the French barracks were also targeted, losing over sixty paratroopers in a separate bombing that day. The explosion killed 241 Marines, sailors, and soldiers. The October 23, 1983 bombing was the deadliest day for the United States Marine Corps since Iwo Jima in World War II.

Santi weighed his options. Finish his enlistment or be medically discharged. With his college degree, he could become a commissioned officer. He could go home to Texas and stay with his mother, a thought he didn't relish. He could do something with his education. Do his best to forget about Marie. That's why he enlisted, for all the good it did.

Another nurse entered the room. As they cleaned the pins in his leg, Santi gritted his teeth and indulged in a bit of self-pity. He tried to tell himself to be grateful. Sometimes that thought process worked. In other moments he felt guilty for being alive, while most of his brothers weren't. There was nothing special about him. Why did he deserve to live and not someone else, like Dugan? His emotions ran the gamut. Most days, he tried to bury his thoughts, and not feel anything.

"You are doing very well, Private Rivera. Doctor will give orders for you to go home soon."

Santi sucked in a breath against the pain the nurses inflicted with their ministrations. "Thank you, I think."

"Your burns are healing nicely," the blonde nurse said. He'd have permanent scarring, but he didn't care.

Later that day, or maybe it was the next – all the days seemed to run into one another - a physical therapist spoke to him about the treatment plan. Santi immediately forgot the man's name after introduction. The therapist reminded him of his Tío Luis, and from then on, that's what he called him in his head. The therapist said he'd be up and walking in no time, with aid, of course.

"Will I be able to ride again?"

"Ride?"

"Horses."

The therapist chuckled. "Let's figure out walking first, yes?"

Santi wondered how he'd be able to move around with all the IVs and whatnots attached to him. The therapist insisted it could be done.

In the following weeks Santi was plodding along the hospital corridor with the aid of a walker. It was almost worse than boot camp. He was joined by a few other servicemen, also in various stages of their physical healing processes. They encouraged one another, and though Santi wouldn't recall their names, their company helped.

"Hey Texas, bets on who makes it to the water fountain first."

"Not there yet, maybe next time."

"Your ass is showing."

"Gotta give y'all something to look at."

He made a few calls to his mother. "*Mijo*, when are you coming home?" His younger siblings also vied for telephone time, all with a million questions about when he was coming home, how badly was he hurt? Did he kill anyone?

Some days he welcomed the sound of their voices, other days, he had no desire to interact with those who cared most about him.

When he arrived home, he had access to a wheelchair, but pushed himself, and tried to avoid using it when possible. He was able to walk with a walker for short distances and take care of his personal needs, but he tired easily. Subsequent surgeries in the months that followed left him weak. Every morning began with prescription meds and strong coffee. As he healed, he began strengthening exercises.

The fracture of the once-close relationship between Santi and his mother was a pervasive undercurrent neither of them spoke of. Despite the underlying tension, his mother spoiled him. He wondered if guilt was her motivation. She made his favorite foods (he'd lost weight she said, too skinny), and doted on his every need. She even tried making some Italian dishes that Marie had shown her how to prepare. Was this her way of making amends? He didn't think anything could heal the harm she'd caused. Perhaps she meant well, but he felt smothered. The younger ones wanted to help. Santi didn't want the attention, preferring solitude.

His brother Erik was sixteen and didn't understand Santi's withdrawal. When he told stories or gave updates about Santi's horse, Rebelde, he seemed disinterested, or became annoyed. Susana was eleven. If she didn't understand her brother's mental state, it didn't deter her. She carried on as though nothing were different, as though he were not different. Whenever he had a nightmare, Susana was the first to enter his room to offer comfort. Worse, was the unanswered question that haunted him; why did he survive, when many of his brothers didn't?

His mother returned to work at the family's small restaurant and the kids were in school. He had the house to himself. He couldn't go anywhere. He sold the Camaro after his enlistment. Rebelde was boarded at Ferguson's ranch. His mom used the pick-up truck for work. He had his wheelchair and his walker. The television was poor company. He didn't watch it anyway. Alone, his mind was left to dig a hole into an abyss. And always, somewhere, there was Marie. He wanted to hate her. Tried to hate her. He couldn't.

None of this was her fault. It was his. He was a coward. He should have fought for her. The last time he saw her, she told him to go to hell. Some days, he felt like he was there. Most days he felt like he deserved nothing less.

He didn't want to be around people, and he didn't want to be alone. Nothing made sense. His old crew visited from time to time. Cowboys, guys he'd worked with on the nearby ranches. They sat around the yard at night, a bonfire burning. They smoked weed and drank and asked too many questions.

"Have you been to the restaurant lately? Your mom's done a lot with it since you've been gone. Business must be good."

Santi knew where the financing came from for restaurant improvements and all the fancy upgrades to the house. In his mind, it was dirty money. He had minimal interest in the restaurant, having worked there for years to help his family. "I haven't been much of anywhere, 'cept the hospital and the doctor's office."

"When you gonna ride again, *mano*?" One of them asked.

Santi sipped his beer, it tasted flat. "Thought I'd do something with my degree. Go to Dallas or Houston and work for a design company. Maybe train horses again. Don't know. Anything but the restaurant."

Armando laughed. "You could become a farmer."

"Mechanical Engineers make decent bank," Sergio chimed in. You'd be set. Get yourself a fine *mamacita*. Get out of this place."

Santi rose from the lawn chair. "Ya'll can stay. I'm headed back to the house. Put out the fire when you're done." They watched him hobble through the yard like an old man.

Armando attempted to follow.

"*Déjalo*." Enrique said. "He needs to get his shit straight. My oldest brother was the same way when he came back. His head's messed up. He'll get right, give him time. Leave him alone for now."

When Santi entered the house, his mother was waiting in her pink flowered robe. A small woman, her dark hair was undone, reaching past her shoulders. Several sparse strands of gray interspersed the raven black waves. Her arms folded across her chest; her chin jutted upward as she met his gaze. *Shit.* He didn't need a lecture, not from her. He was a grown man, even if he didn't feel like much of one.

"This needs to stop."

"What?" he snapped.

"You're wasting your time, your life."

Santi brushed past her, staggering toward the living room. Numbness was beginning to settle in. He could ignore her, maybe she'd go away.

His mother followed him. "I know what happened over there was horrible, but you refuse to speak of it. I understand that, and I've given you space. But I will not stand by and watch you drink and smoke and sink deeper into a place I cannot reach. You are not being true to yourself, Santiago. This is not you."

His jaw clenched. "This *is* me. You don't know, *mamá*."

Erik and Susana crept out of their rooms. Awakened by loud voices, they shared a brief look, remaining in the shadows to eavesdrop.

"I may not understand what you've gone through, but I know what it's like to lose people I care about. I will not lose you, too."

Santi dropped into an overstuffed chair. His mother had redone most of the house while he was away. The chair was new and stiff. His head pounded. "You lost me a long time ago."

His words stung, even if she felt she deserved them. "You haven't tried to contact Marie, have you?"

"Don't want to talk about it."

"Fine. As long as you leave it alone."

Santi lifted his head. "I *am* leaving it alone. That's what you wanted. This is where it got me."

"Things don't always go the way we plan. It's life."

"Or death. Either one works."

"You're drunk talking. It's best left in the past. It's been over a year since you've seen her, Santiago. Time to move forward with your life."

Santi sank deeper into the chair, resting his head against the back cushion, glazed eyes stared unseeing at the ceiling. The buzz was getting to him. Sweet numbness. "That's right, my life. Not yours."

She glossed over his statement. "Your body is getting stronger. You need to work on healing your mind," she tapped a finger against her temple. "You won't find answers in a bottle or a joint. Your father drank himself to death after his cancer diagnosis. Do you want that for yourself?"

He shrugged lazily. "Maybe. Don't know what I want."

"You need to talk about what happened in Beirut. Talk to someone. Doesn't the VA offer counseling? Therapy?"

"Didn't want to go."

"Because you're stubborn."

"Get that from you."

"I had to do whatever I could to raise and care for my children. To survive."

"Even make a deal *con una diabla*."

"Yes, even that." Irma crossed herself, glancing at the small statue of La Virgen de Guadalupe on display in the hallway. Catching a glimpse of her other two children, she waved them back to their rooms.

After a long silence he said, "Heard Ferguson needs a ranch hand, someone to train a few horses."

"You're not thinking of riding…"

"I don't feel alive if I'm not riding." He didn't know if he could sit a horse.

"The doctors said it's too dangerous. If you fell or were thrown… it'll be worse… you could die."

"I'm not living anyway, *mami*."

His words deflated her. A tear slipped. She didn't know how to help her child, how to undo the harm she caused. She was proud of her son. The first in her family to graduate from college where most didn't graduate from high school. He was intelligent, capable, full of life. But that was Santiago before Beirut, before the horrible deal she'd made with Carla Rossi. She didn't know this young man sitting in her living room chair.

Irma Rivera grew up, enmeshed in cowboy culture. She watched her father, her husband and now her son embody the same ride or die mentality. Man up, cowboy up. Be tough. Her son felt worthless, aimless, questioning his own grit and merit. He was floundering, having no sense of place. Much of that was her fault. Calling up this bullheaded attitude could work. Having renewed purpose might help save her son.

"Okay," she relented. "Build your strength. When you're ready, we'll go and see Rebelde. Until then, no more drinking to excess and getting high like this." She turned to leave, looking back over her shoulder. "Promise you'll talk to someone."

He'd say anything to end the conversation. "Promise."

Irma went to her room, pulled out her pearl rosary beads from the side table drawer, and wept and prayed for her son. Yes, she did what she needed to do to secure her children's future. She forced her eldest son to make an impossible choice at great cost to his personal happiness, and to his life. She would spend the rest of her days making it right again. Irma wished she'd never met Carla Rossi, anguishing over the day she made a deal with the devil.

Chapter Three

Chicago, Illinois
Winter 1983/1984

" "Asleep deprived Marie woke to Elton John serenading, *I Guess That's Why They Call it the Blues*. Fumbling with the clock radio, her fingers found the button to silence him. She loved that song. She hated that song. The words made her think of Santi. Marie rolled onto her back kicking away the covers. She lay awake relishing the silence, grateful that Elton didn't wake anyone else. Grace was feverish last night, a side effect of her infant immunizations. They barely slept. The nurse instructed her to alternate between doses of infant acetaminophen and ibuprofen every four to six hours to combat the fever.

Before she could doze off again, Marie slipped out of bed, smoothing disheveled, brown curls from her face. She padded toward the crib, placing the back of her hand over the baby's cheek, and stroking her dark hair. No detectable fever. Marie slipped into black sweat pants and socks, moved to the bedroom window of the downtown high-rise condo she shared with her parents. She swept the curtain aside. It was dark. Snow continued to fall and pile up in the streets below. A blue plow truck pushed the white powdery stuff, clearing the roads before the morning rush of commuters. From this distance above, the snow-covered streets seemed an idyllic, wintry painting, evenly spaced streetlights dotted the networked grid. In a few hours, the roads and walkways would be a slushy, dirty mess.

Marie stifled a yawn, took a quick peek at Grace, headed to the kitchen, and set the coffee maker to brew. She readied a bottle of formula for Grace, then leaned against the counter, her chin resting in hand, staring at the coffee machine.

"Have you thought about attending the fundraiser?"

Marie sucked in a breath, turning. "You startled me. No, I haven't"

Mrs. Rossi, her hair already combed, dressed in her blue satin robe, pulled two thick mugs from the top cabinet. She set about taking out spoons, cream, and sugar. "I think you should go. Lots of important people will be there. Interesting young men."

"You mean, lots of wealthy, eligible bachelors will be there. I'm not interested, ma. Besides, I have a child. I work. I don't have time or energy to get involved with anyone."

"You're pretty and young. Only twenty-three. You've got time. Might make your life easier. You wouldn't have to work."

Marie blanched at her mother's suggestion. "I'm not looking for a meal ticket. I appreciate the help you and dad have given me, allowing me to stay here. But I'm setting money aside. I'll pay my own way, and when I've saved enough, I'll get a place for Grace and me."

A brief look of panic crossed Carla's features, she recovered quickly. "Where would you go?" she scoffed. "You'd be homeless if it weren't for your father and me." Carla's initial reaction to Marie's pregnancy was to banish her from their home. Her husband would not allow that. Carla soon realized that having her daughter at home meant that she could still exert her influence and authority.

"You think I'll move to Texas, don't you?"

"I didn't say that."

"You didn't have to."

Carla lit a cigarette, waving away the smoke with a manicured hand after she exhaled. She poured steaming coffee into each mug, setting one in front of her daughter. "That's a chapter best left in the past, don't you think?"

"You never liked him. Why?" It wasn't the first time she asked the question. Her mother's response was always evasive.

"Look what he did. Left you with a baby, what is there to like?" Carla took a sip of the hot brew.

"Before that. You didn't like him from the start."

Carla set her mug down. "That's not true. I helped his family, investing in their little restaurant. It would've gone under without me."

"Why *did* you help them? How did it benefit you? You think I don't know you, mom? There's an ulterior motive for everything you do."

"That's enough," Carla warned. "Can't I do something out of kindness?"

"All the insults and snide remarks you made in front of him. He may not have cared, but I did."

Carla blew a thin stream of cigarette smoke from her lips. "Don't be so dramatic. I never made any insults. I can't help it if you can't take a joke."

"Remember when you told us about the days after the war, when you first came to this country as a young girl? Your family was dirt poor, you didn't speak a word of English. You were sent to school, bullied, and teased because you were different."

Carla took a seat at the counter. "I remember. I'm proud of my accomplishments. What does this have to do with anything?"

"You dye your hair blonde, stay out of the sun, and speak like a high society woman. There's no trace of peasant Italian left in you."

"Things were different then," Carla defended, aggressively putting out her cigarette in the ashtray. "Back in the forties and fifties, people were different."

"Maybe they aren't. Maybe things are the same, but the players have changed. You don't like Santi or his family. You think they're beneath you. You're doing the same thing to Santi that others did to you. He's not white enough, he's not rich enough. He's not good enough. Should he have died his hair? If he were rich, would that change things?"

"Stop, Marie. You won't like the outcome," her mother warned.

"Are you ashamed of who you are?"

Carla snapped. "I said that's enough! You don't know what I went through. I worked hard to get where I am today. I'm protecting this family! Do you think I want you to live like that?"

"Live like what?" Marie's voice rose to match her mother's. "Santi is more American than you, heck he was born in Texas. Unlike you, he has a college degree, and is probably working a very lucrative job. Are you ashamed of dad, or of Tony and me? Of your granddaughter? Does having lots of money erase your shame? Why are you so concerned with appearances and status? Why do you care so much about what others think?"

"*Basta!*" Her mother turned away, throwing the mug into the kitchen sink where it exploded before exiting the room. Pottery shards and hot coffee flew in every direction.

"Can't hide your Italian temper!" Marie called after her.

"What the hell is going on in here?" Vincent Rossi, groggy from sleep stepped into the kitchen.

Marie grabbed the broom and a kitchen towel to clean up the mess. "Arguing. We seem to do a lot of that. I'm afraid I egged her on."

"Why would you do that?"

"I don't know, dad." As she finished wiping up coffee, she heard Grace crying from the bedroom. "I have to check the baby," Marie choked out, grabbing up the baby bottle, and running from the kitchen, tears of frustration threatened, but she held them at bay.

"Carla!" She heard her father call.

Marie entered the room to find Grace standing in her crib. She stopped crying and immediately reached for her mother. Marie changed Grace's diaper and dressed her in a pink one-piece. "There's my girl. Feeling better? No more fever, yay!" Her daughter's grin and happy squeals made her forget her anxiety. She sat in the over-sized rocking chair and fed her daughter while she hummed that damned Elton John song. The morning sunrise filtered through a slit in the curtains, the only illumination in the dimmed room.

The door opened. Her mother entered. "I don't want to argue with you, Marie." Carla moved to sit on the bed opposite. "You will come to the fundraiser with your family, and you would do well to forget about that boy."

"Mom…," Marie protested.

Carla held up a hand. "Trust me. It's best left in the past. You need to move on with your life."

"Move on with my life. While every day I'm reminded of him when I look at his daughter."

"You wanted to keep this baby. Now you live with your decision. You're strong. You can, and you will forget him." Carla rose from the bed. "We will not discuss this again."

"Fine."

Carla watched her daughter feed Grace. "I've got someone interested in Apollo."

"What? No!"

"You haven't ridden him much, and now with the baby, you don't need him."

"Mom, I take care of him, I plan to ride more often. That's my horse!"

"A horse that I and your father bought and pay to board. It's an extra expense. Now, you need to stop this nonsense about that boy. If he wanted you, he'd be here. Have some pride," she answered in a tense, clipped voice that forbade any questions.

"Don't sell Apollo," Marie pleaded. "I'll pay for his board."

Satisfied, Carla turned to leave. "I'll think about it."

The political fundraiser was held at a lavish downtown hotel ballroom. It was a bore. Marie felt like a holiday ornament in a red low-cut, form-fitting gown her mother chose that emphasized her hourglass figure. Her lips matched the dress, her eyeliner was perfect, and her hair didn't move for all the Aqua Net she'd sprayed. She wished for jeans, a t-shirt and cowboy boots. The dress had the desired effect. Marie received more male attention than she could stand.

"You could smile at least," her mother said after dinner.

"I'd rather be home with Grace. All this talk of Chicago politics and Mayor Byrne and Harold Washington is of no interest to me. The snow is plowed. That should make everyone happy." Marie took a sip of champagne, then grimaced as the bubbles tickled her nose.

"Grace is fine with the babysitter. See that young man over there, the blond?" Carla gestured with her champagne flute. "The one talking to those two older gentlemen. He's the son of one of your dad's business associates. Chicago contractor and real estate developer. His name is Wade Bennet. Superb family, *very* wealthy." Carla peered at her daughter. "He's good-looking, don't you think? Come on, I'll introduce you."

"Ugh."

As the two women approached the men, snippets of conversation filtered through. "Terrible what happened in Beirut. Reagan needs to get them all out of there. We're not doing enough to retaliate. Lots of Marines killed. A damn shame." The young man turned at the approach of Carla Rossi accompanied by an attractive, young woman in a killer red gown. He smiled, revealing perfect teeth. "Hello Mrs. Rossi."

"Hello, gentlemen. Wade. So nice to see you again." Carla gestured, as though presenting a prize. "This is my daughter, Marie."

Wade's green-eyed gaze flitted to Marie's bosom. He extended his hand. "Hello Marie, it's nice to meet you."

"I'll leave you two to get more acquainted." Carla then strode away through a maze of crystal and linen set tables.

Marie shook his hand as the two older gentlemen muttered greetings and lame excuses to take their leave. "Hello."

"So, Marie what do you do?"

She had to admit, Wade Bennet was handsome. He had an air about him that commanded respect. A man who suffered no hesitations or inhibitions. None of it moved her. "I'm a teacher. English Lit at a public high school."

"Ooh, brutal."

"I love it."

"Never had a high school teacher look quite like you, though. Unfortunately for me, most of my teachers looked like my grandmother."

Marie feigned a laugh and fought the urge to roll her eyes.

He nodded, smiled, and waited for her to ask a question. Most women would, simply to prolong a conversation with him. After an awkward gap of silence he said, "Well, it was great to meet you. Hope to see you around sometime."

"Good to meet you, too."

He left to find someone more interesting to talk to. Marie was relieved. She wandered around the banquet hall, looking for a quiet place away from all the hob-knobbing until the night was over. She settled for the lobby area just outside the banquet room, finding a vacant loveseat across from an impossibly tall, gaudily decorated sculpture. She wanted to go home.

"Hey. You hiding out here?"

Marie lifted her head to find her brother, Tony. He was buzzed, his warm brown eyes slightly glazed, his dark hair out of place from all his moves on the dance floor. His tuxedo tie hung open on either side of his neck, the collar open. Her lips curved in a smile. "Apparently my hiding skills need improvement. You found me. How long do you think it took to decorate that?" She gestured toward the sculpture.

Tony gazed at the object, tilting his head to the side like a confused puppy. He couldn't figure out what the sculpture represented. "Too long. Mom and dad will be ready to go home soon. Mom's made most of the rounds, talking to everyone. She's about done."

"Thank God."

Tony sat beside her, swirling the remnants of amber liquid at the bottom of his high-ball glass, then downing the last bit. He was silent for a long moment, staring at the sculpture as though still trying to discern what it was. The things that passed for art these days. "I probably shouldn't tell you this."

"What?"

"I heard something about Santiago."

Marie perked up, stirring uneasily in her seat. "What is it?"

"Just - don't tell anyone I told you, and don't go doing anything stupid."

"I can't promise that."

"I heard that after graduation last year, he joined the Marines."

Marie hesitated, blinking with bafflement. "Why would he do that? He had job prospects lined up, interviews."

"I think I know why. I think he wanted to forget about things, forget about you."

"He left me. He wouldn't have to join the Marines to get over me. That's crazy."

"He didn't leave you, Marie." Tony struggled to maintain an even tone. He knew that his mother would be angry if he divulged any information about Santiago. He didn't wish to upset his sister, but something didn't sit right with this entire situation.

"He did. Told me himself it was over, more than once." Though the hurt of that day lessened with time, it would never fade completely.

"I've said too much already."

"What are you talking about?"

"Don't tell anyone. I'm sorry, Marie. Just, please know that. I'm really sorry for everything. Nobody knew you were pregnant."

"You're not making any sense."

"I'm not saying anything more, so don't ask." He rose from his seat, peering into the bottom of his glass. "I need another drink." He held up a hand and walked away.

"Tony!"

Her brother turned and made the motion of zipping his lips, locking them with an imaginary key and throwing it away. A grown man in a tuxedo, he looked ridiculous. He seemed to know this too, laughed at himself and gave her a thumbs up before returning to the reception area.

Carla cornered her son near the coat check window. "What did you say to upset your sister?"

"Nothing. We were just talking."

"About what?"

"I dunno, stuff. It was nothing. I'm headed to the bar for last call."

She gripped his arm. "Anthony."

He pulled away. "Don't worry about it, ma. It's good. We're good."

Marie's silence on the ride home told Carla otherwise. Whatever her children spoke about, wasn't good.

Before January faded, they celebrated Grace's first birthday. Marie spent most of her days at work or in the downtown condo with her child. When she initially returned to work soon after Grace's birth, her mother insisted they hire a nanny to care for Grace. Marie didn't wish to be indebted to her mother for one more thing. Despite their argument over childcare arrangements, Marie enrolled Grace in a nearby daycare center. The expense was a burden on her teacher's salary, but it was the path to freedom. Freedom. It seemed she spent the better part of her young adulthood searching for it.

Marie loved her work, and her time with students. Planning and implementing lessons became an escape. Other aspects of the job she could do without. They never told her in college that much of her time would be spent on things that had nothing to do with teaching. She developed positive relationships with colleagues, and one or two proved to be invaluable mentors. She learned more from them than any college course.

She moved Apollo to a barn on the opposite side of the city suburbs where the board was less expensive, and the care was better. She filled her life with her work, her child, and her horse. She would never forget Santiago Rivera. A part of her would always love him, but she knew she had to move forward. Once, she tried contacting him, but the number was unlisted, and the DOD would not give out military personnel information to anyone without proper authorization. She called the number of his family's restaurant, asking to speak to Santiago, but employees insisted he no longer came to the establishment. She thought to write a letter, still believing he should know about his daughter, then dismissed the idea. Her mother was right about one thing. If Santi wanted her, he'd be there.

"Let it go, Marie. He doesn't love you. He never did." she admonished herself. She focused on building a life for herself and Grace away from her mother's influence, and a life without Santi.

In February of 1984, President Reagan ordered the Marines to begin withdrawing from Lebanon.

Chapter Four

Spring Branch and San Antonio, Texas
Summer, 1984

"Looking good, Santi," Erik shouted words of encouragement to his brother. Thin, tanned arms clinging on the fence rail, he watched as Santiago sat atop the stocky bay horse, Rebelde, in the large round pen. They walked the wide circle several times to warm up, then jogged.

Santi sat tall in the saddle. The high and tight military cut gone, his hair had grown out, hidden beneath the cowboy hat. Black strands touched the collar of his chambray shirt. Santi asked his horse to lope. He sat the three-beat gait easily, hips rolling with the rhythm of his horse. It felt amazing to be in the saddle again. God, he missed this.

"Please, nothing crazy," Irma called out.

"You got it!" Erik was proud of his brother. Santi looked as though he'd never taken time off or been severely injured. After he was medically discharged under honorable conditions from the Marine Corps., he worked hard to regain strength and build his body. He spent hours at the local gym and worked with a physical therapist. Some days he overdid it and set himself back. Some days his body rebelled against the exertion, but he pressed on. He attended group therapy sessions to assist with his mental state. For years they called it shell shock, combat fatigue, or war neurosis, but now it had a new name: Post Traumatic Stress Disorder, or PTSD. Erik didn't think his brother would ever be the same as he was before Beirut, or after Marie, but he noticed great improvement.

Santiago slowed his horse to a walk and approached his brother. "Open the gate," he asked, gesturing toward it with a lift of his chin.

Erik leaped off the rail to do his brother's bidding.

Irma objected. "You can't ride out there."

"Need to see what I can do," he said. As soon as he was outside the round pen, he urged Rebelde onward into a full gallop, Santi yipped and hollered as they sped off. They disappeared over a distant rise.

"He'll be okay," Erik said to reassure his mother.

Santi knew not to overwork his horse. They galloped for some distance, then slowed. Erik kept Rebelde in good condition, but the warmth of morning would soon turn to the intense heat of day. He walked his horse back to the main yard to help cool him down. Gazing out over the scrubbed lands of the Ferguson Ranch, he couldn't help but think of Marie and the plans they'd made. A pang of remorse hit his gut. He'd been purposely cruel to her, all for a lie that wasn't his. All for the sake of his family's survival. He'd never forgive himself for hurting her.

When Santi arrived back at the round pen, he dismounted, ignoring the tinge of pain in his hip. He still walked with a minor limp and sitting in the saddle didn't help. He handed the reins to his brother. "Never said it before, but thank you for taking care of Rebelde, you done a good job. I owe you."

Unsure of his brother's reaction, Erik reached out and pulled Santi in for a hug. "I knew you'd want to ride again. Had to keep him in shape," he said, his voice muffled against his older brother's shirt.

Santi returned Erik's hug. Guilt washed over him for the way he'd distanced himself from his younger brother and sister since his return from Beirut. He'd forgotten how much Erik looked up to him since their father died. "I'm sorry. Been in my own world for a spell, but I'm trying."

Erik stepped back, wiping tears from his eyes. "I know."

"It's gonna be okay, *'mano*."

Erik nodded. Taking the reins, he led Rebelde away.

"*¿Cómo te sientes?*" Irma asked. Their relationship remained strained, but there had been no major arguments between them. They simply existed under the same roof and acted as though everything was fine, but in the undercurrent of daily life flowed the knowledge that her son had not forgiven her.

"I'm okay, *mamá*," he answered, turning away toward the pick-up truck.

She cleared her throat, stepped in front of him and faced him squarely. He stopped in his tracks. If they hadn't argued lately, they would now. Irma braced herself. "I received a phone call last night. From Carla Rossi."

His dark eyes narrowed. "Don't want to know about it."

Irma grasped his arm to stay him. "She reminded me of our bargain. The restaurant is doing well. Enough to repay her in a few years. Her hold on us will be over."

He shook his head. "And? That doesn't change a thing."

"I was thinking, when the money is repaid, I would sell the restaurant, keep some money for myself, Erik, and Susana. I'd retire, give you the remainder so that you could buy your own land, find a good woman, and settle down."

His anger rose to fore, but he tempered it, keeping his voice low. "I *had* a good woman. Having a spread was *our* dream. Now I've got a whole lot of nothing. You and Carla Rossi saw to that. I can't believe you allowed that rich, bigoted *puta* to wrangle you into something so evil."

"She tricked me," Irma cut in. "I've told you before. I didn't know her plan, you must believe me. I cared about Marie too." She looked away. Not for the first time, Irma wondered how a mother and daughter like Carla and Marie, could be complete opposites.

"You got greedy. You were ripe for the picking. Carla saw a weakness and went in for the kill. That's what people like her do. She's crooked as a dog's hind leg."

She licked her lips, pressing them together to stave off tears. "I will never forgive myself for hurting you. I'm trying to find a way to make it up to you, *mijo*."

"I hurt the girl I love because of your bargain. Broke her heart in a million pieces. How do you think that makes me feel? No. What you both did was rotten. You could've returned the money. Instead, you spent it. I don't know if there's anything you can do."

"I'm sorry…"

"Trying to get my life together. Don't want to hear about Carla Rossi again."

That night he dreamed of riding on the Ferguson ranch. Marie was racing her paint, Apollo, riding toward him, calling out to him. She was beautiful, her face lit with a radiant smile. Sunlight caught the golden

*highlights of brown hair as it flew behind her. He rode
toward her, his heart full. When he grew close enough
to reach for her, the ground shook. The world grew
silent, then exploded in a violent blast. She was gone,
the landscape was gone. There were no horses. He
found himself trapped beneath rubble of concrete and
steel. This time there were no fellow Marines to help
him, no rescue. He felt the weight of debris crushing
him. He couldn't breathe.*

Santi awoke with a start, pushing up from the
mattress, sucking in air to catch his breath. Sweat
beaded his skin. His hands swept his body, checking to
make sure he was still there. He peeled off his T-shirt,
balled it up and wiped the sweat away. His hip pained
him. His leg throbbed. He flipped on the small bedside
lamp.

"Another nightmare?" asked the soft, child's voice.

Santi swung his legs over the side of the bed, away
from her. "It's okay Susana. You can go back to bed.
Sorry to keep waking you." Their rooms were adjacent
and unfortunately, the walls were thin.

She hopped on the bed beside him. "I liked Marie.
She was very pretty and nice to me. She cooked good
too, remember when she made lasagna for my birthday?
That was good as all git out." Susana knew her brother
wouldn't speak about the nightmares, he never did.

"Why are you talking about Marie?" he wondered.

"You said her name in your sleep."

Santi ran a hand through his hair. "Ah. Did I? Well, she liked you too."

"Why aren't you with her anymore? Did you find a new girlfriend? Daniel Fuentes said he liked me, but the next week he ignored me. Now he likes Gloria Ruiz. He's just a butthead jerk."

"Nope. No new girlfriend."

"Maybe you should get one. Or maybe you should call Marie."

If only it were that simple. He nudged his baby sister with an elbow. "Maybe you should steer clear of Daniel Fuentes. Want me to kick his ass for dumping you?"

She stifled a short giggle and bounced lightly on the bed. "Nooo, I didn't like him that much anyway."

"Good. You're twelve. Don't rush it."

"I won't." She slid from the bed, bare feet sinking into the thick area rug. "Feeling better?"

"Yeah, I am. Thank you, Susa. Go back to bed."

"You too. No more nightmares."

"No more nightmares."

Susana padded back to the door. Grasping the knob, she hesitated before turning back to her brother. "Are you gonna call her?"

"Don't think she'd want to talk to me."

Susana's brows creased into a frown. "Why not?"

"Because I'm a worse butthead jerk than Daniel Fuentes."

"I don't think you are."

As the months wore on, Santi rode as often as he could to build back his strength and confidence in the saddle. He spent more time at the gym, cardio, weightlifting, stretching for increased flexibility. Toward the end of summer, he approached Mr. Ferguson for full-time work.

James Ferguson was drafted in 1969. Initially sent to Cambodia, he was shipped to Vietnam in 1970. He served a year in-country until he was wounded. When fully recovered, he became a full partner with his father, gradually taking over the family ranch. He knew the Rivera family well. Worked with Santiago's father, Francisco Rivera, rustling cattle when they were both younger men. Mr. Ferguson was surprised to find the younger Rivera looking for work.

Ferguson was going over the books in his office adjacent to the main barn. A bright room, the walls were lined with photos of generations of both family members and horses with top breeding and award ribbons. A wooden bookshelf boasted several trophies. The strapping, middle-aged man invited Santi to sit. "Thought you'd be in San Antonio or Dallas by now with your young lady, working a fancy city job."

Santi removed his hat, taking a seat opposite. "No sir. Change of plans."

Mr. Ferguson nodded his understanding. He smoothed his graying reddish-brown mustache. "I see that. Your mom told me you were in Beirut. Mess that was. They swept it under the rug, no retribution or answer to the bombing. Then turned around and invaded Grenada days later." The U.S. would launch no serious and immediate retaliatory attack for the barracks bombing beyond naval barrages and air strikes that did little to stop future terrorist attacks. Mr. Ferguson shook his head in disgust. He changed the subject. "How's the riding going? Saw you working with Rebelde. You look pretty good."

"I can ride."

Ferguson tapped the eraser end of his pencil on the desk. "Well, I could use help fine-tuning some new stock and gentling some young horses. You do have a way with 'em, just like your dad. Could use extra hands at spring and fall roundup. You'll always have a job here if you want it."

"Thank you, sir."

They discussed pay and housing, then shook on it. Ferguson wondered what happened to the young lady Santi brought by from time to time but didn't ask. Instead, he said, "Listen, if you ever want to talk about Beirut, we can trade stories."

Most Vietnam veterans Santi encountered never wanted to speak about their experiences. They might share snippets here or there but never anything in-depth. Too many memories, too much pain, trauma, and survivor's guilt. When they returned home, they didn't exactly receive a hero's welcome. Many were ostracized, called baby killers. Some never recovered from their trauma. "Thank you, sir. Appreciate that. I think being here will help." He needed to get away. Needed to be on his own. Needed wide open spaces, work he could lose himself in, and time.

Ferguson understood. No further explanation was required. In that moment they were two soldiers from different eras, different wars with similar internal battles. No words were necessary.

Chapter Five

Chicago, Illinois
Summer, 1984

Marie moved the bite-sized piece of medium-rare steak with her fork. It was delicious, but she had no appetite. The extravagant setting and the expansive, breathtaking views of the Chicago skyline would lend a magical air to any dinner. But she had no part in arranging this date on the 95th floor of the John Hancock building, Signature Room.

Wade Bennet watched her silently for a moment. The small talk consisted of Michael Jackson's one glove to Geraldine Ferraro as the first female candidate for Vice-President. The conversation was now exhausted, pretension peeled away, revealing the awkward situation they'd found themselves in. He took a sip of wine. "Hey, Marie?"

She lifted expressive brown eyes, meeting his green ones. "I'm sorry, I…"

He grinned, loosening his black silk tie. "It's okay. Tell you what, why don't we just cut through the mess, admit that our parents put us up to this, and enjoy ourselves on their dime."

Her response was a watery smile. "Okay."

"If it'll make you feel more at ease, I have a confession." Wade removed the linen napkin from his lap, placing it on the table.

"What's that?"

"I'm in love with someone. My parents don't approve."

Marie let out an unladylike snort. "I can relate."

"Let's just hang out as friends for the evening," he suggested. "No pressure, no expectations."

This new knowledge set Marie at ease. She exhaled, releasing pent up tension. "What's your someone's name?"

"Olivia. I met her in college."

"Why don't your parents approve?"

Wade signaled to the waiter, lifting his wine glass as an indication he'd like another. "Similar reasons. They place a certain, unrealistic value on social class distinctions. I get it, but I don't."

"What will you do?"

"Crazy as it sounds, we may elope."

"Wow, that serious?"

"That serious."

"What would your parents say?" she asked. A waiter refilled Wade's glass. Marie declined.

"Doesn't matter. I'm their only child, sole heir to the Bennet fortune. I've already begun taking over some of my father's business interests. It would harm them financially to disown me. Whom I love and marry is my business, not theirs. Ultimately, they'd have to accept Olivia as my wife."

"And whomever has the wealth, has the power."

"Of course."

She'd saved some money. Her plan was to find her own apartment and move out of her parents' home. His words gave her encouragement and food for thought. She raised her wine glass, offering him the first genuine smile of the evening. "To you and Olivia, and to many blessings ahead."

"And to new friends," he added. Their glasses clinked in a toast. Wade took out his wallet, slipping a business card from it. He handed it to her. "I mean that. If you ever need anything, let me know. If I can't get if for you, I'll know someone who can."

Marie eyed the embossed card, then lifted her gaze to his. "That's very kind of you. I can't think of anything at the moment, but thank you, Wade."

The following day, Marie picked up copies of *The Chicago Sun-Times* and *The Chicago Tribune*. She scoured the apartment ads, circling ones that fit her budget, were within a half hour of her school, and close enough to Grace's daycare. She wanted to wait until she'd saved more money, but her conversation with Wade inspired her to make the move from under her mother's dominion. It was a daunting undertaking. Marie understood that she'd been sheltered most of her life, but for her mother, all that sheltering was a means of control. Marie knew that her dependency on her parents was a tool used as leverage, and emotional blackmail. No more. She had to live her own life, whatever that might be.

After touring several apartments, she found one that suited her needs. Four rooms, one bedroom, one bath, with a large kitchen and combination living room/dining room. Other than her bedroom set and Grace's crib, she had no furniture, no pots and pans, no towels, or any other household items. She could pick up the basics along the way.

Marie took advantage of the help Wade offered. He knew the owner of a local moving company and cashed in on a favor. She promised to pay him, half now, half later. Thankfully the mover was amenable, agreeing to the arrangement. She didn't have much to move, anyway.

Her mother, as expected, was not happy. Carla watched her daughter pack. "You'll regret this, Marie. You can't make it out there on your own."

The mover had already picked up her meager furniture. "I need to try. It's time I got my own place." Marie continued to stuff folded clothes into black plastic garbage bags.

"After all we've done for you! This is how you thank us."

"Mom, I'm twenty-four years old. I'm a mother, I have a decent job. I can't live with you forever."

Resigned, Carla folded her arms over her chest. "Don't expect us to help you."

"I won't." Marie stuffed the last bit of clothing into the bag, and picked up her daughter, exiting the room.

In the lower-level parking garage, she placed the remaining bags into the back of her red Daytona, and made sure Grace was tucked securely in her car seat. She had to meet the mover at the apartment. She had the apartment keys and didn't want them waiting outside for her.

Her father exited the elevator, approaching before she could sit in the driver's seat. "Here, Cookie. Don't tell your mother." He pulled out his wallet and pressed a wad of bills into her hand.

"I can't take this, dad."

He pressed a kiss to her forehead. "Yes, you can. Buy something nice for the apartment and something for the baby. I'll come by sometime next week, make sure you're doing okay. Fix me a nice dinner, eh?" he joked.

She hugged him. "Thank you, dad."

"Don't listen to your mother. You're a good girl."

Marie spent the week unpacking her few items, purchasing necessities, and setting up her apartment. Her brother Tony was a frequent visitor. He helped her put together a kitchen table and four chairs she'd found at a discount furniture store. They ate delivered pizza on the floor from paper plates and laughed over the confusing table directions, written in every language but English. He played with Grace, who adored her uncle.

The three of them were spread out on a blanket placed over the carpet in the empty living room. Tony wore his niece out playing all afternoon. Grace was dozing between them. "Did mom get upset when you moved out?" Marie asked.

"Not too much. But I'm a guy, maybe that's different."

"She's so controlling."

"Everything has to be her way or the highway. I know."

"Why?"

"I stopped asking that question a long time ago. She's not gonna change. Dad just doesn't care anymore. He's away a lot and out of the loop." Tony rolled onto his back. "I think he stays away on purpose. He doesn't want to be around her."

"That's sad."

He shrugged. "It's the life they created. He won't divorce her. She'd get half of his assets, and knowing mom, probably more."

"Thank you for helping me, Tony."

"Anytime, sis."

She hadn't been to the barn in days and needed to see her horse. She knew he was in good hands in her absence, turned out, well-fed and groomed, but he needed exercise, and she missed him. Tony offered to stay with Grace at the apartment while she rode.

Arms loaded with her gear and horse treats in her pocket, she headed for Apollo's stall.

"Hey, Marie." The barn owner, an older, wiry gentleman, was cleaning stalls. He greeted her, his expression quizzical.

"Good morning, Mr. Dunham. Finally had a free moment to spend time with my boy."

Full-blown confusion clouded his features. "I don't understand," he said.

"What do you mean?"

He lifted his ball cap, smoothing his thinning salt and pepper hair. "Well, Apollo's not here."

Marie raced to Apollo's empty stall. Her gear fell from her arms. She whirled on Mr. Dunham, alarmed. "Where is he?"

"Mrs. Rossi was here with a young lady on Tuesday. The girl rode him in the arena, did the barrel pattern. On

Wednesday, a trailer came and picked him up. I thought you sold him. That's what Mrs. Rossi said."

"I didn't sell him." The initial panic turned to anger. Blind rage filled her. Marie ran from the barn, leaving all her gear behind.

"I'm sorry, Marie," Mr. Dunham called after her.

She didn't hear him. She ran to the car, tears of fury and frustration streaming down her cheeks. She sobbed the entire way home, barely able to see the road. Her beloved horse, that she'd ridden since she was a freshman in high school was gone. Her partner in the barrel arena, her solace when she was in despair. Her champion. Gone.

Marie burst into the apartment near hysterics. "She sold him! She sold him!"

"Hey, hey, what's going on? Calm down. You'll wake Gracie." Tony reached for her, but she moved away, pacing the empty living room.

"She sold my horse!"

"What?"

Marie lowered her voice, but the blitz of words held the same fire. "Mom sold Apollo! I went to the barn, and he was gone. Mr. Dunham told me she was there earlier in the week. She sold him!"

Tony reached for her as his sister collapsed against him and wept into his chest. "I'm so sorry, Marie. I'd never believe she'd do something like this."

"I hate her! All the bullshit she's said and done to me. I don't need this. Why? Why?" she sobbed.

"I'll talk to her."

"No!" Marie stepped back, using a wall behind her for support. "This is all part of her game. This is her checkmate. I won't give her the satisfaction."

"It'll be okay. We can find out where he is. Buy him back."

Her tears subsided, Marie slid to a sitting position on the floor, covering her face. There was no way she could afford to buy Apollo back, even if they could find him. He was gone. She lifted her head, staring ahead into nothingness. Her tear-streaked face took on an angry, determined look that alarmed her brother. Her voice became cold, flat. "She's started a war she won't win. I'll never forgive her for this."

Two weeks passed before her father called setting up the day and time to visit and see the apartment. Marie prepared a light lunch, fresh lemonade, bread rolls, garden salad, and a small assortment of cured Italian deli meats and cheeses that her father loved. She set out a bowl of his favorite; marinated green and black pitted olives with red & yellow peppers, sliced garlic, onion, and herbs in water and oil. After the meal, she put on a pot of coffee and set out cannoli she bought that morning from a Sicilian bakery uptown.

"This is nice," he said surveying the room. He took a sip of steaming brew. "Reminds me of the first apartment your mother and I lived in years ago." His expression turned melancholy. He stared ahead, through the kitchen window.

Marie said nothing, knowing he'd continue when he was ready.

Snapping out of his reverie, he changed the subject. "Your mother's been asking about you. Says you won't return her calls. I don't agree with what she did. I know you loved that horse." He paused, shaking his head. "Your mom and I have known each other a long time. She wasn't always like this, you know. I don't know when it all changed, and I'm not good with dissecting people's motives, and worse with emotions. One thing's true. Money can change people. Even the best ones."

Marie tried to recall a time when her mother was not controlling and manipulative. It had to be sometime before her high school years.

"It was different back then. Your mother went through a lot when she was young. Bad things happened to her." Vincent Rossi took a sip off the top of his coffee mug, as though to keep from saying more. He paused for a time, reminiscing. "When we were young, she was driven, worked hard, and helped get the business off the ground. The work was her escape. She really was the backbone of it all," he laughed lightly. "The mastermind. Had her hand in everything. She's a perfectionist and felt that if she didn't take care of it, it wouldn't be done right. It was her brains and my brawn.

I trusted her to make decisions, make connections, rub elbows with the right people. She's good at the game. Me, not so much."

"That's no reason for her to do what she did." Marie said. "I understand that you and mom bought the horse for me. I will be forever grateful for that. But if she wanted to sell him, she could have given me the opportunity to buy him. I could have made payments, some arrangement. She did it deliberately, to hurt me. I can't forgive her for it."

Her father sighed. "I understand. She's changed. Sometimes I don't recognize her, myself. But I owe her, and after that thing happened, I promised her."

Marie couldn't guess what the 'bad thing' was that happened years ago. Her father wouldn't elaborate. But it seemed no excuse for her mother's behavior. "You feel indebted to her, you made promises to her. I get that. I'm not trying to hurt anyone, but I must start living my own life now. I need space and time away from her. I need to find my place, my purpose. Without her influence."

Her father seemed to understand. She loved him for that. He spent the better part of the afternoon with Marie and the baby. After he left, she found a cash-filled envelope on the table. *Get something nice for you and the baby*, was written in her father's hand.

Chapter Six

Spring Branch, Texas
Spring, 1985

"Easy, boy," Santiago crooned. . .Groundwork with the buckskin was coming along, the horse trusted him, accepted physical contact and understood cues and intention. Saddle work was next. Santi had worked on Ferguson's Ranch since last Fall. It was a smaller spread compared to some, but Ferguson, was a fair man, paid fair wages, and offered him free living quarters in one of the trailers on the property.

His mother urged him to find a better paying job in San Antonio, Dallas or Austin and put his degree to use. Santi wasn't ready for that. This is what he needed.

Horses never lied. They taught patience and calm. They showed you who you are, mirroring emotional states. Living on the ranch afforded him time alone. Time to heal.

The sound of crunching gravel on the road diverted his attention away from the buckskin. A white pick-up with a hitched, combination RV and horse trailer pulled up. Santi didn't recognize it.

A young, African American man dressed in blue jeans, dark green shirt and a tan cowboy hat exited the truck, read a slip of paper in his hand, then lifted his head to survey his surroundings.

"Ho-ly shit," Santi muttered. He exited the pen, leaving the buckskin. "Mike?" he called out.

"Rivera?"

The two men closed the distance between them, reaching for the other in a genuine bear hug. Friends who survived boot camp together, survived deployment, survived a horrific bombing. All the unspoken memories and the emotions that accompanied them were poured into their greeting.

"Looking good, Riv, looking good. Been hitting the gym?" Mike said when they separated, wiping his eyes.

"You too, man. It's great to see you. I can't believe it." his voice broke. Santi, too, was visibly emotional.

Mike replaced his hat. "You're a hard man to find. I've been driving through half of Texas. Bev's about to have my head." He chuckled, gesturing toward the truck.

"Let's not keep your lady waiting," Santi said, moving toward the vehicle. Mike noted the slight limp as his friend walked.

Beverly Jones slipped down from the truck seat with her husband's helping hand. Santi couldn't be sure but thought she might be pregnant. She greeted him with a warm, dimpled smile. "Pleased to finally meet you Mr. Rivera. MJ's spoken a lot about you."

Santi removed his hat, "Ma'am". He extended his hand in greeting, but she refused it.

"Can I hug you? I feel like I know you already."

"Call me Santi, and I'd be all kinds of a fool not to accept a hug from a lovely lady."

She laughed and glanced at her husband as she hugged Santi. "Oh, he's a good one. Must be that Texas charm."

"Can't believe you're here," Santi said, then gestured behind him. "Come on down to my place. Got lemonade and water in the cooler and a shady spot to set down."

"Is there a place I can turn my horses out?" Mike asked. "I've got corral panels on the horse trailer. Just need a space."

Santi put the buckskin away, then helped Mike put up the corral panels. They set out plenty of hay and water. "I finally get to meet the famous Blueberry," Santi quipped as Mike led the blue roan gelding from the trailer. Beverly brought out a sleek palomino mare behind him.

A laugh erupted. "This here is the famous Blueberry," Mike introduced his horse proudly. He stroked the animal's dark mane, gazing with pride. "Isn't that right?" He turned to Santi again. "He's a money winner, and a friend too. Got me through some tough times."

"I believe it." Santi understood the presence of horses was good for the soul.

Once the animals were settled and hay munching contentedly, Santi escorted Mike and Bev to a row of several trailers behind the stables. Most were newer models with all the amenities. He lived alone, and his needs were simple. Water hookup, electricity, propane gas. Ferguson had a few of them around for cowhands who needed them. He unfolded a couple of lawn chairs, inviting his guests to sit.

When they were seated, cool drinks in hand Mike asked, "How long have you been here?"

"About six months. Most of the cowhands are out. Springtime is calving season, but Ferguson asked me to train some young stock, otherwise I'd be out there too. That buckskin you saw is gonna make a nice horse. He's got a good mind, smart. Doesn't have a barn name yet. I've been calling him Biscuit."

Mike nodded. "We've just come from Denver. They're starting an all-Black rodeo. Calling it the Bill Pickett Invitational. I've been wanting to rodeo again. I'm getting back into rodeo shape."

"And I'm due in about five months," Beverly chimed in. "I'll need to head home to Illinois before the baby comes."

"So, I've been entering the slack, winning a little money, and moving on to the next rodeo," Mike continued. The slack in rodeo terms were rodeo events scheduled at times outside the main event due to time constraints. Entering open rodeos didn't require an affiliation with any particular professional organization, allowing riders of various skill levels to compete.

"You don't mind traipsing around the country with this man?" Santi teased.

Beverly laughed. "Not at all. I enjoy the travel. Might not get to do much of it later on."

"Riv, what's been happening with you? No señorita? Any bambinos?" Mike asked.

"Nope, just been doing my job here. Don't mind it."

Mike studied his friend. He nodded thoughtfully. "I get that."

"Why don't you ask him?" Bev prompted.

Mike hesitated, then dove in. "Well, I came looking for you, first to see an old friend, see how you were doing. Last time I saw you, you were in a bad way. I'm happy to see you fully recovered and doing what you love. The second reason I came by, was to see if you'd like to join me, thought maybe you'd like to enter a few rodeos, do some team roping."

Santi hadn't thought about the rodeo in a while. It seemed like a lifetime ago. It all reminded him too much of Marie. "I haven't done anything like that since college. Don't know if I'm capable."

Mike swallowed a sip of lemonade. "Only one way to find out."

Santi wasn't sure. He was safe here at the Ferguson ranch. He lived alone, worked well with the other ranch hands, but kept to himself. He did his job. He'd created a nearly impregnable bubble of a world, all encompassing, yet fragile. It was comfortable. Traveling and entering rodeos felt out of his comfort zone. He also knew that at some point, he would need to step out, or the bubble would burst, leaving him no choice.

"Man, I know what you're going through, I know what you've been through." Mike lifted his head, scanning their surroundings. "This is nice. Quiet. Peaceful. Nobody messes with you." He gestured toward the stables. "An entire remuda, all the horses you could ever want to ride, roof over your head." He looked at Santi square. "Let me ask you one question. Are you living or merely existing?"

Santi rose from his seat, turning away. He lowered his head studying the bottom of his empty plastic cup.

He was silent for a time, ashamed to admit that leaving his bubble scared him. Just thinking about it caused his heart to race with anxiety. He closed his eyes, breathing deeply. The words from a therapist came to mind. *Approach things you've avoided. It won't erase trauma, but keeps it from getting in the way of your life.* Perhaps it was time. "How long can you stay?" he asked, then faced his friend. "We'd need a lot of practice. I'll talk to Ferguson. He's a good man. Vietnam Vet. Got a soft spot for vets like us. May let you stay on the property in exchange for helping the crew. Might could let us use some steers for practice. I've still got to finish a couple of horses for him. Gave my word on it."

"We can stay as long as we need," Bev answered, an edge of excitement in her voice.

Mike approached his friend unable to contain his glee. They shook on it. "You won't regret this, man. Thank you."

That evening, a few of the hands sat around smoking, drinking, and telling tall tales. Santi introduced Mike and Bev. They were welcomed. Mike loved to talk, and fit right in. A bonfire was lit. Beverly noticed Santi leaning against a tree, away from everyone. She sidled up to him. "I want to thank you for accepting my husband's offer. When he came back from Beirut, he wasn't right. He saw things that day no one should have to see. So much pain and death. They found Dugan's body in pieces. MJ talked about you a lot. He didn't know what happened to you and was afraid to find out. Felt guilty and responsible for it. I don't understand why he should've, but he did. When you asked me earlier if I minded traveling, I answered truthfully. MJ's passion is horses, rodeo. I knew that when I married him. After Beirut, his light was gone. Just to see him have passion for anything is a miracle. And if allowing him to follow his dream is going to help get my whole husband back, I will do whatever it takes to support him. He'd do the same for me. He's an amazing man."

Santi studied her. Distant firelight danced across her elegant features. "He's a lucky man. He's got you."

Bev's smile was wistful. She wanted to ask who Santi had, but it seemed inappropriate, too familiar. Besides, she already knew. "He wants his own place. After the rodeoing is out of his system, we plan to settle down on some land my family owns."

"It's a good plan. A nice dream."

She knew at one time, it was Santiago's dream as well. "We're going to make it happen."

The following morning, Beverly hopped into the pick-up, telling the boys she had to run a few errands. She headed for the post office in town. What she was doing might be all kinds of wrong. She should mind her business, stay out of other people's affairs. If this went sideways, Beverly would be stepping into a skillet full of snakes. But after meeting Santiago, she couldn't stop herself. She had to right a grave wrong.

Mike saved the letters Santiago wrote in the time span from boot camp to Beirut. Mike's intention was always to return the letters to his friend. He never opened or read them. Then thought he lost them and forgot about them. Call her a busy body. Call her nosy. Call her curious. Bev read them. They were sincere and beautiful, and they revealed an unscrupulous scheme. Her heart went out to Santiago.

Bev arrived at the post office. Placed the worn packet of letters into a large envelope and addressed it using the information Santiago had written there years before. The girl could have moved, gotten married, or be dead. Didn't matter. Bev paid for postage and handed the envelope to the postal worker. It was done. The die was cast. Whatever happened from here, she'd have no problem admitting what she'd done. Right or wrong, she'd stand by her actions.

Marie Rossi deserved to know the truth.

Chapter Seven

Chicago, Illinois
Summer, 1985

T he terrible twos. That's what they called it. Grace sat on the floor, occupied with her blocks, attempting to build something akin to the Sears Tower. She became upset when her blocks fell over. The world would surely come to an end.

Marie was at the stove preparing breakfast for her daughter. A neighbor fixing his car in the alley had the radio blaring. Madonna's *Like a Virgin* filtered through the opened kitchen window. "It's okay, Grace. Mommy will help you."

"I do! I do it!" Grace demanded, when mommy picked up one block and placed it atop another.

"That works too. Here you go, put the block on." Marie handed her daughter the next block.

Grace clapped her hands, pleased. All was right with the world again. "I do, ma."

"Yes, good job, baby. Come on, let's eat." Marie plated her daughter's scrambled eggs, cut the slice of toast into four triangles, because Grace preferred it that way, and poured a bit of watered-down apple juice into a sippy cup. She lifted her daughter into the booster seat. Grace refused to relinquish a block, preferring to keep it with her at the table. Grace was a fairly good eater. When she enjoyed her food, she'd sing, hum, wiggle happily in her seat or talk to herself. This morning was no exception.

Marie warmed up her coffee, topping it off from the pot. She sat next to her daughter, offering to help. Grace shook her head, wanting to feed herself. Yesterday's stack of mail needed sorting through. One particularly large, tattered manila envelope stuck out from the bottom of the pile. It had been through the wringer. Her parent's high-rise address was printed in neat letters, a woman's hand. Who knew where this envelope traveled, or how long it took to get to her, but kudos to the U.S. postal service for forwarding it to the correct apartment address.

Marie took a sip of coffee and nearly choked. The postmark was from Spring Branch, Texas, dated about two months prior. She flipped it over. No return address. Her heart pounded. "It's probably an advertisement. Junk mail," she lied to herself, not believing anything would come from Spring Branch, from Santi. She opened it, pulling out the contents. A short stack of letters. Eyes wide, Marie covered her mouth, stifling the cry of shock that threatened to escape.

She shuffled through the letters, fingers trembling, heart racing. They were dated from September 1982 to October of 1983. The letters were ordered by date. Most were worn, the edges tattered as though someone had read and reread them, folded, and unfolded them numerous times. *Dear Marie, Dear Marie, Hello Marie….* all from Santiago, written in his hand. What was this? Who sent the letters?

Marie pulled the first crisp sheet from the top, braced herself, and began to read.

Hello,

You don't know me, but someone who served as a U.S. Marine alongside Santiago Rivera in Beirut came upon these letters. Santiago was wounded in the bombing of 1983, but is now doing well. He's unaware that these letters were sent to you. I thought you deserved to read them for yourself and make your own decisions.

Signed,

B.

"Who is B?" Marie wondered aloud. How did this person come upon Santiago's letters? Santi was wounded? What was happening? Her breath stuttered as she braced herself. She picked up the first letter.

September 12, 1982

Dear Marie,

Not sure why I'm writing. I know you'll never read this because I'll never send it. Not because I don't want to. Because I can't.

I know I hurt you, and I'll never forgive myself for it. I said things that I can't take back and didn't mean any of them. I think I needed you to hate me, so I'd have an excuse, something to hide behind. Maybe I'm writing more for myself. To try to make sense of everything, or to ease my conscience.

Where do I start? You may not know, but I enlisted in the Marine Corps. I'm sitting on the edge of my rack. My buddy Mike is snoring. He's a good guy. We both love horses. He's done some rodeoing, too. I know you're wondering why I chose this. I'll get to that. (Sorry if I'm all over the place in this letter. I know the English teacher in you, is cringing by now. No matter how tempting, please put the red pen away, haha.).

I think it all started the spring when you stayed in Texas with my family, just before graduation. It was the first time your family could tell that things were getting real serious between us. When your mom and dad came down to meet my family, it got worse.

As you know, since my dad died, my family's struggled financially. (We never had a big fancy house like yours, and most of the profits went back into the restaurant.) The restaurant was falling apart and about to go under. My mom was desperate. If we lost the business, we'd lose everything. Your mom 'graciously' offered to help. She called it an investment. My mom had dollar signs for eyeballs and signed on the dotted line and didn't read the fine print. I blame her for getting into something she had little knowledge of.

Right before our graduation, your mom called on the loan. She told my mother that I had to stop seeing you, have no contact with you, that if I did, she would ruin us. It was a lot of money. Hundreds of thousands. There was no way my mom could pay it or return money she'd already spent.

I didn't want to do it. I refused at first. I wanted to tell you, so that we could talk sense to your mom. Didn't want anyone to tell me who to love and hated being blackmailed for it. My mom begged. Pleaded with me to think of my little brother and sister. I was mad at her, mad at the world, mad at you too, even though you had no part in it. I was just supposed to break up with you, and you'd be none the wiser that it was all part of Carla's plan. (I don't know if your dad or brother knew anything about it, your brother was always good with me, I thought).

I'm no liar. My word means something. That's how I was raised. It tore me up to lie to you. After I broke it off with you, I didn't attend my own college graduation. I drove the Camaro around not knowing what to do with myself. I couldn't call you. Couldn't see you on the sly for fear Carla would find out and leave my family with nothing. I drove for hours. I ended up at a recruiting office in a strip mall. I had nothing else to look forward to. All my dreams blown away on the wind. I had nothing better going, so I enlisted.

I know you loved me. I feel that loss every day. You never thought about the differences in our backgrounds, our ethnicities, our skin tones. You saw me as a man. You saw me. Your mom didn't. She didn't see me as a young man with a college degree. A young man with hopes and dreams who loved her daughter. She saw economic status, she saw someone who looked like a bus boy in a fancy restaurant, or a janitor, or someone who picks the fruit she eats. She has wealth and she uses it as a weapon. Don't trust her, and please don't ever become her.

I have to go. Don't know if I'll write any more. We'll see. I love you. I'll never stop.

Always Your
Santiago R.

Marie felt the tug of tiny hands on her shirtsleeve. "Mama crying?" Grace uttered more words Marie didn't understand. "You crying?" She picked up her daughter and set her on her lap, using a paper napkin to wipe her daughter's hands and mouth of toast crumbs.

Marie brushed away tears. "Yes, sweetie."

"Mama sad?"

"Yes, mommy is sad."

"Aww". Little Grace formed toddler words of comfort, some understood, some not. She offered her mother the building block.

Marie sniffled, grabbed another napkin, and wiped her nose. She accepted Grace's block. "Thank you, baby. I've got to call Tony." She picked up her daughter, leveraging her on her hip. She went to the wall phone and punched the number into the receiver. He didn't pick up. She left a message on his answering machine. "Tony? It's Marie. Please call me back or come over as soon as possible."

December 24,1982

Dear Marie,

Wasn't sure I'd write again, but here I am. Thought I'd tell you a bit about boot camp and training. It's as bad, and not as bad as you'd imagine.

After getting off the Greyhound bus, all new recruits stand on yellow footprints. Makes you wonder about all the men who ever stood on that same ground, in those same yellow footprints before you. After that, we enter a barber shop, where older guys with clippers ask you how you'd like your hair cut. Then they laugh and buzz cut every bit of hair off. We receive Marine Corp issued clothing. You run everywhere.

Reveille at 4:30 am. We've got five minutes to shit, shower, and shave. It's a lot of hurry up and wait.

We run several miles without falling out of formation. Do eighty to a hundred sit ups, pull ups, and push-ups. In the afternoons there's academic classes and marksmanship.

There's field classes too. We learn about camouflage, throwing grenades, hand-to-hand combat, low crawl under barbed-wire, and there's the gas chamber. We march with all our gear plus a seventy-pound pack, canteens full of water, and an M16. Two lines, one on each side of a dirt road.

I'm writing this on Christmas Eve. This isn't where I thought I'd be spending it. I was hoping to give you a ring, and ask you to marry me, but I don't think that will ever happen now. I try to think of a million ways I could have done things differently. I can't think of one. Carla Rossi's got us all by the balls. (Sorry, but it's true). I feel like a coward for not fighting for us.

I hope you're doing well. I hope your Christmas is good. I wish I could talk to you. I have to go. If I write anymore, I'm afraid I'll sink into a hole bigger than Texas.

I love you. I'll never stop.

Always Your

Santiago R.

PS I forgot to tell you I sold the Camaro. Lots of sweet memories in that car.

Tony arrived a few hours later. He could tell that Marie had been crying. "Hey, what's going on, you sounded upset on the phone, is Gracie okay?"

Marie put a finger to her lips. "Shh. She's fine. Sleeping." She gestured toward the bedroom. Marie led him to the kitchen where Santiago's letters were spread out on the table. "Please tell me you don't know anything about this." She handed him Santi's first letter to her.

Tony sunk into a kitchen chair as he read. Marie watched him, attempting to decipher his expression. When he finished the letter, he rubbed his face with a hand. "I'm afraid I can't tell you that. I mean, I didn't know all of it, but I knew some." Tony scanned the array of worn papers on the table. "He wrote all of these, huh? How did you get them?"

Marie ignored his question. "How much did you know?"

Tony averted his sister's gaze. He couldn't bear to see the look of hurt and accusation in her eyes.

"Tony?"

"She didn't think he was good enough for you. She didn't like that they weren't wealthy. She didn't like the cultural differences, and I'm putting that nicely. She was hoping it was just a fling, a phase. She wouldn't be upset if you two broke up. I didn't know about the blackmail, or whatever scheme. I thought she was really trying to help them in her twisted way, even if it was out of pity."

"Yes, she was trying to help them, so she'd have some hold over them. It's her thing. Power. Control. Leverage. Manipulation. Coercion." She turned away from her brother. "I can't believe you lied to me."

He stood up. "Do you think I wanted to? Mom said she'd cut me off if I told you anything. I work the family business, Marie. I'd have nothing."

She crossed her arms over her chest. "Dad wouldn't allow that to happen."

"He might not know. He's so tuned out to anything she does…"

She glared at him over her shoulder. "I thought you were on my side."

"I am."

"I thought you liked Santi."

"I did, I do," he defended. "I don't think like mom does. Santi and I had a lot in common, he's a good dude."

She faced him. "I want to see him. I'm going to Texas."

"You can't do that, Marie."

"Mom has no hold over me. I haven't spoken to her since she sold Apollo. She can't do anything to me anymore."

"He's not in Texas."

"How do you know?"

"You think mom doesn't check in from time to time to see what he's up to? She's making sure he stays away."

"Where is he?"

"I'm not sure exactly. He's rodeoing. He was either in Oklahoma or Nebraska I can't recall which."

"Can you find out? Please, Tony."

"Marie, maybe you should let it go."

"I will not! He has a daughter, and a right to know her. Let him decide if he wants to let it go. A choice like that shouldn't be forced or made by someone else. Our mother has played God with our lives for the last time."

Tony lowered his head. He released a slow breath. "I'll see what I can do."

After her brother left, Marie prepared dinner. She'd have to wake Grace from her nap soon, or she wouldn't sleep tonight. As she waited for the pasta water to boil, she sat at the table, choosing another letter.

June 1983

Dear Marie,

Haven't had much time to write. We've landed in Beirut, Lebanon. Almost like the beach landing on D-Day, they put us out in the water. I'm part of the 24th MAU (MAU stands for Marine Amphibious Unit. Everything in the military is an acronym). We arrived on May 30th, relieving the 22nd MAU. There's lots of media presence, TV news cameras, photographers, and journalists all writing in notepads, and taking photos of us on our patrols. Part of me is excited for new adventure, part of me is determined to do a job, and part of me, I'm not ashamed to admit, is a little bit afraid.

Lots of tension here between different religious groups. We're here to stabilize the region and maintain peace. We're here to protect innocent people. Truth be told, I'm not sure about all of this. It feels like our patrolling is adding to the hostilities, and some locals see us as another faction. I get the sense we're not welcome here. Folks don't appreciate when someone interferes in their business. I agree with Mike. He says there's too much we don't know about the language and culture here to do anything good. Guys don't feel safe because we're under orders not to have any loaded rounds. We must operate under peacetime rules of engagement.

Dugan is trying to read what I'm writing. He's a pain in the hind parts sometimes, but we laugh a lot. I'll tell you more about him next time. I'll try to write more later. I know you'll never see these letters but writing them helps me.

I love you. I'll never stop.

Santiago R.

July 24, 1983

Hello Marie,

I hope you're doing well. Lots happening here. A Lebanese patrol was ambushed by a hostile militia earlier in the month. Yesterday our headquarters in the Beirut International Airport (BIA) was shelled with mortar and artillery fire. Three Marines were wounded. I think about what might happen if I were wounded or killed here. You might never know what happened to me.

Let me tell you about Dugan. He's from California, like a real surfer dude. Talks like one too. He started calling me Texas and now it's stuck. I'm not the only guy here from Texas, but I've been called worse. He's a jokester and if you can't find your boots or your helmet, he's most likely responsible. He's a good guy to have around though, guaranteed to put a smile on your face. We could use that here.

Remember,
I'll never stop.
Santi R.

Aug 31, 1983

Dear Marie,

I hope you don't mind if I write letters this way. Saves paper, and it's easier to keep adding on, as if I'm writing a diary. Earlier this month, about thirty-five rounds of mortar and rocket fire landed on US positions, one Marine was wounded. We've been taking on constant fire throughout the month. Finally, we were able to return fire. Our artillery stopped the attacks for now. We lost two more.

If something does happen to me, if I die, I don't want you to think badly of me. I want you to know the truth. We'd be married by now and working to have our own place. Apollo and Rebelde would be grazing in a field together. It was a nice dream...

Marie set the letters aside, dropping her head in her hands. She closed her eyes, unable to read more. Not now. It was all too much to take. If he died, would anyone have told her? She recalled news reports of the Beirut bombing. He was there. He was wounded. He made it out somehow. He was alive and well and traveling to rodeos. Did he have a girlfriend? A wife? Marie had done her best to move on. Wade Bennet set her up on dates with a couple of his friends, double dates with him and Olivia, but nothing was ever serious. Her focus remained on her work and her daughter. She had little time for much else. Marie had no desire to disrupt Santiago's life after all this time, after all he'd been through, but she had to see him.

.

Chapter Eight

Summer/Fall 1985

Team roping features a steer and two riders. The first roper is referred to as the header, who ropes the front of the steer, usually around the horns. Once the steer is caught, the header must dally, or wrap the rope around the horn of the saddle and use his horse to turn the steer to the left. The second roper is the heeler, who ropes the steer by its hind feet only after the header has turned the steer.

Santi and Mike practiced roping on the Ferguson ranch, working against Bev's stopwatch. They spent hours perfecting their timing with each other and their horses. They switched roles between header and heeler. Since Rebelde was a bit larger than Blueberry, they settled on Santi in the role of header. They would need to bring along an extra horse or two to give the regulars a rest.

Beverly was their cheerleader and secretary. She made phone calls and plotted out their travel. She booked motel rooms if they were affordable. They would otherwise sleep in the RV, or the truck. She sorted the money they pooled together for food and entry fees, hay, and horse feed, creating a budget. She wrote out itineraries. She wouldn't be able to travel with them for the entire duration as she came closer to her due date. All she asked was that Mike return home to Illinois for the birth of their first child.

They stuck to smaller, open rodeos, knowing the payouts would not be as great, but needing the practice and exposure. They did well. As August turned to September, they stopped in central Illinois to bring Bev to her grandmother's house. They would travel west to Iowa, enter the rodeo in Fort Madison, then head back to Texas. From there, Mike would return to Illinois in time for his child's birth.

They arrived at Fort Madison in the evening, pulling into the RV parking area where many other rodeo participants also congregated. MJ and Santi set up the portable pens, then fed and watered the horses. Mike said he was turning in for the night. Santi couldn't sleep. He left the RV and went for a walk. Some folks were out sitting around the RV park drinking, laughing, talking. Music floated in and out. Rodeo people were mostly a good bunch. Although they might be competing for the same prize, they often helped each other, like family.

Santi found a tavern on a main road, took a deep breath, and stepped inside. His therapist would be proud. He hadn't been to a crowded place like this in years. He thought to order a drink or two and head back to the RV. Dimly lit and smoke-choked, it was relatively crowded, humming with rodeo people, cowboy hats and heavily made-up women, several of whom watched him enter, eying him appreciatively. Ronnie Milsap crooning, *She Keeps the Home Fires Burning,* sounded from the overhead speakers. A neon sign advertising a brand of beer he'd never heard of, hung against the mirrored back wall of the bar. Since Beirut, he did his best to avoid crowds, but scanned the area, finding an empty spot with full view of the entrance. Perfect. Santi slid into the empty seat at the end, ordered a shot and set his money down.

"Look it what the cat dragged in. Santi? It's you right?"

He hadn't seen her since she graduated a year ahead of him at Liberty Creek University. "Charlene?"

The pretty blonde looked a little worse for wear. She sidled up next to him. "It's been a while, but yes, it's me. Are you in town for the rodeo?"

He stared ahead, avoiding her gaze. "I am. Here with my heeler, MJ."

"Team roper. Nice."

"You still barrel racing?" He wasn't sure why he asked. A conversation with Charlene wasn't high on his list of priorities.

"Yep." Her ice blue eyes searched the crowd. "No Marie? I heard you got roped with that one."

He downed his drink. "No."

"Wow. What happened?"

He shrugged. "We broke up." The absurdity of the entire conversation was surreal to him. Charlene spoke as though nothing had ever happened years ago, and he seemed to be going right along with it, caught up in a twisted current, as though they had been old friends just casually catching up.

"I thought y'all would be married by now with babies the way everyone talked. Crazy. That might explain it." She finished off her drink and set the empty glass on the bar.

"Explain what?"

"Why she sold her horse. I have him now. He's a money winner. Buying him was the best thing I ever did."

Blood pounded in his temples as he absorbed the stunning news. "You have Apollo?"

"Yup. Running him tomorrow. You should come watch."

He motioned for the bartender, ordering another shot. "Maybe."

Charlene placed a manicured hand on his bicep. "Soo… No girl? No sweetheart for Santi?"

"Haven't come across anyone worth my time."

"Oh, I don't know about that." Her voice lowered, husky and suggestive.

Her words were a cold splash, pulling him out of the twisted current before he drowned. "If I recall, you never had much use for a beaner like me. And Marie was always your competition." He shot her a pointed look. "In the rodeo arena as well as out. Besides, what would your family say? Your brothers anywhere around?"

Charlene's expression deflated momentarily. "That was a long time ago, Santi. Things change. People change. You cared about me once."

Once. Never again. He changed the subject. "When you bought Apollo, did you see Marie?"

"No. Her momma was there. I rode the pattern with him."

"That explains it."

"Explains what?"

"Carla Rossi sold Apollo. Not Marie."

She shrugged. "He's mine now."

"What happened to Cody?"

Her eyes flitted away briefly. "I'd rather not talk about it. Buy me a drink?" Charlene slid her body cat-like against his side. She wrapped her arm around his neck and ran her free hand up his thigh, moving dangerously close to his crotch. She whispered in his ear, her lips grazing him, "Pretty please, Santi? I really need it. You're the only familiar face I've seen in a while."

"You're here with someone," he guessed. No one, especially a young woman traveled the rodeo circuit alone with no help.

"A friend. She's gone off for the evening with some cowboy. Don't mind about that. Come on, Santi," she begged.

"You're buzzed."

"A little. I know what I'm doing. Buy me a drink? Please?"

He'd taken a wrong turn down this road before with her and didn't intend to visit again. He should have bought her a drink and left. It would have been the gentlemanly thing to do. Charlene didn't want a gentleman tonight.

After the way she treated him years ago, he never would have predicted he'd end the night like this. In her RV, making her moan, and call his name as he clutched her hips, pumping himself into her from behind. Charlene never cared for him, outright scorned him, used him. Rich girl just plain did him dirty. He never thought much of her after that. Somehow, they ended up here. Both needing a mindless, meaningless fuck.

When they finished, Santi carefully removed the condom, and went to the tiny bathroom to clean up. Charlene sat up from the bed, hugging a pillow. She watched him dress. Santi had an amazing physique. Lean, well-toned muscles shifted and bunched under brown skin as he moved. "How'd you get all those scars?" she ventured.

"Beirut." At her confused expression he added, "I was a Marine there at the time of the bombing in '83. So was my friend, Mike."

"Oh. I'm so sorry. I didn't know."

"It's okay." He tamped his foot into his boot, tucked in his shirt, zipped his Wranglers, and fastened his belt. Dressed and ready to leave, he faced her. "Look, Charlene... this...," he cast about for words to describe what they'd just done.

She held up a hand, waving it off. "You don't have to say anything. I know what this was. I wanted it." She exhaled, smoothing blonde hair away from her face. She looked down at her hands in her lap. "You know, all those years ago, I'm sorry for what I did to you, all that mess with daddy and my brothers. I was so immature. I was angry at you for rejecting me, even when I was with Cody, and I knew you fancied Marie. I was so messed up." She was quiet for a moment, then lifted sad eyes to his. "Look at us now. I still love Cody, and you still love Marie."

"I'll never stop."

Awkward silence stretched between them for a moment before Charlene spoke. "I need to tell you how sorry I am for the way I acted years ago. I promise you

I'm not that ignorant girl anymore. A whole lot of heartache can change a person."

"The hard way."

"The hard way," she agreed. "Good luck, tomorrow."

"You too." Santi opened the trailer door, grabbed his cowboy hat from the counter, and exited.

Before heading back to Mike's RV, he found Apollo on the opposite side of Charlene's trailer in a portable pen. The horse nickered, approaching him in the darkness. "Hey boy," Santi whispered. "Long time, no see." He ran a hand down the horse's neck. "Charlene treating you well? I hope so." Apollo stood still long enough to allow the young man to rest his forehead against him for a moment. Santi closed his eyes. A last connection. "You have a good run tomorrow."

Mike teased him about coming in late. "'Bout time you got laid."

Santi took it in stride. "Maybe."

"You're alone too much, man. What ever happened to that girl you used to write to? You didn't like talking about her."

"Still don't."

"That bad, huh?"

"Nope. That good."

Mike rolled over onto his back, staring at the ceiling. "The one that got away."

"Something like that."

"I don't know what I'd do without my Bev. She's my rock."

Santi didn't want to think about Marie, afraid to feel guilty about what he'd just done with Charlene, even if they weren't together, even if he never saw Marie again. His heart still ached for her. "It's great to be here with you, Mike. Glad we're doing this."

"I knew it would do you good."

They made their runs the following day with excellent times, they each placed in the money. Santi didn't stick around to watch Charlene ride Apollo. Seeing her brought back a flood of memories. Ones he'd been trying to forget.

The First Part
Second
1980 – 1982
Chapter Nine

Liberty Creek University
Texas
Fall 1980

He nodded politely, tipping his brown cowboy hat in greeting as he passed her in the barn aisle, exiting the stables. Marie caught a glimpse of alluring, dark eyes, and enchanting half-grin. She hoped she wasn't blushing. "Who is *that*?" Marie blurted without thinking. She lifted her stall fork, tossing horse manure into the wheelbarrow, eyes following his retreat, all well-fitting Levi's, and broad shoulders in a gray cotton shirt.

"That's Santiago Rivera," Charlene feigned disinterest, but oh yes. She knew Santiago.

Marie tore her gaze from the empty barn opening where dawning light filtered through. Dust motes shimmered on the air. "He's on the team?"

"He's last year's regional champ. Bronc rider and team roper," Charlene commented absently, tossing more manure into the wheelbarrow they shared. "Highest point earner on our team. I know him." Charlene didn't seem interested in saying more.

Marie wanted more. "He's a senior?"

Charlene shook her head. "Junior"

"That's good for us, then, right?"

Charlene shrugged, flipping her Farah Fawcett hair over her shoulder. "He's here on a scholarship." Charlene was a senior, tall, and blonde with striking blue, cat-like eyes. "I'd steer clear of that beaner if I were you."

Surprised, Marie wondered why Charlene would use a derogatory ethnic slur to describe Santiago, but skipped over it, tossing clean shavings into the stall, spreading them around. "Why? Is he like, a jerk or something?"

Charlene avoided the question. "You're not from around here."

"What does that mean?" Marie heard that a lot. Her Midwestern, Chicago accent always gave her away.

"No offense. Santi's a bit of a player. You'll learn. Besides, there's plenty of available cowboys once we hit the circuit." Charlene gave Marie a once over, assessing her appearance. Marie's petite frame, warm café eyes, and long, brown curls would attract attention. "You'll have your pick, for sure. Nothing serious of course, relationships are hard because we're always practicing and traveling so much. Rodeo dating isn't like regular dating."

Marie wasn't sure what to do with this information. "Good to know. I'll keep that in mind."

After stall mucking, students fed and watered all the livestock, then headed back to the dorms to prepare for 8:00 am classes. Brick and concrete buildings dotted the landscaped, manicured campus. Mature trees and perfectly shaped hedges lined various walkways. A small group of students lounged in the grass around a boom box, laughing and chatting over Crystal Gayle's *Don't It Make My Brown Eyes Blue*. Marie made it to her British Lit class on time. A reading and discussion of *Beowulf*, followed by a response paper due by Friday. Despite her wash-up, she sat in class, noting the faint, lingering scent of horse. She didn't mind it. Horse was a comforting smell. Maybe they should bottle it. *Parfum de Cheval*.

After spending two years at a junior college in Chicago, Marie transferred. The student population at Liberty Creek was unbalanced, with slightly more males than females, and not particularly diverse when it came to race and ethnicity. The majority of about seventy percent of students were white, fifteen percent African American, and about ten percent Latino. The remainder identified as Asian, Native American, or other. At first, Marie didn't think about those things, or what it might mean to the overall culture of a university. She cared about rodeo.

Since she'd enrolled at Liberty Creek, Marie survived Welcome Week, and the Orange Raiders – masked students dressed in costumes who traveled around the campus to promote school spirit. The Liberty Creek Bell loomed above the northeast corner of the campus. Liberty Pond and the Horseshoe all had historical significance and were part of university pride. To an introvert like Marie, all the emphasis on community and school spirit could be overwhelming and strange. Her desire to get away from home, and out of her comfort zone, outweighed any initial misgivings. Liberty Creek University had a first-class rodeo team, that alone sold her. She admitted the reason her parents allowed her to study away from home was because her older brother Tony attended a nearby school. He could keep an eye on her, they'd said.

After classes, Marie headed back to the stables. She wanted to check on her horse, Apollo, and get a little riding time in. A lone horse and rider were in the nearest of the three outdoor arenas. Marie drew closer, grasping the rough wood of the middle rail. The solid bay horse was... *dancing.* She likened it to the movements of dressage horses. Piaffe, passage, pirouette all in a graceful, measured tempo, as though horse and rider danced to a music only they could hear. The rider stopped, spun his horse right, then left. He took the horse around the arena, walk, jog, lope, then galloped and brought the horse to a long sliding stop. This was no dressage horse. This was a cowboy's horse, and at that moment, that cowboy lifted his head, and looked straight at her.

She was so fascinated by the animal that it took a moment to register. The rider was the young man she'd seen this morning. Her cheeks burned. She'd been leaning on the rail staring with her mouth open. He most certainly noticed. Flustered at being caught staring, Marie darted away.

Apollo nickered when Marie arrived at his stall. She greeted him with soft, sweet words and stroked his head and neck before she haltered him and pulled him out into the aisle, attaching crossties. Digging into her stall bag, she pulled out her grooming supplies and went to work.

"Nice lookin' paint." The smooth drawl was like velvet.

Marie turned, surprised to find the rider she'd just admired standing a few feet away, his magical horse in tow. "Oh, thanks. Uh, your horse is beautiful too."

"What's your name?"

His perfect smile was disarming, catching her off balance. "This is Apollo. Oh. My name, sorry. I'm Marie." She had trouble meeting his eyes without blushing. He was better looking than she remembered this morning. She recalled Charlene's use of an ethnic slur to describe him. He was a player, she'd said.

He touched the brim of his hat in a gesture of greeting. "Nice to meet you, Marie. I'm Santiago, but most people call me Santi. This rascal here is Rebelde."

"Rebelde." She imitated his Spanish pronunciation, rolling the first R perfectly. He seemed impressed by this.

"Nice. It means…"

"Rebel," she finished. Offering him a shy smile, she tucked tendrils of brown hair behind her ear. "I have a rudimentary working knowledge of high school Spanish," she said in an awkward rush. It sounded like an apology.

"Let me guess, barrel racer?" Santiago began removing Rebelde's saddle, loosening the cinch, unhooking here and there. Rebelde snorted out a breath and shook his dark mane in appreciation.

"You'd be correct." She grabbed her curry, using it to rid Apollo of excess dirt and hair. She had to keep her hands busy and focus on her task. Santiago's presence made it difficult.

"What's your best time?"

"Hooo, well, 16.3, 15.2 if you don't count tipping a can." Knocking over a barrel added a five second penalty to a rider's time.

Santi set the saddle on the rack, removed Rebelde's leg wraps, and picked up a brush. "Not bad," he responded, sounding genuinely impressed.

"Broncs, bulls, or roper?" she asked, pretending she didn't already know, reminding herself not to talk so much, something she did when she was nervous.

"Saddle bronc and roper. You know, those old vaqueros can go longer than eight seconds on a bronc and rope a chicken's leg on the run."

She couldn't stop the laugh that erupted, imagining a cowboy throwing his rope to lasso a chicken. "A chicken leg?"

He laughed too. "Yup. Not saying I can do it, but I've seen it."

His demeanor was open and relaxed, confident. It set her at ease enough to ask, "How'd you get Rebelde to dance like that?"

"Trained him myself. Old Mexican vaquero secrets. Can't tell ya." He winked.

"You train horses too?" He impressed her even more.

"Yup. Pays the bills, sometimes."

"That's pretty cool," she said, bending to pick up one of Apollo's feet to scrape out any dirt and manure with a hoof pick.

They continued grooming their horses in silence. Santi watched her work for a moment as she wrapped Apollo's front feet with bell boots. "You're not from around here."

"No," she sighed, hefting the pad, then saddle onto Apollo's back. "Everyone says that."

He hoped he hadn't offended her. "Don't mean anything by it. I can hear it in your voice." He finished brushing out Rebelde, tossing the brush into the storage bucket.

"It's okay, it's the Midwestern thing. I'm from Illinois. Chicago." Usually when people found out she was from Chicago, and of Italian descent, their next question would be to ask if her family was in the Mafia. Marie thought it was both funny and ridiculous.

"Big city girl, huh?"

"Yep." Apollo accepted the bit she offered. Marie slipped his ears under the headpiece, adjusted the browband and buckled the throat latch. "It was great to meet you, Santiago. I'm going to take my boy here for a spin," she said, hoping she sounded a bit more Texan.

He tipped his hat, offering her that disarming, boyish grin. "Pleased to meet you too, Ms. Marie."

After she led her horse outside, Santi dawdled, taking his time to put Rebelde away. Kenny and Andrew entered the stables starting a conversation before they reached him.

"You meet the new girl from Chicago?" Kenny asked. Tall and lanky, Kenny's reddish-brown hair was completely disheveled after getting tossed from a bull during practice. His jeans and shirt still bore the dirt and dust as evidence.

"Cute 'lil thing," Andrew added. Shorter than both Kenny and Santi, his stocky build was mostly muscle.

Kenny elbowed him. "Good luck with that. Looks like she's all work, no play. Too serious and wound up tighter than a two-dollar watch."

"She's new," Santi cut in, releasing Rebelde into his stall. "Just shy is all. Give her a minute."

"Santi will get her talking. Bet on it."

"You'd win that bet." Santi couldn't help the smile that curved his lips. "Already did."

"Dang, he moves fast."

Santi shook his head, amused. "No moves. Just talking."

"She's about to make a run. Let's check it out," Andrew urged them all outside.

Curious, Santiago walked with his teammates to the adjacent practice arena to watch Marie ride. She warmed the bay and white paint, putting him through his paces. She was a small thing, but solidly built. When it was time to start her run, she asked, and Apollo answered. Marie sat up straight. As she prepared for the turn, she kept her shoulders up, then raised and extended her inside hand forward to cue her horse to begin his turn. Her outside hand acted as a brace on the saddle horn. After coming out of the turn, she used her body to encourage her horse to move forward to the next barrel. They moved well together, Apollo took her cues and responded to the shifting of her body. Her horse knew his job, and she was a damn good rider.

"Turn and burn!" someone yelled from the sidelines. "Go, go, go!"

"Whooo go, cowgirl!" hollered another.

"Hey, Charlene! Looks like you've got some competition."

Charlene flipped a hank of hair over her shoulder. She'd just arrived and missed Marie's run. "I'm not worried. Four of us ladies will make it to competition. I aim to be one of them."

The exhilaration Marie felt in the saddle was indescribable. It was freedom, joy in its purest form. No one in her family understood her passion, and no one could take it from her. She reined her horse in, and brought him down to a trot, then slowed to a walk. She caught sight of Santiago leaning against the rail. When their eyes met, his mouth spread into a wide grin, perfect, white teeth against bronzed skin. Her heart fluttered. She didn't know whether it was the ride or Santiago, but his smile made her spirits soar with delight. She couldn't help but smile back or keep the blush from her cheeks. She wondered why Charlene would warn her to keep her distance from him. She wouldn't have to worry. He was out of her league. He'd never be interested in her, and Marie didn't have time or energy for entanglements anyway. She had bigger plans.

Chapter Ten

Liberty Creek University
Fall 1980

Homecoming week. It seemed the entire university had football fever. There were pep rallies, and impromptu parades. Students painted themselves orange and black. Marie watched it all from the sidelines. She declined invitations to parties, making any excuse to stay away from awkward, anxiety-inducing situations.

Marie's days were filled with her studies and barrel practice. Coach Bell implemented 6:00 am workouts in the gym, followed by barn chores, classes, and afternoon practices till dark, then evening barn chores. She kept to herself, staying in her dorm room or at the library. Her roommate Luanne rarely stayed in their room. She had a boyfriend and spent most of her time at his off-campus apartment. This was completely fine with Marie.

Four women and six men would be entered into intercollegiate rodeo competitions and represent Liberty Creek. If she were one of the lucky ones, she'd be traveling with the team. She saw Santiago from a distance most days. Most of their conversations were exchanged pleasantries in passing. A saddle bronc rider and team roper, he spent much of his time practicing in areas Marie didn't frequent. So far, he and Cody Reed were the point leaders. Coach wanted them to start roping together as a team.

Few students had classes on Fridays, allowing more time for practice. That morning after barn chores, Marie entered Apollo's stall to halter him, when she heard a group of chattering girls enter the stables. She recognized Charlene's voice, complaining to another student. The words disturbed her. "I can't believe Coach Bell wants Cody to partner with that beaner." Charlene let loose with a few other ethnically charged insults and curse words. Her comments were followed by uneasy silence from the others. A few of the voices admonished her. This didn't stop Charlene. "You know I heard that dog did…" Charlene couldn't finish her insulting comment. Marie exited the stall with Apollo, silencing them.

She heard the entire exchange from inside the stall. She loathed gossip. After Charlene's insulting earlier comment, she'd had enough. Even if Santiago Rivera were the devil himself, it wasn't right for someone to speak in such a way. A combination of anger and fear coiled in Marie's gut. She despised confrontation, avoiding it where possible. She dealt with that enough at home. After a brief awkward moment, Marie's eyes narrowed. Though her stomach coiled in knots, she inquired with feigned innocence, "What *did* you hear? He... does... what, exactly? I'm not from around here. Why don't you explain it?"

The other girls Lacy, Heather, and Bryn turned their heads in Charlene's direction at the same time, awaiting her response. Charlene lifted her chin, whirling away. The others scrambled to fetch their horses.

Marie would never see Charlene in a positive light again. Her insults and gossiping said more about her character than they did Santiago. Charlene's haughty attitude and demeanor made Marie's blood boil.

She groomed and readied her horse, quietly fuming over the incident, then took Apollo into the arena for practice. Nothing went right. They both seemed out of sync, out of sorts, not communicating. Coach was hollering, adding to Marie's anxiety and frustration. After two or three failed runs where they hit almost every barrel, Coach Bell told her to call it quits for the day. "Come back on Monday with your head right! See me in my office after practice!"

As she left the arena, she caught a glimpse of Charlene atop her horse, smirking. Marie led Apollo back to the stable, tying him in the aisle. Pressing her cheek to his shoulder, she closed her eyes. She couldn't screw this up. She'd begged her parents to allow her to attend Liberty Creek. If she didn't make the rodeo team, there was no reason for her to be here. Her mother would insist she return to Chicago to attend a college or university there.

"Anything wrong with him?" Santiago startled her. When she didn't respond, he began to unfasten Apollo's saddle.

"I don't think so. It just wasn't a good day," she admitted.

"He knows you're upset or frustrated about something." He removed the saddle, setting it on the rack.

"How so?" She stepped aside to allow him freedom to move around her horse. Her entire being became acutely aware of him.

"Horses don't lie," he said. "They're like mirrors. They reveal us. If we're anxious, they'll be anxious. If we're scared, they'll be scared. If we're mad, they'll be mad." Santiago ran his hands down Apollo's legs, lifting each foot for inspection.

"How do you know this?"

"Wild horses in a herd rely on the leader to tell them when there's danger, when there's calm. It's a survival instinct. A rider is a horse's leader. If I'm anxious, Rebelde will pick up on that, and think there's something to be afraid of. Whatever mood I'm in, becomes his. If I'm calm, and he knows he's safe with me, he'll usually behave that way too." He continued his examination of Apollo, checking for sore spots. There didn't seem to be any, since the horse didn't react negatively to his touch.

Marie watched his hands, mesmerized. Why did all of her senses seem suddenly heightened when she was around him? "I see."

Santi stroked Apollo's back. "If you're ever upset or mad, take a minute or two to check your mood. Might help him. He needs to feel safe with you, like you'll never let anything bad happen to him."

"I would never let anything happen to him."

Santi's dark, warm, eyes met hers over Apollo's back. A thin crackle of energy passed between them. A hint of a smile turned up the corners of his mouth. "I know. He needs to know it too, every time. Being with you has got to be his best option."

"Thank you, Santiago."

He stepped around to Apollo's head. "So, if I'm not stepping out of bounds, what's got a bee in your bonnet, Ms. Marie?"

She wouldn't tell him about Charlene. "Just, schoolwork. I've got lots on my mind. The upcoming competition, football madness, everything."

"If you can, every so often, take him for a leisurely ride on the trail, or up the road a piece, someplace where there's no pressure. A pleasure ride. It don't always have to be about working. You could even sit with him while he's turned out, grazing, or do a little light groundwork, no pressure. Make a game of it."

"Thank you. I'll do that."

"Might do you both some good to relax a bit." It seemed Kenny was right in his assessment. Santi also got the impression that the pretty Ms. Marie Rossi was usually wound tighter than a tick.

"I appreciate your help."

He tipped his hat. "Your boy seems fine. See how he does next time. Remember what I said."

"Horses don't lie?"

"Never."

She wanted to say something else, ask more questions, if only to keep him with her for a few precious moments, but nothing came to mind. By the time he left, she felt better, her tension eased.

Santi walked out of the stables, heading for the barn office. Coach wanted to see him. He wondered about the new girl, Marie Rossi. She intrigued him. It was rumored that she was from a wealthy family, but unlike some of the spoiled, rich, big city girls he'd met, there was no pretension. She was pretty, but didn't wear tons of make-up, or wear her hair in a crazy style. She seemed reserved, a bit introverted, and didn't dress or act in any way to draw attention to herself. But after last year's incident, Santi had sworn off rich white girls. Still, there was something different about Marie, something inexplicable that drew him. Despite his misgivings and internal warning bells, he wanted to learn more. He shook his head, ridding himself of the thought. Nope, nothing special about Marie. Nothing at all. He'd been there and done that. Got a scar to show for it, too. Santi rubbed his eyebrow, where he'd caught stitches from his scuffle with Charlene's brothers. His mother was right, stick to your own kind. Maybe he'd ask Raquel Sanchez from the local escaramuza team to hang out. He'd call her tonight. Resolved. He opened the office door stepping inside.

Coach Bell was flipping through some paperwork, his reading glasses at the end of his nose. Dressed in a black Liberty Creek rodeo polo shirt, his cowboy hat was tipped back, revealing salt and pepper hair. "Have a seat," he said without looking up. Several moments passed in silence as Mr. Bell signed a few documents. Coach removed his reading glasses and smoothed his graying mustache and close-cut beard. At that moment the office door opened.

"You asked to see me, coach?" Marie entered, surprised to find Santi sitting there. Her expression quizzical, her eyes sought to ask the question burning them both. Santi shrugged. He didn't know either.

"I assume you two are acquainted?" Coach's gaze moved from one student to the other.

They both nodded affirmatively, still confused about why they were in Coach's office.

"Marie, Santiago Rivera is last year's regionals saddle bronc champ. Best bronc rider I've seen in a long while. Our highest point earner, however, he's in danger of losing his scholarship, and his place on the team to…," Coach stopped to peek down at a sheet of paper. "Of all things, a poor Humanities grade? It's an elective class, dadgummit!"

"I can explain that, Coach," Santi began.

Coach cut him off. "I already know. You've got missed assignments, and class absences." Coach fixed his gaze on Marie, who swallowed visibly. She knew what was coming. "Marie, you're in danger of failing your math class. Mr. Rivera here, is an Engineering major. He's a math whiz." Coach slapped the papers down on his desk, rising from his seat. "I can't lose my best." He gestured toward Marie, while pinning Santi with a look. "Ms. Rossi here is an English major; her grades are impeccable. You both want to stay on my team? She tutors you. You tutor her."

"Wait, coach," Santi began.

"Can you do that?" Her panicked eyes darted to Santi. "Can he do that?"

"Already done." Coach Bell rounded the desk, leaning against it. He crossed his arms over his chest. "I spoke to your professor, and she's agreed to give you an extension on missing work. Get it done." Coach eyed the two stunned-faced, speechless students. "Figure out days and times on your own. Now git. We got chores at 6:00 am tomorrow morning."

They filed out of the office in silence. Marie headed back to the barn area, her stride purposeful, sandy earth crunching with each furious step. Santi followed, jogging to catch up. "Hey, look, sorry. You don't have to do this."

"And be kicked off the team before I even know if I've qualified? No thanks. I worked hard, had to convince my mother that I could make it down here on my own." Marie's voice rose in frustration. "If I can't do this, she'll say, 'I told you so' and have me back in Chicago on the next flight," she sputtered, bristling with indignation.

Santi didn't understand what all of that meant. But apparently being here and proving herself was important to her. He could respect that.

Spending time, one-on-one, tutoring or being tutored by Santiago Rivera was the last thing she needed right now. Marie came to a fast halt, turning on him, the defiant gleam in her brown eyes caused him to take a step back, lifting his hands in mock surrender. She released her breath, adjusting her tone. "The truth is, I'm really struggling with advanced trigonometry and analytical geometry," she admitted.

"At the library? Around 7:00 tonight?" he offered the mini fireball in front of him.

"It's a date." Marie froze, her flush deepening to crimson, realizing what she'd said could be misconstrued. "I mean, yes, uh, yes, I'll meet you, first floor study lounge. At 7:00." Marie looked away to avoid further embarrassment but didn't miss the amusement in his eyes or the quirk of his brow, or the teasing curve of his lips. Her ire rose again. "Ugh!" She spun away leaving him to stare after her.

Later that evening, Marie waited in the library. When Santiago didn't show up, she decided to study alone. It didn't help. Her own class notes confused her, the book wasn't much help. She worked several problems, checking the answers. Wrong. Every time. She didn't know why she decided to take this class as her math requirement. It was too late to drop it. After two hours of waiting and math frustration, she left.

The following morning after workouts, Marie went to the stables. She was in rotation for morning chores. She entered the barn on a mission. She was met with the sounds of rustling hay as the horses ate, faint music from a radio, and Kenny telling jokes as he and Santi dished out hay. Her legs propelled her down the aisle as she honed-in on her target. She took up a spot behind him, leaned against a stall post, and folded her arms across her chest. Kenny noticed her first. Santi did a double take.

She spoke before he could utter a word. "I waited in the library for hours." Her words were simply spoken and to the point.

"Shit. That was last night? I'm sorry, I got side-tracked."

Kenny snorted out a laugh. "Side-tracked with Raquel Sanchez." Santi sent him a keep-your-mouth-shut look. Kenny coughed, then cleared his throat.

Marie pushed away from the post with her shoulder. "Maybe if you weren't a walking hormone, you'd be able to pass Humanities class."

Kenny let out with a chortle. They both sent him a murderous glare. "I gotta go check, uh… my horse." He tipped his hat, leaving them standing toe to toe.

Black brows drew together in a scowl. "What's that supposed to mean?"

"Raquel? Does she know she's just a 'side-track'?"

He raised his hands in defense. "Look, I forgot, I'm sorry. Maybe if you went out once in a while, you wouldn't be so uptight."

Her back stiffened, arms rigid at her sides, her voice rising. "Uptight? I'm not uptight!"

Noting her ramrod posture, his eyes blazed with mischief, he couldn't help but stoke her ire. She was in a horn-tossing mood, and he was enjoying it. "Should try letting loose a bit," he said, reaching for a couple of flakes of hay for the next horse. "Do you ever let loose?"

Marie bristled; her annoyance grew. "I don't need to let loose. I need to earn my degree."

"Nothing says you can't enjoy yourself a little along the way. When was the last time you had fun?"

"I *do* have fun!"

"What? Name one thing," he dared. He moved the hay-filled wheelbarrow to the next stall. Marie followed him, pretending not to notice his bicep muscles bunching, peeking from under the sleeve of his well-fitting, gray T-shirt. He faced her, waiting for her response.

"Uh…. I read. Books. You should try it sometime."

"That's it? Come on, Marie."

"I ride my horse. That's fun!" she offered, as though it were definitive proof that she knew how to have a good time. Her mind raced, realizing she could come up with no other immediate options. Marie tempered her emotions, her voice returning to an even keel in a poor attempt to hide her agitation. "We were supposed to help each other. You were supposed to help me. If you don't want to that's fine. Just say so. I'll get tutoring elsewhere. I can't fail this class. I can't."

"Okay. I'm sorry I missed our study date."

"It's not a date!"

A smile quirked his too sensual mouth. "I promise I'll be there tomorrow night. At the library. To study."

"You're sure?" she confirmed.

"Same time. I won't be late."

"No side-tracks?"

He didn't miss the hopeful expression in her eyes. "You have my word," he assured.

"Okay." Relieved, Marie turned, headed for the grain storage area of the barn, to start feedings.

Santi's eyes moved a slow arc as she walked away, unable to keep from admiring the way her blue jeans loved her curves. And then, surprisingly, a warm protective feeling washed over him as he watched her. With a slight shake of his head, he turned back to his task. He couldn't afford to care or indulge himself in emotions that could only lead to disaster.

The following evening, Santi arrived on time as promised. He watched her face, utterly captivated as her eyes moved over the handwritten page in the quiet library space, trying to read her expression. She asked him questions. She circled some things, made comments, changed wording, crossed out and corrected a misspelling, made a notation for a paragraph break. He waited with interest for her reaction.

"This is pretty good," she said. Bringing the teacher to fore, the call to instruct made this entire uncomfortable situation easier. "Just some minor things. I'd add some evidence here, for this point." She showed him the section, marking it off. "Just a few sentences or maybe a direct quote to support your statement, to show why it's important to your thesis."

He looked over her markups, fascinated by how easily she found inconsistencies, fixed, and polished his writing. "Thank you. Never would have thought to make these corrections." He slid the paper into his notebook, then looked up. "Show me the trig."

Marie dug into her bookbag, pulling out her big fat math book and calculator. They spent the next hour going over trig functions. Santi explained it so that she gained a better understanding. For him, it was like solving puzzles. Marie marveled at how easily it came to him. "Thank you. I think I'm getting it, now." Marie stretched, arching her back. She stifled a yawn.

Santi surveyed the library. They seemed to be the only two left. "I'll walk you back to your dorm. It's late." He packed up notebooks, stuffing them into a backpack. Marie followed suit.

Girding herself with resolve, Marie muttered hastily, "You don't have to. I know the way."

He followed her anyway. It was dark. Lamplight illuminated the campus pathways. Marie was unsettled by his presence, and not in a bad way, which bothered her too. It was all so confusing. She didn't know what to talk about. Thankfully, Santi made small talk. "Thank you for your help," he said once they'd reached the entrance of her side of the dorm building.

"Thank you too. It wasn't as bad as I thought," she said, then realized her statement could be interpreted as an insult. "I mean... uh."

Judging by his confident stance, he was too cocksure of his appeal. He grunted a laugh. "You thought being stuck with me in the library would be a horrible experience?" Santi feigned offense, placing a hand over his heart. "I'm hurt."

"Sorry, I didn't know what to expect I guess," she confessed with a slight lift of her shoulders.

"So, next tutoring session?"

"Once a week as needed? Pick any day after practice?"

The corner of his mouth lifted into a lazy half smile. "It's a date." Offering her the slightest, teasing wink, he left her at the building entrance. It was her turn to stare wide-eyed after him. Marie didn't understand why he made her flustered, anxious, self-conscious. Charlene said he was a player. Marie saw the way girls ogled and fluttered around him like hens at feeding time. It was gross. Well, she was no fluttering hen.

She had no time for that. Marie had something to prove. She was here to compete in the rodeo arena and earn her degree. She vowed she'd never be like her mother, who dropped out of high school, worked, then got married and had a baby. Guys were a distraction, and she wouldn't allow anyone to stand in the way of her goals and dreams.

Her way out, her independence from her mother was her education. She'd seen too many young women back home give up their dreams, their friends, their hopes for the future, all for male companionship. That was fine if it worked for them, if that's what they chose, but it's not what she wanted for herself. There had to be balance. Marie wasn't sure she'd find it.

Soon she would be a great teacher, inspiring young minds. She'd be able to support herself. Save up for a small place where she could keep Apollo and maybe a few other horses. She'd get a dog. It would be nice to have a man by her side to share it with, but if she didn't, that was fine too. She didn't need a man.

Thankfully, Marie didn't have to worry about that. She flew under the radar, made herself invisible. She hated attention. Attention brought judgment and criticism. Attention brought anxiety and doubt.

She raced to her dorm room, tossing her book bag on the bed. No sign of Luanne, her roommate. Marie sunk into her beanbag chair, staring at the ceiling. She'd never had a boyfriend. Sure, she played spin the bottle, and truth or dare, and she'd been kissed, but those were fleeting, frivolous games of childhood, and meant nothing. She'd been sheltered and kept such a busy schedule all through high school, that she never had time for dating.

She recalled her senior year of high school. Everyone buzzed about prom. Girls talked about their dresses, hair, makeup, limo rentals. They made plans for going to one of the Lake Michigan beaches or renting hotel rooms for after-parties. As the months drew closer to prom, no one asked Marie to go. When she worked up the courage to ask a classmate, a male friend she'd known throughout high school to senior prom, he said that if he ever wanted to go to a dance, he'd be the one doing the asking. He ended up going with someone else. She was too embarrassed to speak to him when she saw him again.

Marie wasn't sure she believed in love. She'd never seen her parents show affection to one another. They were opposites. Where her father was easy-going, her mother was rigid and unmoving. Her father was a peacemaker, her mother was an agitator. It was a wonder to her that she and her brother were even born. Her parents acted more like friends or roommates who tolerated one another.

Now she was stuck with Santiago Rivera. Rodeo champ, chick magnet, and every time his gaze met hers, her heart turned over in response. Ugh. Just put her out of her misery, now. But she had to pass her Trigonometry class. She should have told Coach Bell she'd get tutoring at the Student Union. Too late. She'd have to find a way to deal with it. Keep it professional. Wear her teacher façade and tutor him.

Santi, the good-looking cowboy would never be interested in her. Thank goodness. She certainly wasn't interested in him.

On Sunday morning, Marie stuffed pens, spiral notebooks, and a few books into her bag. She went to the school bookstore and found a canvas umbrella-type folding chair with the Liberty Creek University Guardians logo emblazoned on the back. Tucking it under her arm, she grabbed a medium coffee at the university cafeteria and headed for the stables.

Santi found her sitting at the edge of the turnout pasture with her nose in a book, while Apollo grazed unconcernedly. Every so often she highlighted a few lines, then switched out the highlighter for a pen and took notes. Apollo became curious and approached her, snuffling her papers and her plastic foam coffee cup with his nose. She laughed and petted him. He bolted, running off, kicking and bucking playfully.

"You're doing homework?" Santi asked in disbelief.

Marie didn't look up. "I'm killing two birds with one stone, as they say." She lifted her head, shading her eyes against the morning sun to see him clearly. Her smile took his breath away. "Is that not allowed?"

He sat on the ground beside her. "It's a start."

"How's practice going with Cody?" she asked, for lack of anything to say. The excited, nervous, feeling she felt in his presence rushed through her. *I am not a hen, I am not a hen. Stop it.*

"Going well. If we both place, we'll team up in competition. I think we could win."

"Of course, you'll place. You're very good."

"You are too."

She looked down at her notebook. "I hope so. Charlene is better, Lacy is awesome too."

After a long silence he said, "Cody and Charlene have teamed up, so to speak."

"They're dating?"

"Not sure. Saw them together at a homecoming party last night. Looked pretty cozy." He didn't tell her that Cody was Charlene's second choice.

Marie tapped the end of her pen against her lips. "Interesting." She turned to him. "Is that a bad thing?" Did Santi like Charlene, she wondered? The idea of them together had her feeling as though an icicle lodged in her stomach.

He thought a moment before answering, not wishing to speak ill of anyone, or reveal too much to Marie, who wasn't aware of all that had transpired the year before. It was best left in the past. "We'll find out."

"Do you like her?" Marie regretted blurting the question as soon as it left her mouth but braced herself for the answer.

He leaned back against the fence rail, and removed his cowboy hat, running a hand through his dark hair. He stretched out his long legs crossing them at the ankles. She admired his comfortably worn-in boots. Santi stared out into the landscape before them, watching Apollo graze. "Don't think much one way or another about Charlene." That wasn't entirely true. At one time he did care for her, until he discovered he was being used in a twisted power-play against her family. Unconsciously, he touched the small scar above his eyebrow.

He also didn't tell Marie that a drunk Charlene made it clear that she was fishing for him last night. She could flirt and smile at him one moment, then insult him the next. As tempting as she could be, Santi wanted no part of Charlene or her game. He wasn't interested in what she was offering, and when he didn't take the bait, she moved on, casting her net on an unsuspecting Cody Reed.

Marie noted Santi's pensive silence. "It's probably best to reserve judgment. People tend to reveal themselves in time," she interrupted his thoughts, unable to bring herself to tell him what Charlene said about him that day in the barn. To do so would feel as though she was stirring up a pot of trouble. Marie didn't want that.

"That's true, enough." Santi stood up, brushing bits of grass and dirt from his well-fitting, faded blue jeans. He looked down at her. "Taking Rebelde for a ride. You're welcome to come along."

"Really?"

He laughed. "Yup. Really taking him for a ride."

She smiled, rolling her eyes at herself. "I meant..."

"I know, book worm," he teased. He flashed her a captivating smile that was both invitation and challenge. "Come on."

He didn't have to ask twice. She didn't know what she was doing, or where this was headed, or why he asked, but - challenge accepted. She gathered and packed up her things while Santi fetched Apollo, leading him back to the stable.

They rode mostly in silence at a leisurely pace. Santi led her through various trails adjacent to the campus. Marie felt as though she were transported to another place and time. She relaxed, taking note of her surroundings. Up and over hills, through shaded areas of cedars, junipers, and the occasional mesquite tree. A red-tailed hawk circled against the sky, then flapped its wings away. They passed a few fellow students out on a leisurely hike, or a morning jog. There was no hurry. No concrete and brick buildings, no students hustling to get to their next classes, no loud music, no raucous parties. No timed events.

When the trail widened, she pulled up next to him. Rebelde and Apollo didn't seem to mind being close to one another. "Your major is Engineering?"

"Mechanical Engineering. When I was a kid, I'd take things apart just to see how they worked and then put them back together." He smiled, recalling something. "Made my mom madder than a wet hen. Especially when she found me on the living room floor with parts of our television scattered 'round."

"Oh no, not good."

He glanced her way, the handsome grin still in place. "I put it right again. Worked better after that, and she didn't miss any of her *novelas*. What about you? What do you hope to do with your English degree?"

"I'm also majoring in History, but I'd love to teach. I'm hoping to teach English or History at the high school level."

He studied her for a time, then nodded. "I can see it."

"Because I'm a book worm?"

"Because you've got the right stuff for it. Not everyone can teach. I know I couldn't. For horses, I've got patience, not sure about it for other people's kids." He thought for a moment, then shrugged. "Maybe." His eyes met hers, a smile quirked his lips. "Ready to kick it up a notch?"

"Let's go," she answered, as they both asked their horses to move out simultaneously. "Let's see what you've got!" Marie whooped as Apollo passed Rebelde on the trail, wind in her face, whipping her hair behind her.

Santi laughed, urging his horse forward. Apollo was fast but used to making short sprints and bursts of speed, not trained for endurance or distance, like Rebelde. After a few moments, Rebelde and Apollo were neck and neck. Santi held Rebelde back, allowing Apollo to pull ahead. Marie slowed her horse to a trot then a walk. Santi was close behind. When they stopped, they were both laughing. Santi thought her smile changed her beautiful face, softened it, adding a touch of vulnerability. "Let's cool them down. We'll walk back."

Marie caught her breath. "See? That was fun, right?" She felt light, free.

"It was," he conceded. They rode in companionable silence for a time.

Without realizing how long or how far they'd gone, they emerged from the trail, the university stables appearing ahead. He'd led them back to campus. The ride ended way too soon. After they dismounted, he asked, "How ya feeling, Ms. Marie?"

"I feel wonderful. Relaxed, rejuvenated. Thank you for allowing me to tag along. I didn't know we could take our horses on those trails."

"Any time. I'm glad it worked."

"Part of your diabolical plan to help me loosen up a bit?"

"Maybe. Sometimes we all need to get back in balance. Horses teach us that too."

You know so much about horses. My trainers never explained things the way you do."

"My father, grandfather, great-grandfather all the way down the line worked on ranches. Back in the days of the old haciendas and latifundios. Vaqueros from California and Texas. Learned from them."

"You had great teachers."

"Yup." Santi didn't seem to wish to speak further on the subject, leading his horse down the aisle, ending their conversation.

He brushed and put his horse away. Marie did the same. She thanked him, said goodbye, then left. Santi stayed behind, deciding to clean his saddle. It wasn't dirty, he simply felt like wasting some time. Marie. He didn't know what to make of her. Didn't want to think about it. A part of him liked being unattached. He didn't want to be tied down. He had to admit that female attention was a huge ego boost, especially after the Charlene incident left him feeling unsure of himself. On the other hand, he longed for connection.

He missed his father terribly. His parents had a good marriage. His dad used to joke, *'Esposa felíz, vida felíz'* happy wife, happy life. There was no denying the machismo of a Mexican cowboy heritage that ran through his veins, but he also knew that if you were lucky enough to find a good woman, someone you could trust with your heart, then you took care of her. His dad would use an old saying, *love isn't looking at each other, it's looking forward in the same direction together.* It sounded better in Spanish, but the sentiment was the same. Deep down, that's what Santi wanted. Someone with similar goals and dreams, moving together toward a future together, building a life together. His dad would say, *'family isn't important; it's everything'.*

Santiago's good looks afforded him the ability to be picky about who he spent his time with. It was a blessing and a curse. He never found anyone worth more than the casual. Most girls he'd met were taken in by his looks or by his status in the rodeo arena. Most were nice girls, but they didn't see beyond the superficial. A few were buckle bunnies; female groupies who followed rodeo cowboys. He had little interest in them.

He hated to admit that the incident with Charlene hurt him. He'd known Charlene or thought he did. She was his teammate. They'd hang out with the group after practices and traveled together on road trips for competitions. He thought she liked him, and what guy wouldn't want to get closer to Charlene? Blonde and blue-eyed, she looked like an angel. Which made him no better than some of those buckle bunnies, he realized. He was just as guilty of not seeing beyond the superficial.

He fell for it, thinking maybe, maybe this is what his *Papi* talked about. Maybe he could find someone with whom he could move forward in the same direction.

Even as he traded fists with her brothers in the dark of the campus parking lot that night, confusion and hurt stung more than any physical blows. The warnings to stay away from their sister. The slurs and insults flung his way. Charlene was from a wealthy family. He wasn't. Charlene was white. He wasn't.

When the campus police arrived, Santi was the one they handcuffed. Charlene looked on. Worry and fear etched on her angelic face. Santi knew in that moment her concern wasn't for him. She realized she'd carried things too far. Charlene cared only for herself.

He didn't wish to psychoanalyze her. Didn't want to know why she'd set him up, using him to get her family involved. Kenny and Andrew said it was for attention, said her family was bigoted too. They placed more value on material things than on each other. Charlene was spoiled, they said. Parents gave her whatever she wanted. Everything except meaningful time and attention. Her home life was fucked up and twisted. If that were true, a part of him pitied her.

Santi didn't want to hear it. He licked his wounds and moved on, grateful that he wasn't kicked off campus and expelled. Charlene, for her part, did the same. They didn't talk about it. Once or twice, she had the decency to look ashamed for the chaos she'd caused. Then last night at the party, she approached him. She was drunk. She admitted she used him and apologized repeatedly. She put her arms around him, tried to kiss him, asked his forgiveness, and for another chance. Santi set her aside gently and walked away. His rejection angered her. He didn't care.

He was here on a scholarship. He couldn't mess that up. He vowed to keep his head down, work hard, and be this year's top point earner. He couldn't afford emotional distractions.

Marie. He could tell she was the sort who deserved a forever kind of man. He was stuck with her for now. But she didn't seem to want to spend time tutoring him either. The pretty, wound-up fireball from Chicago. She didn't seem interested in him. He certainly wasn't interested in her. Santi's musings were interrupted by a nudge from Rebelde's nose. He rubbed his horse's forehead affectionately, put his cleaning supplies away, then left the stables.

During the week of practices, Marie didn't see Santi much. She remembered what he told her, checking her mood before setting foot in the barn. She and Apollo made good times, earning points. With her trigonometry grade slightly improved, she prayed she made the team cut.

That Friday, final team selections were made. Names were announced at the team meeting. Marie couldn't believe her ears when her name was called.

Chapter Eleven

Liberty Creek University
Fall/Winter 1980/1981

The team traveled together to save money. They all shared driving duties, set up horse trailers, packed gear, put up pens and fed and watered livestock.

Santi was right. Cody and Charlene were a couple. It was nauseating. There was no in-between for them. They were either all over each other loving it up - or arguing. Even Lacy and Bryn found them exhausting.

They arrived at their destination early Saturday morning. Trailers filled the lot. Other college rodeo teams would compete over two days. Lacy parked the truck, green eyes searching the lot for their teammates. She spied them pulling up one row over. "I hope Barbie and Ken over there can keep their heads in the game," she muttered, indicating the couple with a nod of her head. They watched as a group of five piled out of Cody's truck. Santiago was among them. From a distance, Marie thought he looked agitated.

Bryn chuckled from the back seat. "Barbie and Ken?"

Marie turned sideways in the passenger seat, surprised by Lacy's comment. "I'm sure they'll be fine. If nothing else, competition is important to them."

"I hope you're right." Lacy turned her head to wake Andrew and Kenny, who'd fallen asleep in the back seat on the ride, heads tipped back, mouths hanging open. "Guys, wake up."

When there was no response, Bryn, seated next to Kenny, smacked his thigh. "Wake up, cowboys. We're here."

"Okay, Okay, I'm awake!" Kenny elbowed Andrew. "Crazy women," he muttered, nudging Andrew out of the truck.

Lacy hesitated a moment, as they walked around the horse trailer to the rear. She stopped, reaching out to stay Marie. "Hey, listen. I know you've been spending a lot of time with Santiago, studying together. Just want to say, I don't agree with what Charlene says about him. You know they dated for a bit, then some shit went down with her family last year. Plus, she's mad he turned her away at the homecoming party. Sour grapes and all. Saying nasty things about him. I'm half Mexican. She doesn't say shit to me. Nobody else cares or even thinks about it. Charlene's mad and hates what she can't have. He's one of the best on our team. I'm sorry I didn't speak up before."

"She used him," Kenny popped up from behind the trailer, his bag in hand. "Just tell it like it is. Used him to make her daddy mad and get attention. Had her brothers fist fighting and everything."

"That's crazy." Marie eyed her teammates, unable to hide her shock at the revelation. Charlene and Santiago dated in the past. Apparently, up until recently, she was still interested. He never mentioned it. Not once. A fist fight? "He turned her down at the homecoming party?" Not that it mattered to her, of course.

"Guess you didn't know." Lacy said, unsure whether she should have mentioned it.

Marie shook her head. "No, I didn't."

"Yup." Bryn added. "Charlene was drunk, trying to be all over him. He wasn't having it but didn't want to make a public spectacle. Lots of people already know about what happened last year."

"Charlene almost caused a scene, called him names. Anyhow, we don't want any mess with Charlene to interfere with our competition."

"We're a team." Kenny added. "Santi's a good dude. Didn't deserve what Charlene done."

They all seemed sincere in their defense of Santi, but Marie didn't understand why her teammates felt it was important to tell her all that transpired the year before. She wondered why Santi left that bit about Charlene out of their many conversations. It was all a confusing mess.

"Let's get these animals settled in. I'm hungry. I also need to find a bathroom," Bryn said.

"I told you not to drink so much coffee," Lacy chided as they walked away together.

They unhitched the trailers, left their horses in a designated area, then headed for the nearby hotel. After dropping off their belongings, they picked up eats at a fast-food restaurant. The team had a short practice, then returned to their rooms to dress for competition. They wore black cowboy hats, blue jeans, white long-sleeved shirts, and black vests with the LCU Guardians Rodeo logo embroidered on the front left lapel area. To keep with rodeo superstition, the girls traded clean socks so that they all wore miss matched pairs. They checked their pockets, making sure they were empty, free of money. Not one hat was tossed on a bed. The girls vied for mirror time, trying each other's make-up, and hair spray. Marie bit every fingernail, Charlene painted hers. The excitement of competition permeated the team. Santi was quiet and contemplative, Kenny and Andrew talked too much, Cody was a rock, anchoring them all.

They entered the arena. The various teams stood in groups and watched the opening ceremony. A lone rider with an American flag started off the opening of the rodeo. The large flag rippled and waved as the horse cantered around the arena and the national anthem boomed over the sound system. A drill team then performed to music, and the various rodeo teams were presented to the crowd. Marie participated in rodeos before, but never anything on this scale. She took it all in, the lights, the crowd, the energy.

When opening ceremonies ended, the field opened. "Let the games begin!" Kenny hollered as the crowd clapped and cheered.

After the days' competition, the group celebrated their standings. Coach Bell warned them not to overdo it and reminded them that any drugs or alcohol at a school sponsored event was grounds for expulsion from the team, and possibly the university. After he and two assistant coaches went to their separate rooms for the night, the team pooled their cash. Kenny and Andrew went on a liquor run. The men's team shared a room farthest from the coaches. They'd be quiet, besides there were other rodeo students at the same hotel, coach wouldn't know the difference.

Charlene downed a shot. It was about four or five too many. She stared at Santi, contempt quietly brewing as the others talked and laughed in various places around the room. "Your Englishsh is really good, Ssan-tiago," she slurred loudly, silencing everyone. "Must be all that gooood tutor-ing you're getting from Marie. How long have you, have you lived in the U-nited Ssstates?"

Santi sat on the floor, his black brows knit, wondering what she was on about. He shook his head dismissively, refusing to respond.

"How long have you lived in the U. S., Charlene?" Marie asked from her side chair. The alcohol buzz infused her with some courage. She heard someone giggle in response to the question.

Charlene stood up, swayed, then plopped down in her seat. "I wasss born here, I'm…. an Amer-ican," she slurred then giggled.

"Your English is really good too. Congratulations." Marie deadpanned.

Everyone laughed but Charlene, who pouted.

"That's great, we can all speak English. What's this all about, Charlene?" Cody asked, his blue eyes narrowed, his irritation growing steadily.

Charlene stood up, teetering. She pointed to herself before speaking. "I don't feel com-fort-able," she pointed a finger at Santiago. "With him around." Her attempt to drunk-whisper the last part failed miserably.

"Oh, come on, Charlene," someone said amid other murmurs of disapproval. "Get over yourself, girl."

"Leave it alone, it's all water under the bridge," Kenny said.

"What?" Cody was incredulous. "You better think well on what you say next, you're about to cross a line."

"Oh Cody." She knew he was angry, and coupled with the group's censure, she became sweet and kittenlike, even batting her eyelashes. "I'm drunk. Can you, can you… take me back to the roooom?"

"Come on before you make a bigger fool out of yourself." He glanced at Santi. "I'm sorry, man. She's not acting right."

Santi said nothing. He watched Cody help a staggering Charlene out the door.

Lacy rolled her eyes. "Great. If he ends up staying in our room with her, where will we sleep? I'm not about to walk in on them. Coach won't be happy about this if she can't run tomorrow." She took a seat at the edge of one of the beds.

"Someone can't handle her liquor," Bryn said.

"I'm not a fan of it myself," Marie took a sip from her cup and grimaced. "I mean, it doesn't even taste that great."

"That's because Kenny and Andrew bought the cheap stuff," Lacy hiccupped, then giggled so hard, she leaned sideways, falling over into the bed.

"Hey now, next time we'll let you ladies make the liquor-run," Andrew defended good-naturedly.

Kenny finished his beer, crushing the can. He let out a long, exaggerated burp. "Don't listen to Charlene, Santi. She doesn't know what she's talking about."

Andrew raised his plastic tumbler, "To Santiago! Highest point earner for the LCU Guardian Rodeo team." Everyone joined in the toast and downed what was left in their cups.

"Ugh, I need some air," Marie rose from her seat, tossed her cup into the trash bin, and exited the room. She needed to be away from all the Santiago and Charlene drama.

After a beat, Santi stood up. "I'll make sure she's okay," he said, following not far behind.

Bryn and Lacy exchanged knowing looks. "I think someone likes someone," Lacy sang.

"Who? Someone likes me?" Kenny asked.

"Nobody likes you Kenny," Bryn laughed as she presented him with her cup. "Pour me a drink."

"Hey Bryn, anyone ever tell you, you look a little bit like Linda Ronstadt?"

Marie left the chatter behind. She breathed in the cool night air. It helped to clear the fuzziness in her head and ease her tension. The night was filled with sounds of crickets and the few vehicles that drove by the main road, along with distant voices of hotel guests, and the twang of some country song. She leaned against the brick wall, away from the bright utility light over the hallway exit. Santiago and Charlene. Marie wasn't in the same league as someone who looked like Charlene. Not even close. Marie never got noticed. Most days she was okay with that. She preferred solitude, preferred flying under the radar. There was a kind of freedom in it. Freedom from judgment and censure. It's why she needed to escape her mother. But this felt different.

Learning there was a history between Charlene and Santiago left a bitter feeling in the pit of her stomach.

Marie took a deep, cleansing breath and peered up at the starry night sky. "It doesn't matter. He's just a friend, that's all."

The glass exit door opened. It was Santi. "You're not gonna be sick?"

Recovering from her surprise, Marie laughed. "No. Are you?"

"No. Just came to see that you're all right." He leaned against the wall next to her.

"I'm okay, just fuzzy. Fuzzy and buzzy."

Silence stretched between them before he said, "Thank you. You didn't have to say anything to Charlene. I know she's drunk."

Marie turned to face him, pressing her shoulder against the wall to hold herself up. "Drunk is no excuse. She shouldn't have insulted you like that."

He mirrored her stance. "Truth is my family's probably been in California and Texas since before the Mayflower, before Hernán Cortéz, before Columbus. Technically, I'm more American than she is. Some Spaniards mixed with some *indios* a long time ago, and here we are, *mestizos*, Mexicans. Texicans my dad used to say."

"Used to?"

He looked away, hesitating before he answered. "My dad died two years ago."

She touched his arm briefly in a comforting gesture. "I'm so sorry."

"I miss him. It was his wish that I go to college. Didn't want me to end up as a ranch hand like him or working in the family restaurant."

"Your family has a restaurant?"

"Yup. It's a little place, nothing grand. Worked there a lot as a kid. Still do sometimes. It's why I missed classes and had missing assignments. I had to help my family."

How she'd misjudged him, just like everyone else. She felt like apologizing, thinking he'd been flunking his class because he wasn't serious about it, or because he was side-tracked with a girl. She'd labeled him too, and was ashamed at her insulting remark about tempering his hormones that day in the barn. Marie's head spun from whatever she drank. She took in another lung full of cool night air, hoping it would help. "My family owns a construction company in Chicago. I never worked it." She burst out with a little laugh at the thought. Her laughter grew uncontrollably at the image of herself as a little girl working on a construction crew, over-sized work boots, yellow hard hat, and why not throw in a jackhammer too.

Her laughter was infectious. He joined her, both doubled over, the alcohol buzz making it all seem much more hilarious than it was. "Don't think they let little kids do that kind of work nowadays."

"Child labor," she began, but couldn't finish her thought, unable to breathe. Marie laughed so hard; she swayed, falling against him. Santi wrapped an arm around her shoulders to steady her. To his surprise, she stayed there, settling against his chest.

When their laughter subsided, they stood together wrapped in contented silence. Her cheek pressed against him, he felt solid and strong. Safe. Marie wrapped her arms around his waist. After a few beats, she seemed to remember herself, and stepped back. Santi let her go. "I'm sorry about your dad. He'd be proud of you."

"Hope so."

She asked the uncomfortable question hanging between them. "Why didn't you say anything about what happened with Charlene? I mean, not that it's any of my business, sorry."

He shrugged. "Nothin' to tell."

"Hmm." Marie was unconvinced. Lacy and Bryn said there was a relationship of some sort.

How could he explain it to her? Charlene saw him as beneath her, but worthy of conquest. Santi heard and saw a lot growing up. Some people argued that Mexican immigrants, and Mexican Americans took jobs, increased illegal drug and crime levels. This is what Charlene's family believed. It's what she grew up with. Her attraction to Santi created a cognitive dissonance of sorts, causing discomfort and confusion for doing or wanting something that contradicted what she believed.

When her family discovered a budding relationship between them, they intervened with violence. Charlene garnered attention from them. It was enough to temporarily satisfy her need, filling a void. She didn't want Santiago to be hurt but knowing her brothers cared about her enough to come after him gave her a twisted sense of belonging. It was proof of their love for her. She felt protected. Important. "Charlene is... she sees something she thinks she wants for all the wrong reasons. To her, I'm forbidden fruit. She has no genuine interest in me. Made her daddy and brothers mad, though. Mad enough for a fight."

"Kenny says, she used you?"

"They told you that?" His shoulder lifted in a light shrug. "Maybe we used each other. Don't need those kinds of complications, though. Had enough."

Marie recalled Charlene's warning to steer clear of Santiago. "Forbidden fruit and sour grapes." Maybe things were starting to make sense.

"Something like that."

"If that happened to me, I don't know if I could be around that person. How do you manage it? Being around her?"

"I don't care enough to, I suppose. Not giving a shit has its benefits."

Santi didn't want to let Marie go, but knew they had to return to their rooms. He placed a gentle palm on her shoulder. Dark eyes searched her face. "You okay? We should get back. Another long day tomorrow."

"Yup," she smiled up at him, sleepy-eyed, imitating his use of the word as she nodded. She knew she had more questions for him but couldn't recall any of them. "I think I'm starting to feel it now, but I'm okay."

He wanted to say that he was starting to feel something too, but it had nothing to do with the effects of alcohol. He pushed those thoughts aside. Instead, he led her back to the room where the others were winding down, singing a drunken version of *Blue Bayou*. Within an hour they were all asleep sprawled in various positions and spaces around the room.

The following day, Marie, Lacy, and Bryn placed ahead of Charlene, who spent most of the morning hung over. She blamed her teammates for getting her drunk. Santi and Cody won first place in men's team roping, Kenny placed 3rd in the bull riding, Santi placed 2nd in saddle bronc riding. Overall, the team points put them at second place for the competition.

*   *   *

Study sessions at the library were going better than expected. As long as she wore her teacher mask, Marie found she could get through it. She looked over his psychology essay. The theme was identity. The topic brought them around in deep conversational circles.

They talked for hours without notice of the passing time. They discussed the many contributors to one's identity.

"How do you see yourself?" he asked. "In three or four words."

Her head tipped, thoughtfully. "Hard-working, driven, nerdy?"

"How do you think other people see you?"

"Plain, boring, awkward. No one special. What about you? How do you see yourself?"

Surprised by her self-deprecating answer, he thought for a moment. "Hard-working. Stealing that one from you. Goal oriented. Analytical. A dreamer. But people see me as some kind of skirt-chasing Mexican cowboy Lothario who doesn't take anything seriously except horses."

"Ooh, Lothario, that's a big fancy five-dollar word, let's use it." Marie jotted down some notes. She lifted her chin to better study his face. "Are you? Are you a skirt-chasing Lothario? I've seen girls batting their eyelashes around you a lot."

An embarrassed, muted laugh escaped him. "Not really. But sometimes the attention is nice?"

"I hate attention."

"Sometimes it's all right. A little boost when you're down. But it doesn't last, because they don't know who I really am. They see what they want to see. It's a label. They don't see me, not what's inside. Sometimes it's easier to let people believe the façade. Safer. Can't always rely on other people for confidence."

"I don't mind not being seen."

"Try to get used to it. You're a good barrel racer, a good rider. People are going to notice."

Marie was silent for a time. She stared down at his notebook in front of her. Santi knew how it felt to be misjudged, criticized, labeled, unseen. Maybe they weren't so different. A wave of empathy wrapped itself around her heart. She lifted warm brown eyes to his. "I see you."

His expression grew soft, his dark eyes moved over her sweet face, thoughtful, appreciative. "I see you, too, Ms. Marie."

Marie went home for winter break. Rodeo teammates who lived near Liberty Creek University offered to take care of Apollo for her. She felt especially comforted that Santi would keep an eye on her beloved horse. Her brother Tony picked her up at her dorm room. She thought that most students would welcome the opportunity to return home for Christmas. Marie wasn't looking forward to it.

They took turns driving to Chicago. Got stuck in a snowstorm in central Illinois. Tony talked about all the new girls he'd met at school, Marie talked about her rodeo experiences. She didn't mention Santi, or their Sunday morning rides and tutoring sessions, keeping her growing friendship with him to herself. Her brother insisted they play John Lennon, or old Beatles cassettes, all the way home. Tony was a huge fan and was devastated when one of his musical heroes was killed earlier that December.

"You know how old people say they remember what they were doing the day President Kennedy was shot?" Tony asked.

"Can't say I've heard that."

"Well, I'll never forget what I was doing when the news came on that John Lennon was shot."

"What were you doing?"

"Sitting in my dorm room, doing biology homework with the radio on. As mundane as that is, I'll never forget it."

They arrived at the empty downtown condo. Tony raided the refrigerator. Marie went to unpack.

"Marie, I'm glad you're home. We've got lots of Christmas shopping to do," her mother said as she swept into Marie's bedroom moments later. Carla offered her a stiff half-hug, like the ones she gave to false friends at high society parties. The kind that are for show or out of obligation, lacking warmth, and sincerity.

"Hi mom," Marie returned the hug in kind. "I'm pretty tired after the drive. Can I rest first?"

"You could've taken a flight, but you and your brother stubbornly refused." Carla watched her daughter unpack. "Looks like you're eating a little too well on campus. Watch what you eat, you'll get fat. You can't afford those extra pounds, especially with your full hips and backside."

Marie felt the flush of humiliation creep up her neck. She changed the subject. "I've placed first in barrels for our rodeo team," she said brightly, moving to the dresser, laying folded clothing into a drawer.

"Barrel racing won't get you far in life. Keep your grades up. Rest for an hour or so, I'd like to get to the shops. Your hair could use a trim, I'll make an appointment at the salon." Her mother left the room. Marie sat defeated on the edge of her bed. She reached for a stuffed pink bunny, holding it to her breast. She fell backward, bouncing lightly on the bed. No, she didn't relish coming home at all.

Chapter Twelve

Liberty Creek University
Winter 1981

Marie arrived the Friday before the new semester classes began. Her brother Tony helped her bring her bags up to her room, then drove to his university, about an hour away. After she unpacked, her first stop was the barn. She loved Apollo. She missed him. When she found him in his stall, he was clean, groomed, and munching on hay. She stroked his head and shoulder, then laid her head against him while he ate. She closed her eyes, breathing in his horse scent. Peace settled in her soul. After the winter break spent at home, she needed a little peace.

Her parents bought the horse for her six years ago, when she expressed an interest in barrel competition.

Carla Rossi thought her daughter should take up dressage lessons, and she did for a while. Sometime before her freshman year of high school, Marie watched a rodeo competition on television. She fell in love with barrel racing. Carla would not allow it. Vincent Rossi had the last word. That summer they found a western barn, and a beautiful bay and white five-year-old registered American Paint Horse named Apollo. He'd been started on barrels and had great competition potential.

Marie and Apollo worked with a trainer. They competed in small locally sponsored rodeos. They were good, earning points and prizes. Her father and brother usually attended these events, acting as her own personal cheering section. By the time Marie graduated from high school, she and Apollo developed a beautifully, intuitive partnership. He was a part of her.

"Hey! How was your Christmas?" Marie lifted her head to find Bryn's smiling face, peering into the stall. Whoever said it was right, she did look a bit like Linda Ronstadt.

Marie returned the smile. "It was okay, how was yours?"

"Oh, same ole thing. But it's always nice to get a break and spend some time with my family."

"Thank you for taking care of Apollo for me while I was gone. I appreciate it. I owe you."

"I didn't have much to do with it, Santiago looked after him, mostly."

"Have you seen him around?"

"I think he was here earlier, but I haven't seen him. I'm going to fetch Snickers, take him for a ride. Want to meet up later? We'll grab some food with Lacy."

Marie thought about her mother's incessant reminders about eating and hips and not getting fat. She grinned. "I'd like that, thanks."

Marie didn't see Santiago that day, or the next. On Sunday morning she went to the barn to spend time with Apollo. When she entered, she found her horse in the aisle saddled and ready to go. She walked farther inside, her eyes searching the barn as she drew closer. "Santi?"

He emerged from a stall and into the aisle with Rebelde, grinning. "Thought I forgot?"

A smile lit her face. "I wasn't sure. Haven't seen you."

He adjusted his cowboy hat. "Had to go home and help out for a spell."

"Thank you so much for taking care of Apollo while I was gone. Bryn told me. If there's anything I can ever do for you, just say the word."

"No problem," he shrugged. "I was here anyway."

"How far away do you live from Liberty Creek?"

"About an hour. Two hours both ways. You ready? Bridle up."

She bridled Apollo, then took him outside.

Santi led her along a different path this time. "Never been this way before," he said.

A ping of apprehension filled her. "What if we get lost?"

"Horses know the way home. Besides, these trails aren't that big, they're just winding. Makes them seem longer." He turned to her. "We can always turn around and go back the way we came."

Marie felt ridiculous. "That's true." After a moment she asked, "How was your break?"

"Not bad. Things have been tough since... well, since my dad's been gone. Holidays are hard without him. Nothing feels right. My younger brother and sister look to me now. Mom does too. Not sure what I'm doing. Just try to be there for them, I guess. How 'bout you?"

Marie was ashamed of her own sour thoughts of her mother. How could she admit them when Santi was mourning a parent? Compared to some, Marie lived a privileged life. She stared at the trail ahead, humbled. "Your family appreciates you. It's good to spend time with them. My dad always says that family comes first."

"My dad said the same. Family's everything." Santi noticed that she didn't answer his question. He changed the subject. They talked about movies and music and other interests and hobbies. The conversation meandered to what classes they were taking, and the upcoming competitions. The mood brightened considerably, and when the ride was done, they both felt lighter.

As the semester wore on, Marie dove into the daily grind of classes, homework, tests, late night essays, and early morning workouts, care of the livestock, rodeo travel, and more practice. She had to keep her grades up, she had to keep her practice points up, she had to keep her weight down. She had to get everything done and done well. She had to be perfect. Perfection avoided criticism. She placed first on her team in intercollegiate rodeo competitions.

By mid-semester, Marie's anxiety levels skyrocketed. Sunday rides with Santi helped but weren't a cure-all. Their study sessions continued out of habit, though neither of them needed to tutor the other, having passed the prior semester's classes. Santi found it helpful to show her projects he worked on, explaining them to someone who had little knowledge of his field, while Marie was grateful for his ear and his feedback when bouncing ideas around for a paper.

Marie woke up late on Monday with a headache. She dressed, packed her gear, and rushed to the 6:00 am workout session. She felt weak, sluggish, lightheaded. After showers, the team headed to the barn for morning chores. One minute she was doling out horse feed, and the next, she found herself on the ground. Santi's handsome face, pinched with worry, loomed above her.

Confusion and panic set in. She attempted to rise.

Santi pressed her shoulder gently. "Don't move, Marie." He touched the back of his hand to her cheek. She felt warm. "Why didn't you say you weren't feeling well? We'd have done your chores. We're gonna get you to the med center."

Charlene stood by, silent, her arms folded across her chest as she watched Santi and Bryn kneeling over Marie. Witnessing Santi's care and concern for Marie left Charlene burning with an odd feeling. Jealousy? Regret? She couldn't name it or examine it further. She had Cody now.

Lacy came running back into the barn with coach Bell. "Campus police are on the way, already called for an ambulance."

Marie sat up despite her friends' protests. Her head pounded furiously, her face and hands felt numb. Spots and auras formed, swimming before her eyes. "I'm fine, Santi. I don't need an ambulance," she protested weakly, as her body began to sway sideways.

Santi caught her, wrapping a steady arm around her shoulders, cradling her protectively against his chest. "Let's get you checked out. No harm in that."

Paramedics arrived, stabilized her, and took her away. Hospital staff did a battery of tests, took blood samples, and switched out her I.V., and gave her pain medication for the severe headache. She would be kept overnight for observation. Her family was notified.

When a young doctor entered her room the following day, he explained that Marie had an electrolyte imbalance, and asked about her eating habits. She was dehydrated. Her potassium and magnesium levels were low. He asked if she'd ever experienced migraine headaches.

"I get so busy sometimes, I forget to eat." That was partly true. The part she didn't mention was her mother's voice in her head warning her about gaining more weight.

"Humans can survive for long periods without food, however, doing so can cause an imbalance of important minerals our bodies need to function properly. Always make sure you're hydrated. If you haven't eaten, grab an electrolyte drink, plenty of water, and then eat sensibly, limit sugar, easy on the salt, and no junk food."

He asked questions about school and home and her levels of stress. Marie admitted that she worries a lot about, well, just about everything. He offered her some tips to deal with stress including breathing exercises, taking a walk, reframing her thoughts, meditation. "Sometimes when our mind does too much, or we have too much on our plates, our body will find a way to stop us and tell us to slow down."

She was given pamphlets and health literature, offered the option to speak to a counselor, told she was being released and that she could get dressed. Two young men were waiting to take her back to campus. She never expected Santi and Tony to enter her hospital room together.

"How you feeling?" Santi asked, relieved to see a healthy glow returned to her features.

Her lips formed a shy smile. "Much better, thank you. Tony, this is Santiago. We're on the rodeo team together. Santi, this is my brother, Tony."

"We met in the waiting room when the doctor came out to talk to us," Tony said. "Dad told me to drop everything and come get you." He gestured toward Santiago. "Santi seems to have it covered." He placed a hand on Santi's shoulder in a friendly gesture. "Thanks for looking out for her."

"Anytime." Santi's gaze shifted to Marie, turning affectionate. "I'll go pull up Lacy's truck. She let me borrow it. Nice to meet you, Tony." They shook hands.

"Same here." When he left the room Tony asked with a half-nod of his head toward the door indicating the departing Santi, "Boyfriend?"

"He's a teammate. My friend." Marie turned away to gather her belongings.

Tony wasn't completely convinced of the friendship status. Something more was there. "Seems like a cool guy. We talked a bit outside while the doc was in here. Told me what happened. He's worried about you."

"He is a good person, a friend."

"Want me to call mom and dad, let them know you're okay?"

Marie sat on the edge of the bed, slipping her feet into boots. "I'll call them. Thank you for coming, Tony."

"Of course. You're my baby sister."

She stood up from the bedside, approaching her brother. "I'm sorry you came all this way." She wrapped her arms around him.

Tony returned the hug. "Don't even think about it. It's just an hour. You'd do the same for me. I know it's easier said than done but try not to worry and stress over things." Tony stepped back, his hands on her shoulders, eyes focused on hers. "Do what the doc says, take breaks, breathe."

She nodded. "I will."

"School will be out soon. We'll get to relax, hang out more." He hugged her again. "Come on, your *friend* is waiting."

"Tony," she whined. "He really is a friend."

"If you say so. I'm a guy. I know how guys look and act when they like a girl."

She offered him an indulgent smile. "If you say so."

"Trust me, he's got it bad."

A blush crept up her neck. She punched his gut playfully. "He does not," she protested.

They said goodbye to Tony, who when Santi wasn't looking winked at Marie. She returned it with a scowl. Santi helped Marie up into the truck. She was quiet at the start of the ride back to campus. The voice on the radio reported the biggest recent news stories: Ronald

Reagan's inauguration, and the release of U.S. hostages from Iran. Santi reached for the volume knob, turning it down. He glanced her way. "You okay?" he asked.

"Better. Thank you for being here, for coming to the hospital." She wondered if her brother's speculation was accurate. Could Santi have feelings beyond friendship? No. She didn't think so. She reminded herself that she had no time for entanglements. Marie bit a fingernail, watching the scenery from the truck window, as the last rays of sunset spilled color over the western sky.

"If you're ever feeling overwhelmed, you know you've got friends."

She turned to him. "Thank you. That means a lot." Marie remained silent for a time, hesitant. "I feel guilty for saying it, but sometimes I feel like there's so much pressure on me." Marie looked down at her hands. "My mom... she expects perfection. Get good grades, don't gain weight, act this way or that way. Nothing I do pleases her. I'm never good enough. It makes me feel like everyone I meet thinks the way she does and judges me. When I try to make my own decisions or have my own ideas, she dismisses them, or guilt trips me."

"Why feel guilty for saying that?"

"I know how much you loved your dad, and how much you miss him. Doesn't seem right for me to complain."

"Loved my dad, but he wasn't perfect. No one is." Santi was quiet for a moment, concentrating on the road.

"Toward the end, he wasn't exactly the ideal father. He drank a lot just before he died. Like he knew he was dying and wanted to be numb so he wouldn't think about it. We watched him fade away, not able to do anything about it. Just felt helpless."

"I'm so sorry."

Santi acknowledged her sympathy with a nod. "Kind of makes sense," he mused aloud.

"What does?"

He shrugged. "The whole thing with your mom. Always thought you were wound like a top." He took a quick glance at her. "Don't mean that as an insult. Just an observation."

"No offense taken. You're not wrong. I act like I've got all my shit together, but inside I'm one unbalanced brick away from toppling over. I don't know how to change it." Marie looked out the window. "I don't ever want to be like her, and I'm afraid I'll end up the same way. It scares me."

"Don't have to turn out that way."

Marie sifted through the literature the doctor gave her. "I could try some of this stuff, I guess. Sometimes I think the only way is to distance myself from her. Does that sound bad? It sounds bad, doesn't it."

"Sounds like you need to find your own way. Be your own person. Nothing wrong with that. Family comes first, but not if they're harmful to your well-being. The love and loyalty has to go both ways."

Santi pulled into the campus parking lot. He helped her out of the truck, then walked her to her side of the dorm building, surprised when Marie wrapped him in a hug.

"Thank you, Santi," her voice sounded muffled against him. "I didn't mean to unload on you like that. You must think I'm crazy."

Santi's arms came up, enfolding her. "I don't think you're crazy. Just someone who expects perfection from herself and stresses herself out too much. Don't ever be sorry. I'm here because I want to be." It was true. When Bryn hollered from the barn that Marie was unconscious on the ground, he'd run like the devil was at his heels. Every nerve in his body shrieked to get to her. When he found her crumpled on the dirt floor of the barn aisle, his heart stopped. It was at that moment he realized how important Marie had become to him. If anything happened to her, he didn't know what he'd do. Up to now, he'd held himself back. Past experiences, past mistakes, the whole mess with Charlene. None of that mattered. Only Marie's well-being.

Marie stepped back, taking a breath, fortifying herself. She squared her shoulders. "I'll be fine."

"Get some rest. Don't worry about Apollo, I'll take care of him."

"Thank you. See you tomorrow?"

"Yup." Santi watched her walk away, his heart tagging after her. It was going to be a long spring break.

Chapter Thirteen

Liberty Creek University
Spring, 1981

"Those two seem cozy." Charlene watched from the rail as Santiago coached Marie from the ground. Practice for the evening ended, yet they lingered in the arena working. Marie sat atop her horse, hanging on his every word like he spoke the gospel.

"So?" Cody answered. "We're all teammates. Nothing wrong with helping each other out. I've helped you."

Charlene's ice-blue eyes narrowed. It mattered to her that Marie might have a competitive edge. She vowed to beat Marie's barrel times. Charlene would be graduating in May. She wanted to go out a winner. What made it all worse was that Santiago was the one giving Marie pointers.

She didn't understand Cody's, or the rest of the team's complete acceptance of Santiago. So, maybe she thought she liked him at one time. Maybe he wasn't like her daddy said, but still. After the fight with her brothers, she thought everyone would take her side. No one did.

Cody urged her away from the rail. "Come on. Let's get some food before they close the dining hall for the night. It's getting late and I'm hungry."

Santi looked up at Marie, sitting astride Apollo. "The lighter you pull, the lighter you'll have to pull. The harder you pull, the harder you'll have to pull. Meet your horse where he's at but try to start using less and less effort to get the horse to yield to pressure."

Marie walked Apollo off again, stopping him with her seat, and the slightest pull on the reins. She turned her head, seeking his approval. "That was better, right?"

"Yup." Santi walked up to Apollo petting the animal's neck and shoulder. "In the old days, vaqueros didn't start their horses until they were four or five years old. Took years to train them. Some of the methods weren't always humane, like soring." Soring was the practice of purposefully inflicting pain on a horse in order for the horse to perform a specific gait or movement. "The way I was taught was to use a horse's natural instincts. Pressure and release. The idea is to get our horses to respond with the lightest touch using hands, legs, seat. If you think it, your horse will do it. He'll sense your body movement before you ask him. You've probably experienced that with Apollo already."

"I have. There's times when we're so in-tune it's crazy. It's like he can read my mind."

"That's what you want all the time. When you're working cows, you've got to always pay attention. Anything can happen. Horse has to move and turn on a dime if necessary. He's got to read your mind, so to speak. They call that a centaur wish – to be one with your horse."

Her lips spread into a sweet smile. "Works for barrels, too."

"It does." Santi held her gaze, hesitant for a moment before he asked, "You eaten yet?"

"No," Marie answered as she dismounted.

"I'm gonna grab something, if you'd like to join me."

"Yes. What did you have in mind?"

He took the reins, leading Apollo back to the barn, Marie beside him. "Been hankering for some Italian food."

"Hankering?" Marie laughed. "What passes for Italian food on this campus is a poor substitute." She glanced at him. "One day, I'll make you some real Italian food."

He grinned. "Might hold you to that."

When they arrived at the campus dining hall, Santi chose chicken parmigiana accompanied by fettuccini in a marinara sauce, Marie settled for a dinner salad. Cody saw them and waved them over, inviting them to sit at the same table. Charlene was seated next to him.

Santi glanced at Marie. "It's up to you," he shrugged.

"You have more reason to avoid Charlene than I do," she said.

"Don't care."

"It's fine, I guess," Marie answered, watching Charlene kick Cody under the table, displaying her displeasure over the invitation. "You and Cody would probably like to talk. Charlene's not happy, but I won't let that stop me."

Immediately after sitting across from the other couple, the young men began talking strategy, and how best to beat opponents. They were paired up again this semester for team roping. Marie focused on her salad, listening.

Charlene rolled her eyes. She could feel herself fuming. It might have to do with the closeness she'd witnessed between Santi and Marie. She didn't understand why it should matter to her. She didn't like it. Charlene leaned over the table, eyeing Santi's food, loudly interrupting the boys' conversation. "What, no beans, Santi? I thought you people always ate them." Everyone within earshot looked at her as though she'd grown a second head.

Santi didn't miss a beat. "What are you eating, Charlene? Crow? Humble Pie?"

A piece of lettuce threatened to choke Marie. Cody laughed.

His words stung, because up to now, Charlene boasted that it was her senior year, and that she'd leave all the other barrel racers in the dust. As of today, she was the lowest point earner, in danger of losing her place on the team. "You gonna let him talk to me like that?" she demanded of Cody, affronted.

"You asked for it, he dished it," Cody chuckled. "Don't play if you can't pay."

"I'm not hungry anymore," Charlene stood up. "I don't sit with his kind. After what he did to my brothers? You got a lot of nerve sitting here."

"Woah, woah, hold up now, Charlene. Your brothers got some licks in too." Cody grasped her arm. "I asked him to sit here. What's wrong with you? Can't be mad if his joke was better than yours. Leave it be, it's in the past. Over and done." They were drawing attention from others in the dining hall.

"Let go of me, Cody!"

"Sit down." His voice was a low growl. "Please," he added more gently. The last thing he wanted was a scene.

Marie stood up. The desire to punch Charlene in the face became overwhelming. Santi followed suit, unsure what might happen next. He needed to be ready in case one or the other girl started swinging. Cody remained seated, gripping Charlene's wrist.

Marie's voice was low and dead calm. "Thanks for inviting us, Cody." She acknowledged Charlene with a nod. "Charlene." Her manner was reserved, but underneath lay an edge of fury and frustration, her whole body felt as though it shook with rage. "Looks like you two would like to be alone. We'll sit somewhere else."

Cody got Charlene to set her butt down. She clamped her mouth shut. Cody addressed Santi, his expression apologetic. "I'm sorry, Santi. We'll talk later."

Marie picked up her food tray and walked away. She didn't hear Santi's response or know whether he followed. She had to get away from Charlene before she forgot herself and went full-on Italian mobster movie. Marie wound her way through a maze of tables, heart pounding, cheeks flushed from anger. She found a spot near the far end of the dining space, near a large window overlooking a manicured flower garden. Santi wasn't far behind.

They sat in silence for a moment, their food untouched. Marie watched as Cody and Charlene left, arguing on the way out. She tried to focus on her breathing, a practice that helped her anxiety sometimes.

"Cody's a decent guy. Don't know what he sees in Charlene," Santi said as he watched them exit.

Marie pushed a cherry tomato around on her plate, too wound up to eat. "You saw something in her once. He sees a pretty girl, with a great body. Isn't that what most guys see?" She lifted her eyes to his.

Santi wanted to tell her that she was prettier than ten Charlenes. Instead, he said, "Attraction is important, sure. But the most beautiful woman in the world tends to lose appeal after a while if she's got an ugly heart." He cut a piece of chicken, spearing it with his fork. "Thought I'd have to hold you back for a second."

She offered him a thin smile. "You almost did. But after my hospital incident, I've decided to try not to let things like that affect me so deeply. It's not healthy. It's not always easy to keep in check. I'm still shaking."

"Don't let her get to you."

"I'll try not to," she promised. "There's obviously some strong feelings there. Maybe she still likes you?"

"Don't know. Don't care." Santi was quiet for a moment. He knew Marie was asking him to divulge more of last year's incident with Charlene. "We don't exactly run in the same social circles, you know? Two older brothers came looking for me, threatening me... well, it got physical. When the police arrived, they hauled me off in handcuffs. Let her brothers go, even though they started it."

"That wasn't right."

"Nothing happened. Nobody pressed charges, no one filed a report. I was released."

"What did Charlene do? Did she speak up for you?"

"Nope. Did nothing. Said nothing. The next time I saw her she acted like she didn't know me. Acted like it was all my fault. We usually avoid each other."

"That makes no sense."

"Makes sense if that's what she wanted to happen."

"You think she orchestrated all that?"

"Not sure. Maybe some of it." The night of the homecoming party, Charlene confessed to using him. To what end, she didn't say. He didn't stick around long enough or care to ask her why. He wasn't interested in any explanation she might give.

"But why would she do that?"

"Why does anyone do anything? She got something out of it. Attention? Acknowledgement from her family? A chance to rebel? Only she knows. Learned my lesson after that."

"Which is?"

Santi chuckled. "Don't date privileged rich girls with crazy families?" The moment the words left his mouth, he knew it wasn't the right thing to say.

Marie smiled anyway. "Oh. I guess?" She looked down at her salad. It was suddenly unappealing. Her family was wealthy, and they were sort of crazy. Well, her mom was. Marie supposed that was a disqualifier.

"Like I said, outer beauty doesn't mean much if your ugly on the inside. Maybe that's the lesson."

"I don't understand people who think like Charlene."

"She heard it, learned it, believed it. Maybe something happened to her, or her family and they judge anyone who isn't like them."

"You're too understanding."

"I've lived it more than you."

"True, you have. I'm sorry some people are so ugly."

Marie loved history. If she didn't teach English, history was her second choice. She knew something of Mexican American discrimination and anti-sentiment. It was nothing new. When the U.S. won the Mexican-American war in 1848, The Treaty of Guadalupe Hidalgo granted vast Mexican territories to the United States. Mexicans who inhabited that land became U.S. citizens.

In the 19th century, with increased political unrest in Mexico, emigration to the U.S. grew. American businesses and corporations took advantage of the cheap labor Mexican immigrants provided. As immigration numbers rose, so did anti-Latino sentiment. They were prohibited from white establishments and segregated into poor barrios. Though many of them were American citizens, they were often discriminated against for their language or darker skin. Santi and generations of his family were not spared this treatment.

Santi was comforted by Marie's empathetic nature. It was one of her many traits that he admired. Her sincerity, her compassion, her heart. His voice broke into Marie's thoughts. "Lots of people have their prejudices and biases about things, even you and me. Can't fight everybody. Gotta pick your battles, as they say. If I got mad every time, I'd never have any peace. Gotten into my share of scraps, but Charlene doesn't bother me. Don't care what she thinks because she's not important to me. She has no power, no authority. Don't care what she thinks because I'm not what she thinks. Get mad when it matters."

Marie considered his thought process. Santi was so laid back, yet direct, no-nonsense, and open. She found a kind of security in his calm, assertive energy. Marie wondered if this had anything to do with his time spent gentling and training horses. While her first response to conflict or strife was inner panic, his was measured and thoughtful. He acted, but never an overreaction. If he fought with Charlene's brothers, self-defense was a damn good reason for it.

She watched him struggle with fettuccine noodles, trying to cut them with a fork. "Let me show you something us Italians do." She picked up a clean spoon from his tray, motioning for him to give her the fork. "May I?" He handed it to her. "Put the spoon here, pick up your macaroni like this," she said, demonstrating how to twirl his pasta with the fork against the spoon base. She handed it back to him.

"Whenever I make spaghetti, I just break it up, so it fits in the pot and easier to eat."

She sucked in a breath, eyes wide, feigning shock, and horror. "Don't tell me that."

He laughed, then attempted her pasta trick. "I've twirled before. How'd I do?"

"You're a natural twirler. Don't ever break up your spaghetti again, and please don't tell me you like pineapple on your pizza, or that you've ever used ketchup as sauce. I don't want to know."

He noticed she hadn't touched much of her salad. "Is that some kind of cardinal sin?"

"Most definitely. *Nonna* would chase you out of her kitchen with a wooden spoon."

Sounds like *Nonnas* and *Abuelas* have something in common. 'Cept *Abuela* would use a *chancla*."

"What's that?"

"A lethal weapon," he laughed, then went on to describe it as a flip flop, sandal, hard slipper or basically any easily removable footwear used to discipline unruly children with pinpoint accuracy. "Didn't even use it. Just showed it. Set us straight every time."

Marie laughed too. "Who knew grannies were so violent?"

When their smiles faded, he asked, "How's life at home? You haven't said much about it. How was your spring break?"

Marie sighed. She didn't tell him about the family trip to Italy to visit relatives. "Mom and I argue more often because I've been pushing back recently. She's not happy about my little acts of rebellion. When we're not fighting, it's because I keep to myself. Tony is great, though. I think he tries to be the peacemaker. My dad is oblivious sometimes, but he just wants everyone to be happy and for life to go smoothly. How about you?"

"Did some ranch work, started a few horses. Helped at the restaurant. Hung out with friends. Same ole thing. Pretty uneventful."

She envied him. "Uneventful can be a good thing."

*   *   *

After practice the following evening Marie was surprised to find Cody at Apollo's stall. "Hey Marie."

Marie's brow quirked in surprise. "Hey, Cody."

He removed his cowboy hat, fumbling with the brim. He ran a hand through his blond hair. "Look, just want to say I'm sorry about Charlene. I don't know what gets into her sometimes. She's not a bad person. Just has some crazy notions about things."

Marie put Apollo into crossties and began unsaddling him. "That's not your fault, no need to apologize for her."

"Thought maybe you could give me some advice."

"Advice? I'm the one who fell apart before spring break. I'm hardly the person to ask for advice."

"You're a girl."

A short burst of laughter erupted from her throat. "Thanks for noticing."

Cody leaned against the stall door frame. "I mean, maybe you could give me some girl advice."

"Okay?" Marie set the saddle on the rack, picking up a brush. "I'm listening."

"I mean, I know Charlene and Santi have a bit of history, but that was last year. I know Santi, and it doesn't bother me one bit. But every time she acts like that, I don't know what to do. I just get mad. Santi's never done anything to her that I can tell. They were never serious, and it ended when her brothers tried to beat him up. Her family didn't want her dating him. That's not his fault. I don't understand her sometimes."

"Have you asked her why?"

"She comes up with all these things she's heard from her daddy."

Marie brushed out her horse. "People's beliefs can be very ingrained, especially when learned at a young age. It's not easy to change minds. Sometimes people learn things the hard way, through experiences. If they change at all."

"You don't think it's possible to change a person's beliefs?"

"Oh, I do. But it takes time, or an event, an idea, something that makes them see the world in a different way. An open mind, a desire to change. It won't happen overnight. How much patience do you have?"

Cody pushed away from the wall, allowing her room to maneuver around her horse. "That's just it. It's wearing thin. She's not just like that with Santi. It's other things too. She could start an argument in an empty house."

Andrew and Santi entered the far end of the barn. They stopped for a moment to watch Cody and Marie talking in the aisle. Andrew indicated the two with a lift of his chin. "Wonder what they're chatting about."

Santi shrugged. "No idea."

"Better make your move. Looks like Cody's got his eye on Marie," Andrew chuckled with a good-natured clap on Santi's back.

He knew Andrew was joking. There was nothing romantic happening between Cody and Marie. "I'll make a move when it's right," Santi assured him. He studied her as she moved about her horse and talked to Cody. Since he met her, he noticed she'd grown more open and relaxed around others. She smiled more, she talked more. She grew more beautiful to him with each passing day. When she wasn't with him, he'd often wonder what she'd think about an issue, idea, or event. He valued her thoughts and opinions. The harder he tried to deny the truth, the more it persisted. When she wasn't with him, he felt an emptiness, an aching void. There was something special about her from the very beginning. She saw him, knew him. *I see you too, Ms. Marie.*

Andrew cut into Santi's reverie. "Don't wait too long. Someone might beat you to it, and if not that, you'll always just be *the friend.* I know, I've been there."

Santi knew he wouldn't wait much longer. Marie was nothing like Charlene or any other girl he'd ever met.

Chapter Fourteen

L acy and Bryn convinced Marie to attend her first college bash. It was well-deserved, they said. She'd aced all her finals, summer break would be starting, and she was the barrel racing point leader of their team. Marie ran out of excuses not to attend. Too embarrassed to tell them how awkward and self-conscious she felt in these situations, she sucked it up, and told them she'd go. It was about time, she reasoned. She had to push herself out of her comfort zone. She could do this.

It took them two hours to get ready. "Blow dryers, curling irons, make-up, hairspray. I think we're ready." Bryn said. She threw an assortment of clothes on the dorm room bed. "I think you'd look great in this, Marie." She held up a black, off-the-shoulder crop top.

Marie eyed it. It was tiny. "I don't think it'll fit."

Bryn tossed it to her. "Of course, it will. Try it on."

Marie tried on the shirt. Thankfully, it had some stretch to it. With form-fitting, high-waisted, tapered leg jeans, it wasn't so bad, if she didn't mind feeling a bit exposed. Lacy tossed her a pair of black, high-heeled pumps, and large gold hoop earrings completed the look.

When they finished, all three crowded the bathroom mirror. "We got it going on, ladies. Like *Charlie's Angels*, or something." Bryn said.

Loud music pulsed; the sound filling the night air from the street. Within minutes of entering the large, off-campus brick home, they were each handed a drink. Marie lost sight of Lacy and Bryn amid a throng of wall-to-wall people. She sniffed the contents of her cup. It was strong. Certain it contained an unknown alcoholic concoction unsuitable for human consumption, she set the cup down on an end table, and stood near an open window in a living room corner, not knowing what to do or where to go. She calmed her nerves by breathing, and distracted herself, eyes sweeping the room, observing everyone. A group to her left played a drinking game, another group went outside to smoke weed, conversations drifted in and out, someone lamenting the recent death of Bob Marley. A few toga-wearing students were dancing. She wondered what was happening in the rest of the house.

"Hey there gorgeous, where've you been hiding?" Marie realized it was a bad idea to stand in a corner. A drunk young man in a bed sheet for a toga, green eyes glazed over, drink in hand, crowded into her personal space.

Marie's eyes darted left and right, searching for an escape route. It arrived unexpectedly.

"There you are!" Lacy threaded her way through clusters of people, reaching for Marie's wrist. "Come with me." Lacy and Bryn led her through the house, past the crowded kitchen and out to the backyard, brick patio. Relief. At least the air was cooler, and there were less people, and noise. A bonfire blazed in a stone pit, illuminating the area. A boombox played the latest tunes.

"Santi's here," Bryn whispered in Marie's ear as they grew closer to where the others congregated. "Wait till he sees you." She waggled her eyebrows, comically.

Why Bryn's statement should affect her, she didn't know. Marie's anxiety level rose to eleven. Any thread of confidence she possessed upon arrival, fractured. It became difficult to walk in high heels. "What?" Suddenly she wished to go back to the safety of her dorm room with her books and comfortable clothes.

She turned panicked eyes to Lacy, who smiled as though she knew a juicy secret. "You look beautiful. It'll be fine."

Marie wondered why they would think anything was going on between her and Santi. "We're just friends, really," she protested.

"Uh huh," Bryn responded, unconvinced. "All those Sunday morning trail rides?"

"All those study dates?" Lacy added.

The study time together. The Sunday morning rides. A ritual they continued when the team was not on the road competing. Those were treasured. It's where Marie learned that his favorite ice cream was butter pecan, that he was a closet AC/DC fan, but that the greatest album ever made was Stevie Wonder's *Songs in the Key of Life*. He hated the disco craze but liked to dance, he loved fast cars and motorcycles. His favorite food was Italian.

Santi learned that she loved to cook and bake, her favorite color was purple, her favorite bands were Journey, Queen, and Earth, Wind, and Fire. She loved to read, wrote bad poetry, didn't like roller coaster rides, would never jump out of a perfectly good airplane to skydive, and had never been on a motorcycle in her life. And how crazy was it, that her favorite food was Mexican.

Realization dawned like a glimmering light beneath a lifting fog. Santi was her best friend. Always there for her. Her calm in a storm, her anchor. How simple would it be to slide into a physical relationship with him. She often reminded herself that she had no time for romantic attachments. Yet the hours she spent with Santi were filled with discovery. She learned not only about him, but about herself as well. Did he feel the same? She didn't dare believe. She didn't think she could put herself in a position to find out and risk embarrassment and shame if he didn't.

"Woah, ladies, lookin' sharp!" Kenny boomed, raising a beer can in salute.

"Damn, look who's here. Our very own rodeo queens," Andrew added. He walked over, removing his cowboy hat offering them an exaggerated bow. "At your service." Bryn and Lacy laughed. Marie offered him a smile.

Cody and Charlene were on a blanket in the grass, making out some distance away, too occupied to greet anyone.

Several unfamiliar people also milled about, talking, laughing, drinking. Marie spied Santi surrounded by three girls she didn't know. For all she dreaded seeing him, protested anything but friendship between them, her heart sank into her stomach. Santi and one of the girls seemed engrossed in deep conversation. The other two stared, dazedly hanging on his every word. The girls giggled at something he said, then one touched his arm in a flirtatious, too familiar manner. Marie looked away, as an unwanted thought entered her brain. *Don't touch my man.* She told herself, it was none of her concern. Santi was free to speak to and flirt with whomever he wished. She had her answer. It was safer not to reveal how she felt. He was her friend. Nothing more. *I am not a hen.*

Bryn went to the ice-filled metal tub, fishing out bottled wine coolers from it. "This is more my style." She handed a cold, dripping wet bottle to Marie, and one to Lacy. Unscrewing the lid, she took a sip. "Now that's good, like sparkly juice, and it won't get you shitfaced, drunk."

They moved closer to the bonfire, all three taking seats along a brick ledge. Marie was quiet, watching, listening to the various conversations, taking small sips of her wine cooler. She avoided looking for Santi, afraid of her own emotional reaction to what she might see. She wished she could leave. She couldn't be like other party goers and didn't understand why she felt so out of place. It wasn't that she didn't like Bryn and Lacy or even Kenny and Andrew. She did. Except for Charlene, who chose to isolate herself with Cody, they'd all become close over the past year. She enjoyed their company. She considered them friends.

It was the need to be in control of herself, her actions, her surroundings. The notion that she needed to be perfect at all times, and that others would judge her if she wasn't. Maybe she was more like her mother than she cared to admit. Marie had never been out of control.

Never let loose. Riding her horse was her freedom. Reading a book was her escape.

"Evening, Ms. Marie." Santi saw her from a distance when she first arrived. She took his breath away. He couldn't excuse himself fast enough from conversation with a classmate who could talk the hide off a cow. He'd always thought Marie was pretty, but he'd never seen her dressed and made-up like this, surely the influence of Lacy and Bryn. She was a stone-cold knockout, all bared shoulders, and a hint of delectable cleavage. But Santi saw beneath the made-up façade. He knew every expression of her face. Knew her well enough to see that she was anxious, and unsure of herself. A beautiful fish out of water.

His disarming grin made her smile. "Hello, Santi."

"We're here too, Santi," Bryn feigned offence.

Santi tore his gaze away from Marie for a fleeting moment. "Hello ladies. Ya'll look beautiful this evening."

"Nice recovery," Lacy quipped.

"Such a gentleman," Bryn moved over, nudging Lacy to give Santi space to sit next to Marie.

He didn't sit. "Marie, come walk with me?" He extended his hand, palm up, an invitation. "I need to talk to you about a paper I have to write."

Her brows knit. Visibly deflated, she asked, "A paper?" Why would he need to discuss that now, at a party?

Lacy and Bryn giggled at Marie's confusion. Santi trying to be smooth, all right.

Marie hesitated, set down her wine cooler, then placed her hand in his.

He pulled her up, his eyes raked over her from head to toe. "Not used to you being this tall."

She glanced down at her feet. "It's the heels," she responded, stating the obvious.

"Long as you can walk in them," he grinned. Maintaining his hold of her hand, he led her away.

Marie looked back to watch Bryn and Lacy making silly faces and giving a thumbs up.

They left the yard, heading toward the front of the house to the street. "Where are we going?" she asked. They passed a few other party-going students on the sidewalk. Voices, laughter, and music floated on the night breeze.

"Nowhere special. Figured you needed to get out of there for a minute."

"What about your paper?"

"There's no paper."

She understood now that he used the excuse to get her away from the crowd and to allow her to save face. "How well you know me. You can tell that bad, huh?"

"Yup."

The shoes pinched her feet and rubbed the backs of her heels. She stopped near a streetlight under the lacy canopy of a large oak. He released her hand. "This.

This isn't me." She gestured to herself, referring to the sexy snug-fitting outfit. She kicked off the high heels, and removed the earrings, placing them in her little shoulder bag. Her voice deflated. "I'm sorry, I thought I could do this." She pulled out some tissue to blot the bright red lipstick from her mouth. "I don't know why I thought I could pull off the charade. I don't know what's wrong with me." She covered her face, ashamed of her own breakdown, and perceived imperfections. Why couldn't she be like everyone else?

Santi reached for her, encircling her in his arms. "Hey. Hey nothing's wrong with you," he soothed. "Not every day feels like a frat party. It's not everybody's cup of tea."

Marie stepped back, collecting herself. She felt foolish. "I'm sorry. You didn't need to leave the party because of me. We can go back."

Santi thought she apologized too much for things that were not her fault, or out of her control. "I want to know who's telling you you're not beautiful." To anyone who didn't know her, there would be no reason for her to feel awkward or inadequate. Someone, somewhere put that notion in her head. He suspected it was her mother.

Her brows furrowed, confused by his statement. "I don't know what you mean."

His expression stilled and grew serious. "You're the prettiest, sweetest girl at that party," his voice was tinged with wonder, as though it were so obvious, that anyone could see it but her.

"Don't say that."

She didn't believe him. He turned away, looking back at her over his shoulder. "It's true. Don't need to be perfect, Marie. Just need to be you. That's more than enough. You're more than enough."

Marie drew close, placing her hand on his arm. "Thank you, Santi. I know you're being a friend, trying to make me feel better, but you don't have to-"

Santi reached for the small hand on his arm, holding it. He faced her, pulling her toward him with the movement. "Not trying to be a friend, Marie." His eyes held hers. He lifted the opposite hand to cradle her cheek, smoothing the hair back from her face.

His touch caused her to lose all thought. She tried to throttle the dizzying current racing through her. Her skin tingled. Her eyelids fluttered closed as he lowered his mouth to hers. Parting her lips, she raised herself to meet his kiss. His kiss was warm, gentle, exploring, tongue rimming her lips. He brought her hand to rest over his shoulder. Her fingers threaded the hair at the nape of his neck. Delicious sensations coiled in her belly.

Raising his mouth from hers, his eyes searched her face as though he could reach into her thoughts. "Been wanting to do that for a while."

"You have?" she asked, breathless.

"Yup." His lips recaptured hers, more demanding this time. Her response was sweet as wild honey. He pulled her close, hand resting at the curve of her waist where the crop top exposed smooth skin.

"Really? Since when?"

"Since I saw you sitting in the pasture with your nose in a book."

"That was fall semester."

"I know."

"You're very patient."

He shrugged lightly. "We didn't know each other well, and some things are worth waiting for. You weren't ready. Maybe I wasn't either."

"And we are now?"

He kissed her with a hunger that belied his outward calm. His long slow kisses clouded her brain. They parted a few inches. "You tell me."

Marie was surprised at her own eager response. She drew his face to hers, pressing her open lips to his. "Yes. Yes, yes," she whispered between kisses showered around her lips and along her jaw.

They broke apart as sirens sounded in the distance, followed by the appearance of flashing lights. Three squad cars, coming in fast. Cops were about to bust up a party. "Come on," he grabbed her hand, pulling her with him.

"Wait!" Marie ran back a few steps to retrieve the discarded high heels. "They're Lacy's."

He pulled her along at a run for a short distance, until they reached his car.

"I get to sit in the famous Camaro?" she joked. It was a beautiful car, a 1976 model, blue with two thick, white racing stripes down the hood.

He chuckled. "Get in, girl." He opened the door for her, then trotted around to the driver's side. Once settled in, they watched as police vehicles came to a screeching halt, and groups of students ran helter-skelter from the direction of the party.

"I hope our team is okay," Marie said, rubbing her foot. She brushed away a tiny mark of blood where she'd stepped on a pebble. She longed for her tennis shoes or riding boots. She glanced at Santi, "Should we leave?"

"Not yet. I love this car, but it's a cop magnet, especially when they see me driving it." His eyes met hers. "Worse if they see you in here with me, right now."

Marie didn't need to ask why. She must look a disheveled mess. She imagined smeared make-up and runny mascara from crying. It might give cops the wrong impression, especially if they were looking for wayward college kids. "I'm sorry."

"Not your fault." He reached for her hand, threading their fingers, noting the differences between them. Her hand was small and pale, his larger, darker than hers. He stroked the back of her hand with his thumb. "Someone

called in about the party. Best for us to sit tight a bit."
He leaned over the center console between them, tipped
her chin, pressing a soft kiss to her lips.

"I'm going back to Chicago tomorrow."

Santi touched his forehead to hers. "I know. My
timing is shit."

Marie smiled. "No. You were right. I wasn't ready.
Your timing is fine. I'll miss our Sunday rides. I'll miss
you."

"Stay in Texas over the summer."

She lifted her head. "How would I explain that to my
parents?"

"Tell them you found a job here, working at a Tex-
Mex restaurant."

"But, my mother... I don't always have a choice."

"There's always a choice."

She sighed. "You don't know my mother."

He sat back, contemplative. He had a pretty good
idea about her mother. "Since my dad died, my mom's
had to run the show. It's not always easy. If the
restaurant doesn't do well, it affects my whole family.
It's all we've got left, so I help when I can. Family
first."

"Not only does my mom run the show, she tries to run
everyone else's show too. If she ever got into politics,
I'd be afraid."

Santi didn't doubt her mother's stringency and authority. He didn't want to talk about their mothers. He wanted to kiss her again. So, he did.

A frantic rapping on the window jolted them apart. "Santi! Santi! Open up!"

Marie swung the door open to find Kenny, Andrew, Lacy, and Bryn. Pushing her seat forward, they all piled into the back, a tight squeeze. They each began talking at once.

"Oh man," Kenny was out of breath. "Thank you."

"They almost got us!" Bryn cried.

"These two hid in the bushes," Andrew said referring to the girls. He laughed. "It was crazy!"

"They busted somebody for pot, closed the whole party down."

"Some underaged kids got picked up too."

"We're not interrupting anything, are we? We saw your car, figured we could get out of here," Lacy added.

"They were working on Santi's paper," Bryn joked.

"What's your paper about?" Andrew asked. "Biology? Anatomy?" His question brought another round of hoots and laughter. Everyone knew what Santi and Marie were doing.

Marie had to smile too. "We were waiting for the cops to leave," she responded innocently.

"That's smart. They should be cutting out soon. Shook most everyone down or ran everyone off."

"You guys left at the perfect time."

"What happened to Cody and Charlene?"

"No idea. We hid, and then took off when we had the chance."

"Shit, here they come, here they come," Lacy panicked.

They all hunkered down as the first squad car passed. Santi rolled the window down a crack, as the inside of the car became stifling. Marie did the same from the passenger side. The other two police cars passed. Still, they waited.

Santi started the Camaro, pulling away from the curb.

"Drive nonchalant-like." Kenny urged.

"How does one drive nonchalantly?"

"Ya'll know what I mean."

Santi's nonchalant driving got them all back to campus without incident. They said their goodnights and good-byes. The girls exchanged phone numbers, wished each other a great summer, and would keep in touch until they saw each other again in the fall.

Santi walked a barefoot Marie back to her dorm room. He faced her, capturing her hands in his. "So…."

"So…." Marie looked down at her bare feet. "It's going to be weird not seeing you."

She felt Santi's arms come up, enfolding her. Marie wrapped her arms around his waist, melting against his chest. They stood this way for a time, each silently relishing the moment.

"Give me your pen, and something to write on."

She fished out a pen from her little purse but had no paper. She held out her hand. He took it, writing the numbers on her palm. "That's the restaurant number. Sorry to say I don't know about a working home number. Sometimes we have one, sometimes we don't."

She reached for his hand and did the same. "That's my home phone. If I'm there, I'll answer."

He pulled her close, pressing soft lips to her forehead. "You could come up to Chicago."

"I could. Would your parents let me stay at your place? I don't know anyone else living there."

"I don't know. If I stayed in Texas for the summer, I might be able to ask Bryn or Lacy. Would your mom let me stay at your house?"

He shrugged. "Don't know. She might be more open to it."

Ultimately, they both knew they'd spend the summer apart, and count the days until they could see each other again.

Marie watched him leave. Before she could open the door, he'd turned around, trotting back.

He wrapped her up in his arms, kissing her long and hard. He left her senseless. "That's one to go home on."

Chapter Fifteen

Liberty Creek University
Fall 1981 – Winter 1982

S ummer passed too slowly. All Marie cared about, all she wanted was to see Santi again. They were able to keep in touch sporadically over the summer. A few long nights spent talking on the phone about anything and everything, until one or the other fell asleep. Her mother asked questions, Marie answered them as vaguely as possible. She was talking to friends. She didn't lie, she reasoned. Santi was her friend. A friend who had the ability to make her heart do backflips, a friend whose kisses made her head spin and her knees weak.

This year, Marie would have more freedom. Her brother graduated. Her mother didn't like not having him in Texas to keep an eye out for Marie. Tony never interfered, but Marie admitted it was comforting to know he was nearby. Arrangements were made to have Apollo sent to the university before Marie's arrival. She arrived on campus Thursday afternoon before the start of the new semester. She put her bags in the dorm room and headed for the barn, nervous excitement filling her every step. She saw him at the far end of the aisle grooming Rebelde. He lifted his head, stopping mid-motion. Tossing the brush, he stepped out in front of his horse, waiting for her. Marie ran past wheelbarrows, blurting quick greetings to rodeo teammates as she passed them. She flew into Santi's arms as he swept her up, lifting her off her feet.

She kissed and kissed him. "I've missed you."

"I missed you too," he murmured between kisses.

"It's about time!" Someone shouted.

"Woohoo!"

"Hey, don't be like Cody and Charlene!" Loud guffaws of laughter followed. Cody and Charlene graduated last May.

Marie smiled against his lips. "Goodness, no."

Santi set her on her feet, both arms holding her against him, as he lifted his head to address their teammates. "All right folks, show's over!" He called back, grinning from ear to ear.

"Dang, it was just gettin' good!" Kenny hollered.

Santi looked down at her, dark eyes bright with adoration. "Hello, beautiful. How you doing?"

Marie warmed under his regard, cheeks flushed crimson. "Hello. Much better now. You?"

"I'm so happy right now, if I felt any better, I'd think it was a setup."

Marie laughed. "No set up. Just me. How long have you been here?"

"Got in yesterday. There's some new blood trying out for the team. Coach asked me to help show them around."

"How's the new blood look?"

He laughed. "Same way we did when we first arrived. Green."

"You were never green. I need to check on Apollo."

"He's good, settling in. I put him in the stall next to Rebelde."

Marie haltered Apollo, then led him out of his stall. "Thank you for always looking out for him."

"Always." Santi finished brushing out his horse, returning him to the stall. "There's a shindig over at Ferguson ranch on Saturday, would you like to go with me?"

"Is that where you work?" Marie picked up a rubber curry comb and began grooming her horse.

Santi grabbed a tail brush and joined her. "Yup. If you don't mind hanging around some cowboys and families. We don't have to stay long."

"Sure, I'd love to. We can stay as long as you'd like. I'm working on the whole weirdness about large gatherings. This will be an opportunity to practice."

"Let me know if you feel uncomfortable."

"I need to get over my anxiety about such things. I'll be fine."

"Just the same, if you're not enjoying yourself, let me know."

"I'm responsible for my own good time."

He flashed a grin. "Yes, ma'am." After an indecisive pause he added, "My family will be there."

Marie stopped the brush mid-stroke. "Your family? Your mom?"

"Yup. Brother and sister too." A fleeting look of apprehension crossed her features. Santi rounded Apollo's backside reaching for her, touching soft fingertips over her cheek. "I'd like them to meet you, that is, if you're okay with it."

Her mouth formed an uncertain smile. "Oh boy."

"You trust me?" He asked on a half-whisper.

She bound her gaze to his. "Yes."

Santi pulled her in for a quick kiss on the lips. "Don't worry."

Marie agonized over what to wear. If she were to meet Santi's family, she wanted to make a good impression. Jeans and boots? A dress? Santi wasn't helpful, suggesting she wear whatever made her comfortable. Marie chose the jeans with a button-down cream blouse. She opted for keeping her hair loose, light makeup, and simple earrings. She learned that his family would be there setting up their own catering canopy, offering a sampling of dishes from their restaurant, *La Frontera*.

They arrived at the Ferguson ranch before noon. The grounds around the main ranch house were flurry of activity and people. Long tables were arranged with folding chairs near several canopies along the edges creating an outer rectangle-shaped perimeter. There were barrel type grills billowing smoke, the scent of roasting meats wafted on the air. A large area in the center of the rectangle was sectioned off by portable livestock panels for the upcoming rodeo demonstrations.

It wasn't as horrible as she feared. Santi prepared her. Not to be alarmed by multiple questions from his mother, it was normal mom being mom. Expect to be asked to dance by any male, even if you don't know them or the dance steps. Expect loud music, loud talking, loud laughter. She reminded him that she was Italian. He introduced her to the family and countless other people, ranch workers and even Mr. Ferguson, the ranch owner. She knew she'd never remember everyone's names. She thought his sister Susana might be eleven or twelve, his brother Erik, possibly fourteen or fifteen. Once food was dispensed, they all sat together at one of the long tables, enjoying a meal.

"Where are you from, Marie?" Santi's mother asked after swallowing a forkful of rice. She was a small woman, middle-aged. Her hair was dark, interspersed with gray strands. It was tied neatly in a spiral bun at the back of her head.

"Chicago, born and raised."

"And your family?"

"Ah, well my parents are originally from Naples, Italy. They arrived in the U.S. as young children."

"You speak Italian?"

"A little. Not very well. I understand most of it, though."

"Spanish and Italian are a little bit similar. Years ago, I had an Italian work friend. I could understand many words."

"Santi says you're a good barrel racer," his brother Erik chimed in. "Best on the team."

She blushed. "I try to be," she shrugged. "Takes lots of practice, and Santi gives me pointers."

"What does your family do?" Irma Rivera cut in.

"Do?"

Santi sent his mother a look that asked her to go easy on Marie. "Her dad owns a construction company, *mamá*."

Mrs. Rivera seemed impressed by this, offering Marie a nod and a small smile. "Good." She motioned to the rice, beans, and cheese quesadillas. "I hope you enjoy them. Made from our restaurant."

"Delicious. It's my favorite."

Mrs. Rivera asked more questions about what Marie was studying in school and what she hoped to do after graduation. It felt like a job interview. Marie answered every question politely, even if she felt a bit unnerved.

After the feasting, the rodeo demonstrations and mini competitions began. Santi was part of it. He didn't wear the traditional sombrero or charro costume, opting for his usual cowboy hat, but he did wear a brightly colored serape shawl over his vest. Marie cheered along with the crowd when he and others showed off their dancing horses, performing much like she'd seen him that first day. She learned that there was a slim difference between a vaquero and a charro. A vaquero was a cowboy who worked cattle. A charro was one who competed or performed in a *charreada*, a Mexican rodeo. Charros were also highly skilled horsemen. They usually wore costumes and sombreros, performing with lariats, demonstrating their roping skills. They rode broncs, and bulls. The two words had grown to become interchangeable at times.

Marie especially loved watching the local escaramuza team perform. Eight women dressed in identical, colorfully hand-embroidered, flouncy Mexican dresses rode their horses side-saddle in a choreographed display of difficult riding maneuvers. Like a drill team, they came together, separated, turned, spun, all in synchronized movements performed to music. It was beautiful to watch.

As afternoon turned to evening, the dancing began. The corral panels were removed, and the demonstration area was dragged. Some couples joined up on the makeshift dance floor, which consisted of spliced together pieces of finished plywood set out over a section of the former arena. Marie watched as Susana grabbed her eldest brother's hand, leading him out onto the dance space. She'd never seen Santi dance before, clapping and laughing as she watched him twirl his little sister.

Irma Rivera wasn't sure what to make of this girl, but Santi seemed to care for her. He'd never introduced a girlfriend to the family before. She knew he met Marie at school, and that they'd kept in touch over the summer, but it seemed this young woman had stolen her son's heart. It made her happy and sad all at once. She nudged her son Erik, motioning for him to ask Marie to dance.

When Erik offered to escort her to the dance floor, Marie froze. "I'm afraid I don't know the dance steps," she said.

"I'll teach you. This is a cumbia. It's pretty simple, come on," he encouraged.

They took up a spot next to Santi and Susana. Marie followed Erik's instruction. Right foot back on a pivot, then back to center, left foot back and repeat. One, two three, slight pause on four, five, six, seven, pause on eight. After a few missteps she got the hang of it. Erik and Santi switched partners. Santi grasped her hands, holding them between their bodies.

"No fancy turns, I can't do that yet," she laughed.

He returned the smile. "You're doing great."

They returned to their seats at the table for a brief respite from dancing. Santi offered to get Marie something cool to drink. As he made his way to the area where ice chests stored a variety of beverages, a familiar face greeted him.

"Santi, you forgot about me?" Hand on her hip, she was still dressed in her escaramuza performance costume. A pink flower in her tied-up hair, her make-up perfect. She and Santi got together a few times when neither of them had any other attachments. The arrangement suited them both. No strings, no questions.

"Hey Raquel, it's been a long while, sorry."

"I can see why." Raquel indicated Marie with a vague motion of her hand and a slight tilt of her head.

Santi's eyes followed where she indicated before turning back to Raquel. "That's Marie. She loved your performance. Thinks y'all are amazing."

"Hm. Is it serious?"

He glanced back at Marie, who had moved onto a corner of the plywood dance floor. Susana and Erik were teaching her new dance steps. Erik twirled her, she hesitated in her step, then laughed at her own clumsy movement. He loved seeing her relaxed and carefree, even if for a moment. She was beautiful. Facing Raquel he said, "Yes."

Raquel watched him watching the girl, Marie. His handsome face softened, a slow smile turned the corners of his mouth. The look of adoration in his eyes as he focused on Marie was unmistakable. He never looked at her that way. She realized he never would. "Be careful, Santi. Remember what happened last time?"

He knew she was referring to Charlene. "I'm not worried."

She lifted her shoulder, her disappointment, evident. "Guess I'll see you around."

He tipped his cowboy hat, offering her a brief smile. "Thanks, Raquel."

Santi brought Marie a bottled Coke. She accepted it gratefully, taking a few sips before a slow song started. "Come on." He gave her a second to set the bottle down. He took her hand and drew her close, swaying her into a dance. Marie's brain didn't know what to do, but her body did.

Other couples joined them on the dance floor. Marie noticed a group of young women, dressed in colorful Mexican costume. The escaramuza team. They appeared to be milling together at the opposite end of the dance floor, watching Santi and Marie, talking, giggling, gesturing. Marie grew uncomfortable.

Santi took her hands, placing them up over his shoulders, intimately he pulled her against him until their lower bodies swayed in unison. "Don't worry about them. They've got nothing better to do but *chismear*."

She guessed at the meaning of the Spanish word. "We could give them something to talk about," she suggested.

A soft, short laugh burst from his throat. "I would, but my mother's right over there." He pressed a kiss to her forehead. Innocent, sweet, but enough to let everyone know their relationship status.

As the night wound down, Marie helped the Rivera family put away and pack up their catering tent. When the pick-up truck was loaded and ready to go, Santi and Marie prepared to return to Liberty Creek campus.

"It was nice meeting you, Marie," Susana said, offering her a shy, one-armed hug.

"It was great to meet you too. Thank you for the dance lessons."

"I'm a better teacher than Erik," she joked.

"Hey, I'm a great teacher," Erik defended.

"Erik, Susa, in the truck you two, time to go." Mrs. Rivera approached Santi and Marie. She eyed them for a moment, before reaching for each of them in a warm hug. "Be safe driving back to school."

"I will, *mami*."

"Watch out for each other." She opened the driver's side door. "Call me at the restaurant tomorrow, *mijo*. So I know you got back safe."

On the drive back to campus Santi reached for her hand, interlacing their fingers.

"How'd I do?" Marie asked.

He grinned. "You worry too much. They like you," he assured her.

"How can you tell?"

"Never brought any girl to meet them before. They know you're special to me." He kissed her deeply at the first stop light. "Been wanting to do that all day."

Just before they reached Liberty Creek, Santi pulled the Camaro into an area just off the beaten roadway. There was a lagoon and a walking path, but no one was out walking at this time of night. It was known as a make-out spot, and three or four other cars were already parked. They moved to the back seat.

Marie's heart pounded as they settled in, his kisses drugging her. Their hands explored and caressed over clothing.

"I've never….," she whispered as his lips blazed a trail down to the pulse at her throat, a gentle hand caressed a breast over her blouse.

"It's okay. We don't have to do any more than this," he breathed against her skin. He set her at ease, resting his head against her breast. Marie stroked his hair.

They held one another, kissing, touching, talking into the night.

Days fell into a routine, early morning workouts, practices, late nights at the library, or in the back seat of Santi's Camaro. Those nights were filled with kisses, caresses, and intimate conversations.

Marie went home for Christmas. Weeks spent away from Santi were agonizing. The new year came and went. Marie dreamed of a time when she could be on her own, independent, able to live her life as she wished. Upcoming graduation would set her free. Free to be her own person, free to be with Santi.

Chapter Sixteen

Spring, 1982

Tony watched television in the dimness of the living room, wearing comfortable track pants and a t-shirt, stocking feet poised on the coffee table. "No way," he said to the news anchor. John Belushi had died of an overdose. Thinking his father was in the kitchen, he pushed himself up from the sofa. His dad liked Belushi. "Hey dad, did you hear about…?" His voice trailed off, finding his mother instead talking to someone on the phone.

Carla was agitated. "What do you mean you're not coming home for Spring break?" She paced in the kitchen as far as the cord would allow, cigarette smoke trailing her.

"Is that Marie?" Tony asked.

Carla held up a hand to silence him as she listened. "But… you'll be working at a restaurant? Santiago's family. No, Marie. I won't allow it. You're coming home for Spring break, and that's final."

"Ma," Tony interjected.

Carla pressed the receiver against her chest to muffle her voice. "Tony, this is none of your concern."

"I've met Santiago, he's a good guy. It's her boyfriend. Let her stay in Texas."

"I know he's her boyfriend and it's inappropriate for her to stay there with him. Her family comes first." Carla returned the receiver to her ear. "I *am* listening." After a moment of silence, she continued. "I'll speak to your father about this." Carla hung up the phone none too gently. She turned to her son. "Looks like we're going to Texas next week." Carla then pivoted, storming out of the kitchen. "We'll see what this Santiago business is all about. Should have never allowed her to go away to school."

Marie hung up the restaurant phone. "She's not happy."

"Did you invite them to visit down here? Meet my family?"

"I did. She's not happy." Marie's throat burned as she held back tears. Santi wrapped his arms around her. "Nothing I do or say makes her happy."

"You can't make people happy. It's a choice they make for themselves."

"And I'm choosing to do what makes me happy. She hates that."

"It's a change for her. Nobody likes change."

"It's control. She doesn't like not being in control."

"Hm. Sounds familiar."

Marie lifted her head from his chest and let go with a short laugh. "I'm not that bad, am I?"

"No." Santi wiped her tears away with his thumbs. "Let's see what happens. They'll come down; we'll show 'em some Texas hospitality. They'll enjoy themselves, and everything'll be hunky dory. They might even like me a little bit."

"My brother likes you."

"See? We've got this."

Vincent, Carla, and Anthony Rossi flew down to San Antonio the following week. Marie was nervous, certain her mother would find fault in anything and everything.

*   *   *

Santiago never brought girls around the house, though Irma was certain that with her son's looks and charm, there was no shortage. Marie seemed a sweet girl if not a bit shy. Not someone Irma expected her son to date.

Marie proved to be helpful and kind. Irma discovered that the girl loved to cook, and they spent a few evenings in the kitchen together teaching each other either Italian or Tex-Mex dishes. Marie offered to help at the restaurant, surprising Irma, since Marie didn't expect payment. Spending time with Santi seemed enough. Marie was eager to make a good impression. Eager to please.

When Marie's parents arrived, Mrs. Rivera believed she'd seen a glimpse of the girl's home life. After witnessing the interaction between mother and daughter, Irma came to a decision.

It was agreed to use the restaurant space as a gathering for the first dinner together. Marie was grateful, and anxious. She helped with food prep, teasing Santi about how well he knew his way around a kitchen. Of course, he knew. He'd grown up with it.

Carla Rossi stepped into the entryway of *La Frontera,* surveying her surroundings. The place was quaint, decorated with Mexican and cowboy regalia, colorful Mexican tapestries adorned the walls. Mexican Talavera tiles trimmed the arched entryway. Not overstated but dated. Furnishings were worn, but the terra cotta floors were clean, and everything appeared neat and orderly. Soft Latin music played from hidden speakers.

A young Mexican man exited the double doors of the kitchen area, approaching her with a handsome smile. "Hello Mrs. Rossi, Mr. Rossi. Hey Tony. It's great to have you here. Please come inside." He gestured to the long table, set meticulously. "Sit anywhere you'd like. Marie's in the kitchen. I'll let her know you're here."

Carla bristled. "In the kitchen? Hm. Are you a waiter here? I'd like to see my daughter, please."

"Yes, ma'am. Forgive me for not introducing myself. I'm Santiago Rivera. My family owns this place." He extended his hand to her. Carla ignored it. She scrutinized him. He was tall, good-looking. She knew his type. So, this was Marie's boyfriend. A waiter. A cowboy.

"Hey Santi," Tony stepped up, and the two shook hands. "Good to see you again. Nice place you have here."

"Good to meet you Santiago," Mr. Rossi moved forward, shaking the younger man's hand as well. "Smells heavenly in here. I'm starved."

"Nice to meet you too. I hope you enjoy our specialties. Marie's been looking forward to having us all together." Anxious was more like it, but Santi kept that to himself.

"Please tell Marie we're here," Carla said. Santi left. Carla turned a slow circle, her heels clicking with every step, scrutinizing the place while Mr. Rossi and Tony took seats at the table.

"How do I look?" Marie asked. She removed her apron, then smoothed her hair.

Santi pressed a quick kiss to her lips. "Beautiful."

"Hey, none of that in the kitchen," Irma chided playfully. "Come let's go meet your family. Erik, Susa, *vámonos*."

Irma swept into the main dining area, her smile bright and genuine. The kitchen crew consisting of her children and Marie filed out behind her. "Mr. and Mrs. Rossi, Mr. Tony, welcome to *La Frontera, es un placer conocerles*."

As the group exited the kitchen, both Rossi men rose from their seats. Mr. Rossi didn't miss a beat. He took her hand in greeting, his smile warm. "*Il piacere è nostro, signora*."

"Ah! I understood that!" Mrs. Rivera laughed. "Spanish and Italian. I think we can understand each other a little bit, no?" She turned to introduce Erik, Susana, and Santiago. Greetings were exchanged all around.

Carla managed to smile. "It's a pleasure to meet you, Mrs. Rivera. Good to meet all of you."

Marie stepped forward to hug her parents. Her mother's stiff body posture contrasted with her father's warm, genuine embrace.

Irma directed them back to the table. "Please, please. Have a seat. Food will be coming."

Susana and Erik brought out quesadillas stuffed with cheese, green chiles, and onion, served with guacamole, sour cream & tomatoes. Main courses included grilled fajita steak and chicken served with flour and corn tortillas, Mexican rice, and refried beans. Everyone passed serving plates and made jovial small talk.

"This is delicious, Mrs. Rivera. I love Mexican food." Mr. Rossi said.

"It's Tex-Mex, actually. There's a little bit of difference," Irma responded. "I'm so happy you like it."

"Marie's been eating too much Mexican food," Carla commented absently.

Marie swallowed a bite of her steak, then placed her fork on her plate, silent.

"Her weight fluctuates so much," Mrs. Rossi continued as though she needed to further explain her comment.

"Ma," Marie muttered. *Please stop.*

"She's perfect. Healthy," Santi chimed in.

"Leave her be, Carla. Let's enjoy this feast, and good company," Mr. Rossi defended.

Carla decided to change the subject. "Tell me, Santiago, what do you plan to do after graduation? Wait tables?"

"No ma'am. Got some things lined up. Potential employers looking for engineering graduates. Technology is advancing at a fast clip. They need engineers from all fields."

"And where do you plan to live?"

"I'm flexible. Haven't thought about it, but anywhere Marie is, and my family. That's what's important."

Mr. Rossi raised his sangria glass. "Nothing more important than family."

"Exactly," Irma raised her glass as well.

Carla pinned her daughter with a look. "Surely you're not thinking of staying in Texas after graduation, Marie."

"I'm applying for teaching licenses in both Texas and Illinois. I have to pass licensure exams."

Carla's thoughts turned sour. No. This would not do. Her daughter would not stay in Texas for a boy. She belonged in Chicago with her family.

"I'm hoping to save enough money to buy my own land. That way I can still work with horses as a side job."

"He's very good!" Susana piped in.

"Just like his *papá*," Irma added.

Carla wasn't impressed. Maybe down here in Podunk Nowhere, Texas being good with horses meant something. Where she was from, it meant nothing. She didn't like where this relationship was headed. Marie should be married to a young man of means and wealth, not a penniless immigrant who waited tables and trained horses. A cowboy. He'd probably fed her with his delusions about owning land. Anything involving horses was a sure way to Marie's heart.

Marie lost her appetite. Santi noticed that she hadn't touched any of her food, since Carla's comment about weight. He reached under the table, giving her hand a gentle squeeze. She returned the gesture, offering him a soft smile of gratitude.

Irma observed the interaction between mother and daughter. The way Marie minimized herself in her mother's presence. The shyness, the occasional awkwardness, and the people pleasing character. It made sense. She'd learned to navigate emotional mine fields in order to avoid anger, judgment, and censure from her mother. Irma's heart went out to the girl, and from that evening onward, she decided that no matter what happened between her son and this young woman, she would take Marie under her wing.

Marie's parents remained in San Antonio for a few more days. Tony and Santi bonded over cars, baseball, and soccer. Tony took the Camaro for a spin. They spent an afternoon in the garage giving it an oil change and a tune-up. On the last day, the Rossi family stopped by the house to say good-bye. Mr. Rossi and Tony sat in the rental car they'd take to the airport waiting for Carla, who stayed behind for a few moments. Carla thanked Irma for her hospitality. She asked about the restaurant and whether she'd consider investors. The food was amazing, but the place could use an upgrade, and business could be improved. Irma confessed that they were struggling.

"I can help," Carla said.

"How?"

"Consider me as an investor."

"I don't know what that would mean."

"It means I invest in your restaurant, like a partnership or even a loan. You use the money to make the necessary upgrades, advertising, marketing. I'd receive a small percentage for my investment. Think about it. I'd really like to help. Or, better yet, we can arrange a loan you can pay back in installments. Once the restaurant is profitable again, you'll be able to pay it off in no time."

Irma wasn't sure. Of course, she could use the help. *La Frontera* was floundering. "I'll think about it. Thank you."

Irma went over the books three times that night. They wouldn't survive much longer. She didn't know what to tell her children. If *La Frontera* went under, they'd lose everything, the restaurant and possibly their home. She fished out the slip of paper from her pocket, picked up the phone and dialed the number written there. "Hello, Carla? It's Irma. Yes. I've decided to accept your offer."

Chapter Seventeen

Spring, 1982

They seized any free moments they could to spend alone. The first time wasn't what Marie expected. Santi was gentle and slow, but aside from all the delicious kissing and touching and caressing, there was nothing pleasurable about it for her. He apologized profusely for hurting her, kissing away her doubts, fears, and pain. He promised it would be better. He didn't lie. Each time was better than the last. He showed her how to touch him, she showed him what she liked. Together they explored and learned one another's bodies. They couldn't get enough of one another. Urgent and passionate or slow and sweet and everything in-between.

"Is it always like this?"

"It is when you love someone."

"Are you saying you love me?"

"Reckon so, Ms. Marie."

"I love you, Santi."

"I love you, too."

They talked about the future, about the land they would buy. They could raise quality horses and someday have children. Marie didn't want children right away, she said. She wasn't sure she was ready to be a mother. Those nagging feelings of losing her identity, her independence crept in. She wanted to be her own woman before she had children. She needed to see who she could become.

April gave way to May. Rodeo practice, competitions, parties, and friends would soon be left behind. Marie, atop her faithful Apollo, was the top point earner that year. Liberty Creek barrel champion. For once, she enjoyed the adulation and attention. Santi was proud of her. Graduation approached. Santi was on top of the world. He retained his championship status and had several job interviews lined up. The restaurant was doing well and bringing in more money than ever. His mom was able to afford upgrades to kitchen equipment, furnishings, and décor. A new logo and outdoor signage adorned the building's façade and updated menus. They even had a local radio station advertisement. He felt good about his family's future and stability. Marie was finishing her student teaching assignment and was in touch with nearby Texas school districts looking to hire new teachers. They could build their lives together.

When he entered the house, he found his mother in the kitchen, staring out the window. When she turned to face him, he could tell she'd been crying. "What's wrong, *mamá*? *¿Qué pasó?*"

Irma wrung her hands, then rubbed her face. She took a seat at the table, movement pained her. "*Siéntate, mijo*. Please sit down."

His brows furrowed in confusion, but he sat at the kitchen table, watching her. His beautiful mother looked tired, as though she'd aged ten years overnight.

"Santiago. I don't know how…" she paused, searching for words. There were no words in Spanish or English that would help. "Do you remember when Marie's parents visited?"

He watched as she fidgeted with a crumpled tissue between her fingers. "It wasn't that long ago. How could I forget?"

"Carla approached me with an offer to help."

"Help?"

Irma plowed through. "She offered to invest in our business, and because we were in need of the help, I took it."

"Okay…," he wondered where this was going.

"She lent us money. Lots of it. I signed papers without consulting a lawyer or anyone." Irma covered her mouth with an unsteady hand. "Oh *mijo*, what have I done?" She sniffled, wiping her nose.

"What happened, *mami*?" Santi didn't understand her upset.

Her voice caught in her throat, anguished. "We will lose everything. The restaurant. Our house. Unless…"

Santi was growing anxious and impatient. "Unless what?"

For the first time, she looked him in the eye. "You have to stop seeing Marie." She braced for his response.

Santi rose from his chair. "Why? No. Not happening," he said flatly.

She went to his side, tears in her eyes. "I'm sorry," she wept. "I know you care about Marie, but maybe she's not for you. There are other girls, your own kind."

"How can you say that? How can you know what is for me? I don't understand this at all. I'm not breaking up with Marie."

"Think of your family. Erik and Susa. We'll be out in the streets with nothing. If you don't break it off with Marie, Carla will ruin us. Call on the loan."

"Let me see these papers."

"It's no use."

"I can't believe you. Why didn't you talk to me? Talk to a lawyer, someone, anyone, before you signed papers? You run a business. This makes no sense."

"I was desperate. We didn't have much time before *La Frontera* went under. Weeks, a month or two at most. I trusted that she acted in good faith."

"You should have told me," he accused, his voice rising. "*¿Por qué no me dijiste nada?*"

Irma wiped away her tears. "You have to let her go, or we'll have nothing."

"I won't. No. I'll talk to Marie. She'll talk to her mother. We'll fix this."

"You can't. If you tell her, Carla Rossi will ruin us."

"I'll talk to Carla, myself. She can't do this."

"It doesn't matter. Nothing you do will change her mind."

He extended his hand. "Give me her number."

"Santi."

He waited until his mother handed him the slip of paper.

Irma gave it to him. "She doesn't want her daughter with you, y *esa mujer maldita* will do anything to keep Marie away."

It wasn't the first time he'd heard similar words. A different voice, a different girl, except this was different. It was déjà vu all over again, but much worse. "I'm supposed to leave the girl I love for no reason? None of this makes sense!"

"I am so sorry. Please think about this, about us," she begged.

Santi couldn't respond. He left the house without a word. The sound of the screen door slammed, reverberating in Irma's ears.

Santi drove to the nearest payphone. He pulled up to a gas station not far from his house, dug into the center console of his car, searching for change. Deposited the required amount and punched in the number.

"Hello?"

Santi tempered his voice, remaining calm. "I'd like to speak to Carla Rossi please."

"This is she."

"Mrs. Rossi, this is Santiago. I just spoke with my mother."

"Ah, yes. Then you know."

"Mrs. Rossi, I'm not going to stop seeing Marie. I love her."

"I'm sorry, Santiago. The relationship between you and my daughter is completely unacceptable. If you don't break it off with her, I'll demand full repayment of the loan I made. Your mother signed papers for a call loan, which gives me the right as lender to mitigate risk."

Santiago was speechless. "Why?" He truly did not understand any of this. "I'll tell her what you've done. She won't agree to this."

"Tell her, and your family is ruined. I trust your family is important to you? Unless you want to see them suffer, you'll break off the relationship and have no further contact with her."

"How can you do this?"

"I can claim that your mother's collateral has lost value, or that she'll be unable to make payments in the future. It's a bit more complicated than that, but I have lawyers at my disposal who will help enforce the contract. Goodbye, Santiago." She hung up.

It wasn't the question he asked, and not the answer he wanted. Santi searched his jeans pockets for more change, dialed again. No answer. He slammed the receiver down, nearly breaking it. Shock fused with hurt, becoming rage, turned into pain. He didn't know what to do with himself. He returned to his car, his spirit as broken as his heart.

*   *   *

It was selfish of him. He knew what he was about to do but he wanted, needed to make love to her one last time. Her dorm room bed. They were squished but neither of them cared. Marie stroked the muscles of his chest, peaceful and languid after lovemaking.

"What's wrong?"

"Nothing's wrong," he lied.

"You're quiet tonight."

Santi slipped from beneath her, rising from the small bed. He searched for discarded clothing and began to dress. Silence weighed heavily between them.

Marie sat up. "Santi?"

"Gotta go." He avoided her gaze. He couldn't look at her, seeing her hair tousled, her beautiful, sleepy face. It would kill him.

Marie turned on the desk lamp. "You've been acting funny the past few days. What's going on? Is everything alright? Did I do something wrong?"

He stopped buttoning his shirt. Of course, she would think she was at fault. Hatred for her mother burned his chest. He reached out to touch her cheek. "No. You didn't do anything wrong." Touching her, looking at her was a mistake. He moved away, slipped on his jeans, then sat on the empty bed opposite. He had no idea how to do this. He didn't want to do this. The anguish inside threatened to burst.

"Then talk to me."

He didn't know what to say or how to say it. He'd broken up with girls before, and he'd been dumped. None of it was pretty. This was different. This hurt like nothing he'd felt before. This was Marie. He loved her, would probably always love her. He felt as though his soul were wailing at the injustice that brought him to this moment. His voice remained devoid of emotion. He stared at the floor. "Been thinking, you know. Since your parents were here and all. Maybe we're just too different. I don't think it's going to work. I don't think we're going to work."

Marie stood up, covering herself with a sheet. "What do you mean? Are you breaking up with me?"

Santi closed his eyes. He loathed himself at this moment. She might as well hate him too. He'd give her a reason. He'd make her hate him as much as he hated himself.

"Santi?"

Unable to meet her eyes, he looked out through the slit of her flowered curtains that hung from the dorm room window. The graying sky mirrored his insides. "Been feeling... I don't know. Suffocated. I'm just not cut out for this, being in a relationship. It's not my style. Don't want to be tied down." *Lie, lie, lie.* How the words stuck in his throat. At one time the words might have been true, but not with her, not with Marie.

"Wait, what?" Marie gathered her clothes, stuffing her head into her Liberty Creek t-shirt. Suddenly aware of her nakedness, and vulnerability, the need to cover herself, and hide away became urgent. She slipped on her blue jeans. "You came here tonight to fuck me, and then tell me you don't want to be with me?"

He looked down at his feet. He wanted her to be angry, his mini fireball. "Pretty much."

"You said you loved me." Her voice broke, wary, and uncertain, laced with accusation.

He offered her a brief glance. "I said a lot of things, didn't I?"

"I don't believe you."

"Believe it or don't. We're done." He rose from the bed, heading for the door.

"Why? I don't understand. The things we talked about. The future. All of it. Was that a lie too?"

"Told you. It won't work. I can't do it. There is no future for us."

Marie stepped in front of him, blocking his path. "Look at me. Santi. Look at me and tell me you don't love me."

Santi braced, forcing himself to look down at her. His dark eyes were cold, empty. "Thought you knew. I'm nothing but a player, Marie. A Mexican skirt-chasing Lothario. You fell for it." The look on her face couldn't have been worse if he'd driven a knife through her heart. It killed him, tore him apart. He knew he would regret his lies, his cruelty to the woman he loved till the day he died.

His voice was absolutely emotionless. It chilled her. Hurt and anger nearly blinded her. A dry sob burned her throat, but she refused to let it escape. "Get out. Go to hell. I never want to see you again!"

He left. Left the dorm. Left campus. Drove for hours. When his father passed away, he could be strong, brave for his younger siblings. He had to be the man of the house. He didn't cry. Why then, could he not keep his tears at bay now? Santi pulled over to the side of the highway, unsure of where he was. He wept. Wiping his eyes, it occurred to him. Now when he'd found Marie, someone he could see a future with, someone he loved, a woman he could spend his life with, moving forward, looking in the same direction, it was gone, taken from him, from them both.

He was numb. He could do nothing. Santi composed himself, revved the Camaro and pulled onto the highway again. He didn't know where he was going. He didn't care.

When he arrived home the following morning, his mother rushed to the door. He looked haggard. Neither of them slept the night before.

"It's done," was all he said, his voice cold, hard.

"Where have you been, *mijo*. I was worried."

"Were you?" he asked, the sarcasm in his voice, so unlike him, took his mother aback.

"Of course!"

He handed her a thick envelope she hadn't noticed before. She opened it. "United States Marine Corps? What is this? Recruit training?" Irma didn't understand. She followed him as he lumbered to his room. He needed sleep. "Santiago. College graduation is next week."

"I won't be there."

When he left for thirteen weeks of U.S. Marine Corps recruit training, the only way Irma could contact her son would be through letters or post cards. That's if he wrote to her first with address information. She'd have no idea where her son would be.

*   *   *

Marie was miserable. A raw and primitive grief overwhelmed her. She didn't see Santi again. Graduation day came but neither he nor his family were present at the ceremony. She found his name among the list of graduates on the commencement ceremony program. When she went to the stables to load Apollo on the trailer for home, Rebelde was gone. There was no trace of the horse or of Santiago. She said quick good-byes to her fellow teammates, unwilling to say more or linger any longer than she had to. They traded vague promises to keep in touch. Marie knew she wouldn't.

Everything she thought about herself turned out to be true. She wasn't good enough, pretty enough, smart enough, thin enough. How could she have believed that Santiago ever loved her? Now she could add foolish to her list of faults.

"Aren't you glad you didn't stay down in Texas?" her mother remarked on the drive home.

Marie didn't respond, her mind languid, without hope.

"Give it time. You'll be fine. He wasn't what you thought. Consider it a lesson learned and move on."

"I don't want to talk about it, mom."

"You're better off without that boy. He had nothing to offer you."

"You didn't know him."

"I know his type."

Marie didn't care to argue. She stared out the window as the landscape rolled by.

In the summer of 1982, Marie interviewed for several teaching jobs and received an offer from a public high school. She'd start in September. She thought it must be the summer heat and humidity of Chicago causing her nausea. She'd vomited again. This didn't go unnoticed.

Marie flushed the toilet and wiped her mouth with a tissue.

Her mother's voice sounded from just outside the door. "Marie, what's going on?"

"Nothing. I think it's the heat. I'm not feeling well."

Considering the condo was air-conditioned, Carla suspected something else. "Are you pregnant?"

Marie swung the bathroom door open. "What? No!" She proceeded to her room to dress for the day. Her mother followed at her heels.

"When was your last period?"

"I don't know, March? April? I've never been regular," Marie answered, opening drawers, pulling out a clean shirt.

"I'm taking you to the clinic."

The test was positive. Her mother berated her on the ride home. When they arrived at the condo, Marie headed directly to her bedroom to avoid more lecturing and yelling from her mother. It didn't work. Carla blocked her path.

"We sent you to school to get an education. Not pregnant! *Desgracia. Puttana.* Do you hear me?"

Marie was unfazed. She felt numb and empty. Dead inside. "Yes. I'm a whore. I opened my legs willingly. That's what whores do. I'm a disgrace. Thank you, mother."

"We'll take care of this. You'll get rid of it. I'll not have people talking behind my back."

"People will talk anyway, what does it matter?" Marie countered.

Carla slapped her.

Now Marie felt something. Defiance, anger, rage. "You can't control this, and it's eating you! You hate it. I'm keeping this baby. I don't care what you do." Marie pushed past her mother, ran to her room, and locked the door.

She landed face down on her bed, burying herself in a plush pillow. Anxiety like a snake coiled in her gut. The conflict with her mother did nothing to allay her fears about her pregnancy. Not once did her mother ask how she felt.

Marie had compromised herself too much. She'd forgotten her staunch determination to be independent, self-reliant. She let Santi in. He'd broken down her barriers, to use her and tear her heart to shreds.

Marie rolled over onto her back. She placed her palm over her lower abdomen. Her mother wanted her to get rid of it. Truthfully, that would be the best course of action. She could carry on as though nothing happened, and most of all she'd be free of any reminders of Santiago Rivera.

For the millionth time she asked herself how she could have been so stupid, so naïve, so in love. His hurtful words still echoed in her heart. The ache would not leave.

She was having this baby. She'd defy her mother, defy the odds against single motherhood. Defy the gossipmongers and naysayers. Fuck them all. And Fuck Santi too.

Was it selfish? Foolish? Maybe. It didn't matter. She vowed to hold onto her goals and dreams. She vowed to be a good mother to her child. She'd create a life for herself and her baby.

Hours later, a soft knock woke her. Her vision blurred, eyes puffy from crying, Marie fumbled her way through the darkened room.

Vincent Rossi had been here before. This time it was his daughter. He took a seat at the edge of her bed. He had to ask one difficult question. "Your mother told me. Looks like we've got ourselves a situation," he said quietly.

Marie sat next to her father. New tears fell. She said nothing.

"I've gotta ask, sweetheart. Did he force you?"

She inhaled a shuddering breath. "No, daddy. I loved him. I thought he loved me. He didn't force me."

"Okay." Vincent exhaled audibly, relieved. He didn't want his daughter to experience the same pain and trauma Carla had gone through, years before. "Your mother says you're intent on keeping the baby. You know what this means. It won't be easy for you."

"I know. Maybe if I talk to Santi, let him know…," her voice trailed off. Would he care?

"Mom doesn't think that's a good idea, and not sure I agree but for now, I'll go along with it."

"Why is she like this?"

Vincent paused. What happened in the past was best left behind. He couldn't burden his daughter, and he'd promised Carla years ago that he'd never reveal secrets. "Your mom and I grew up in a different era. I'm not saying that excuses everything but try to understand where it comes from. She wants what she thinks is best for you. She doesn't want you to go through things she experienced. She's been through a lot. She's a tough cookie."

"I have to experience life for myself. She can't shield me from everything. Where's the line between protecting your child, and controlling them? She has to let go and allow me to make my own decisions and mistakes, even if they're difficult or painful. I have to be my own person."

"I'll talk to her about loosening the reins. How's that for a horse analogy?"

"Thank you, dad."

"In the meantime, we'll do what we can to help."

"As soon as I'm able, I'm moving out."

Vincent embraced his daughter. "Dinner's been put away, but if you're hungry, there's leftovers in the fridge. You should eat." He left her, but Marie wasn't ready to leave her room just yet.

Marie continued to work throughout her pregnancy. She saved as much money as she could on a starting teacher's salary. Aside from her car maintenance, and paying an agreed upon rent to her parents, most of her expenses were minimal. Her relationship with her mother remained strained. Instead of talking to her mother or sharing the experience of pregnancy, like she thought most young women would, Marie read books about it, or conferred with her doctor.

She loved her school. Her colleagues were welcoming. A few veteran teachers helped her immensely, since there were too many procedures, policies, events, and classroom scenarios for which her college education did not prepare her. Were it not for their support, Marie didn't think she'd last her first year. While she still sought to inspire and motivate her students, her naivete and dreams of changing the world were quickly tempered with a dose of reality. Teaching was more difficult than most people thought.

Marie didn't want to know the sex of her baby. She wanted to be surprised. As her due date grew closer and her belly swelled, she arranged for a leave of absence from her job. When her water broke on a January afternoon on her way home from work, Marie didn't panic. She remained oddly calm, recalling something Santi told her to do when interacting with horses. She heard his voice in her head, calm yet assertive. She breathed, talking herself through it, driving herself to the hospital as contractions seized her.

The Third Part Last
1986 – 1988
Chapter Eighteen

San Antonio, Texas
Winter, 1986

D^{*ear Marie,*}   *October 21, 1983*

We've been under near constant indirect fire attacks the past month. A cease fire was instituted and so far, held until a few days ago, when a U.S. convoy was attacked wounding four Marines. A remotely detonated car bomb was parked along their route. We continue to do our jobs. Every day it feels like something big is brewing. We're all on edge, like waiting for the other boot to drop, but we go on with duties.

I miss you. Don't regret enlisting, but I thought it would help me not think about you. Instead, I'm writing letters to you. You fill my heart, my mind. Not worried about dying. Worried about dying and not seeing you one last time. Worried about dying and you believing all the lies, and hurtful things I said, letting you think I didn't love you or want you. Don't mean to sound all dramatic, gloom and doom. Guess being in a war zone gets you thinking about things differently. I hope someday you can forgive me. I hope you have a good life. I hope you find happiness. I want that for you.

I love you,

Te quiero, te adoro, te amo.

Pienso en ti siempre.

Santi

Marie pulled into the graveled driveway, parking in front of the attached garage of the single-level ranch home. A red oak stood adjacent, providing shade. She turned her head, checking on Grace, asleep in her car seat. Marie lowered the front windows halfway, as the day was mild, a gentle breeze lifted wisps of dark curls from Grace's forehead. Satisfied her child would be fine for the moment, she breathed deeply, gathered courage, then exited the car.

"Marie?" It was Susana, a bit older, a bit taller, but recognizable.

"Hello, Susana." Marie was uncertain whether her reception here would be favorable.

"Marie!" Susana rushed to meet her, hugging her warmly. "Oh my gosh, it's so great to see you!"

Marie smiled, relieved at Susana's welcome. "It's good to see you, too. You've grown up."

The metal screen door opened. "Susana? *¿Quién es...?*" Irma Rivera stepped out onto the front step. She halted, shocked. "Marie?"

"Hello Señora Rivera. I'm here to visit with all of you, but I need to speak to Santi."

Irma stepped forward. Her manner was guarded. "Marie. I never thought to see you here." Her gaze surveyed the area, as though she expected another person. "I'm sorry but I don't think you being here is a good idea."

Marie stood her ground. "I think that's for Santiago to decide."

"I don't agree. You should have left things alone."

"I know everything Mrs. Rivera. I know what my mother has done. To you, to Santi, to me."

Irma swallowed hard. "Then you know what she'll do, if she finds out you've come."

"What's this all about, *mami*?" Susana asked.

"Coercion." Marie answered. "Plain and simple."

"You know this could ruin our lives," Irma said.

"I'm not here to ruin anyone's life. If you'll listen to me, I think I may have a way for all of us to escape Carla Rossi's hold."

Irma was silent for a time. "I'm listening."

"I must speak to Santiago first, there's something important he needs to know." Marie opened the rear door of the rental sedan, leaning in to unfasten the toddler car seat belts. Grace moaned in her sleep. "It's okay baby."

"*Ay, Diós mío*," Irma whispered.

"Oh my God," Susana echoed.

Marie pulled out her sleepy toddler, holding her close. "This is Grace Rossi-Rivera. Your granddaughter."

Irma held onto Susana, for fear she'd fall over in a dead faint. There was no mistaking her son's child. Tears came to Irma's eyes, a trembling hand lifted to cover her mouth. "Why did Carla never tell me? She never once told me." In all their phone conversations, every time Carla called to check on Santi's whereabouts, she never mentioned the child.

"I'm so sorry," Marie answered. "She's done too much harm to all of us. I'm hoping we can change that." Grace was waking up now and began to cry as she found herself in unfamiliar surroundings, with people she did not know. She clung to her mother as Marie tried to soothe her.

"Please, come inside," Irma gestured toward the door. "We'll talk to Santiago but come rest for a moment."

"Is he not here?"

"No. He lives on the Ferguson ranch now. I'll take you there. He was on the road with a friend, came back about a month ago."

They entered the home. Marie spotted a framed photograph of Santiago in Marine dress blues placed on an end table in the living room, alongside another of his university diploma. Irma offered her a seat at the kitchen table, then set down glasses, filling them with a cool fruit drink. She couldn't take her eyes from Grace. "I know that's my son's baby. It's unbelievable how much she looks like him at that age." Irma slumped into a chair and wept. "*Mi nieta*, I want to hold her, but she doesn't know me."

Susana put her arms around her mother. "She will *mami*, that's why Marie is here," she looked up, hopeful. "Right, Marie?"

"Yes, but I'm here to see Santi. To give him a chance to make his own decision about whether he wants to be in his daughter's life. My mother took that away from him."

"She took away a chance for me to know my own granddaughter," Irma wiped her eyes.

"That too. But we can talk about Carla Rossi after I know how Santi feels. Either way, my mother no longer has any control over how I live my life. But I do understand the control she has over all of you. I hope to fix that."

"Of course, Santi will want his daughter."

Marie nodded. "I'm sure he will." But would he still want her? That was the question weighing like a stone on Marie's heart.

"You know, he was a Marine in Beirut when they bombed the barracks. He's much better, but has not been quite himself since he returned. He's not the same Santiago you knew."

"An anonymous person sent letters he'd written to me. That's what brought me here. Was he badly injured?"

"Yes. He's had surgeries to repair his leg and hip. Scars from wounds, burns and skin grafts." She sniffled. "He's gone through an emotional wringer and come out a different shape."

Marie couldn't help herself. She had to ask. "Is he… does he have a wife, or a girlfriend?" she ventured.

"Not that I'm aware of. Seeing you will be a shock to him, but in the end, it will be good. He's never forgiven me for what happened."

"It wasn't your fault," Marie said, holding the glass for Grace as she slurped fruit juice. "You did what you thought you had to do. You believed my mother's intentions were honest. She wasn't."

Irma's expression relaxed, relieved that Marie understood. "I meant no ill toward you. My son loved you. You were good to him. He was happy. It's all a mother can ask for."

Irma and Susana piled into Marie's rental car. Susana gave directions to the Ferguson ranch, while Irma engaged with little Grace in the back seat, talking to her and singing songs. Susana offered Marie a compassionate smile. "It'll be okay. He didn't forget you."

When they arrived at Santi's trailer, it was deserted. "Must be gone out with the other hands," Irma said. "There's no way to reach him. We may as well wait."

"I need to change and feed Grace. She's doing well with potty training but has the occasional accident," Marie said. Unpacking the tote, she dug out a toddler disposable diaper and cleansing wipes. Grace was dry. She changed her daughter's clothes, dressing her in a pink shirt with an embroidered pony on the front, and a pair of elastic waisted denim pants. She wanted Grace to look like a cowgirl when her father saw her. When Grace was settled Marie pulled out the cooler, offering her some finger foods, cut up fruit, crackers, and cheese bites.

"He's coming," Susana shaded her eyes against the setting sun, pointing to a group of men on horseback in the distance.

Marie's heart leapt. His silhouette was unmistakable. He was the rider she remembered long ago who rode a dancing horse. She watched him until he was out of sight as he entered the barn area. After some time, he and the others emerged. She noted the slight limp as he walked toward the trailers. Marie could do no more than stare wordlessly at him, her heart pounding.

"Looks like you got company, amigo," one of the hands said as they approached. The others headed for their trucks to drive home, or respective trailers to wash off the day's work. Santi spied a vehicle he didn't recognize parked next to his blue Ford pickup.

As he drew closer, he stopped, noticing his mother first. "Is everything alright, *mamá*?"

"Yes *mijo*," Irma began, but never finished her statement.

Santi saw her. She looked the same, but different, more beautiful than he remembered. The sun in the western sky caught the golden highlights of brown hair that curled past her shoulders, her large brown eyes asking, pleading with him for something, anything. In her arms was a child, a little girl with dark hair. He couldn't breathe. He stood frozen, speechless. Conflicting emotions whirled through him like a tornado on a prairie.

Marie was no less moved at the sight of him, as she stepped closer, she noted a new scar above his left eyebrow, and another thin scar over his left cheek, a mark on his chin. Sparse facial hair formed stubble, dark hair was longer, the ends fell over his collar, touching his shoulders. He seemed taller, broader, stronger, grown from a handsome youth to a handsome man. Had it been almost four years since she'd seen him last? "Santi?"

Santi couldn't speak. He looked to his mother, then his sister, then back to Marie. He hadn't imagined what would happen if he saw her again. Hadn't counted on taking one look at her and getting slammed in the chest with a sledgehammer. "Why are you here?" he asked in wonderment. "How?"

"We need to talk. Please."

Irma placed a gentle hand on his arm. "*Está bien, mijo.* Talk to Marie. Take her and the baby inside. Susa and I will wait here."

Santi couldn't take his eyes from Marie and the child. He took a moment to temper his emotions, then walked to the trailer door, opened it, and motioned for Marie to enter.

"Horsey, mama!" Grace pointed to a group of horses grazing nearby.

"Yes baby, horses." Marie went up the steps and into the dimly lit trailer.

"I wan horsey. Horsey pitty."

"I think horses are pretty, too."

Santi followed behind her, tossing his hat on the counter, flipping on lights, rounding up clothes, and tossing them into a laundry basket. He picked up pieces of mail, magazines, and newspapers, clearing a space for Marie to sit on the couch.

They sat at opposite ends, staring at one another as Grace babbled and talked to her stuffed pink bunny.

Words and emotions remained unsaid, filling the space between them.

He broke the silence. "Never thought I'd see you again."

"Someone sent your letters, anonymously. That's why I'm here."

He lowered his head, shaking it. "Those damn letters. Never knew what happened to them after Beirut."

"I'm glad I got them. I know the truth about my mother's awful scheme. And now you must know a truth."

Grace fidgeted, grunting, and groaning, and arching her back to slide from Marie's lap.

She didn't have to say it. He nodded toward the squiggling toddler. Swallowing back emotion, he said simply, "She's mine."

"Her name is Grace Rossi-Rivera." Marie answered, allowing Grace to stand and wander over to the pile of magazines to look at the pictures of pretty horses, her pink bunny dragging behind.

Santi braced elbows on his knees and lowered his head in his hands. He released a quivering breath. Tears welled in his eyes. "Knew as soon as I saw her," he choked. "You gave her my name."

Uncertain, Marie hesitated before scooting closer. Fighting against her own tears, she reached for him. Wrapping him in her arms, relief flooded her when he turned into her embrace. She felt him tremble against her. "I don't want to cause trouble for you. She's yours, you had a right to know and a right to decide whether you want to be a father to her."

His forehead pressed against Marie's shoulder, voice laden with anguish, he asked, "When's her birthday? When was she born?"

"January 23, 1983."

Santi sat back, sniffling, wiping his face with his shirtsleeve. "Was in a damn warzone, not knowing I had a baby girl. This is too much," he said, as he watched a beautiful little girl with dark curled hair and olive skin, talking her toddler words and touching a little finger to the glossy horse photos. She'd just turned three.

"I'm sorry, Santi. I wanted to do what I thought was right. I know this is all overwhelming."

"Not her." He turned back to Marie, his eyes hard. "Carla." He stood up, went to the kitchen sink, washed his hands, then splashed his face. He dried himself with a nearby dish towel. A small hand touched his knee unexpectedly.

"I din wa-er, pease?"

He looked to Marie for translation.

"She wants water, do you have a small cup?"

Santi grabbed a ceramic coffee mug from the cabinet above and filled it halfway. "Can she drink from a cup?" He knew nothing about toddlers.

"Yes, she does well."

He handed Grace the cup, holding the bottom for her. She took three fast, slurpy gulps, then handed it back, smiling, and breathless, she wiped drops of water from her lips. "Dank-oo!" she sang.

"You're welcome, Grace." He watched his daughter giggle and run back to Marie. His daughter. He could not fathom it. He leaned back against the counter, staring down at his boots.

"I understand if you need time to digest all of this," Marie began.

"Might. But I lost enough time. That's my daughter. A daughter who doesn't know me because one person thought I wasn't good enough and had the power to keep me from her."

"I want her to know you."

"She will." He faced her, silent. They studied one another for endless moments from across the room. Finally, he said, "What about you, Marie? Do you want to know me too? I've changed some. I'm not the same as you remember," he gestured to himself. "But I'm still somewhere inside here." And though he felt he had no right to ask, he did anyway. "Do you have a man?"

"No. There's only one I've ever loved." Since he asked, she would as well. "Do you have a woman?"

"There's no woman. But we can't pick up where we left off, act like nothing ever happened. We can't get back what we lost. I have nothing. Nothing to offer you." He lifted a hand to indicate their surroundings.

"What you see here, this... this trailer doesn't belong to me. You deserve more, Marie. My little girl deserves more."

Marie stood up, setting Grace on the seat. Sensing his growing agitation, she approached him. "I know we can't just pick up where we left off. We're both different people. You may think you have nothing to offer, but if you can give her a father's love that's enough."

"Not for me. I take care of what's mine." He took a dig at her. "As you can see, I'm not rich. Looks like you're both screwed."

"Santi, I didn't come here to ask you for anything. I've been taking care of Grace by myself just fine. I thought that... never mind." Marie turned away from him.

Santi stopped her, turning her to face him. He wanted to kiss her until she was senseless, he wanted to hate her. He could do neither. "Don't misunderstand me and then walk away."

"Then explain so that I can understand."

He released her arm. How could he explain when he couldn't put his thoughts and emotions into words? "Where are you staying?"

Marie hesitated, confused by his question. "The Fairmount Hotel in San Antonio."

"I'll pick you up tomorrow evening at the hotel. Need time to sort my head, first."

She nodded. "That's fair."

"I'll be there at six. We need to talk alone, not in front of Grace. Will she be okay with my mother or Susana?"

"She should be. Shouldn't we ask them first?"

"I'll ask. *Abuela* won't say no to a chance to get acquainted with her granddaughter."

Marie retrieved Grace, who was now opening bottom cabinets and investigating the contents inside. "Come on, baby, let's put these back. Don't forget Pink Bunny."

"Bunny!" Grace grabbed the floppy stuffed animal's foot and reached for her mother's hand.

As they neared the door, Santi crouched down to his daughter. "Nice to meet you, Grace." He held out his hands in a gesture that asked her to come to him, but she refused, clinging to her mother. She hid her face against Marie's leg. He didn't expect her to react differently but took a shot anyway. "Got my work cut out," he mused aloud.

"You can tame wild horses. I'm sure you'll be fine."

"Somehow I think this will be ten times harder." He lifted his eyes to Marie. "I'm up for the challenge, though."

"What would you like her to call you?"

Santi rose to full height, his gaze on the little one peeking at him from behind her mother. "What I am. *Papá.*"

That night he slept little. Images of a little girl with dark curls and eyes like his own floated in and out of his mind. His daughter. None of it seemed real. And Marie. So beautiful, and confident. She was always stronger, braver than she gave herself credit for. It was always inside her.

He pulled his drifting thoughts together. He could not deny that he loved her still. He wanted her. Seeing her awakened something in him, bringing a flood of emotions he hadn't felt in years. What to do? Had she forgiven him? Did she still love him, want him? If she did, could he function as a partner and father? Santi wasn't sure, but for the first time there was hope. A way forward from the mental and emotional stagnation he felt for so long. No matter what they discussed tomorrow evening, or what they decided, Santi felt a warm glow flow through him. Tonight, there were no shadows on his heart.

Chapter Nineteen

San Antonio, Texas 1986

M arie was nervous. It wasn't a date. It felt like a date. "It's not a date," she chastised herself as she looked in the bathroom mirror, applying the last bit of light make-up. She smoothed her curls, unable to tame them completely in this weather. She'd forgotten how much warmer it could be in Texas, and so took Grace to shop for lighter clothing earlier that day. She picked up a knee-length flowy fit-and-flare dress for herself, white with soft pastel flowers, and two little cotton dresses for Grace. Flat, strappy sandals completed their outfits.

There was a change of plans. It would be easier to meet at Irma's home, since Marie had the car seat, and meeting there to drop off Grace would involve less driving for each of them.

Santi was waiting for her as she pulled up into the driveway, next to his truck. She exited the car, opening the rear door to retrieve her daughter. Holding Grace against her hip, she reached down, picking up the heavy baby bag. "I got that," he said taking the bag from her. "You look beautiful."

Marie brushed strands of hair back from her face. "You clean up pretty well yourself," she smiled. He was clean shaven and wore a crisp indigo pearl snap-button shirt, faded Levi's, a leather tooled belt, and cleaned boots.

"Didn't have time for a haircut," he said, running his fingers through shoulder-length hair, pushing it away from his forehead.

"I like it. Looks good on you." She turned to Grace. "Say hello."

Grace became bashful in front of Santi.

"Hello Grace, I like your dress. You look as pretty as momma."

Grace giggled, covering her face, and throwing herself back against her mother. At Marie's gentle urging, she sat up, concentrating. "Hel-lwo, Hel-lo *Pa-Apá"* she waved a little hand. "Hiii."

Santi was visibly affected by his baby's use of *Papá.*

"We practiced a little. I hope that's okay."

His voice came out unexpectedly gravelly and broken. "Yup. Let's go inside." He didn't trust himself to say more.

They greeted Irma and Susana. Erik was there too. The brothers embraced. Marie hadn't seen him since he was about fifteen. He'd grown so much.

"Hey Marie," Erik offered her a genuine hug.

"It's good to see you. You've grown so tall." He must be about eighteen or nineteen by now. *How quickly time passed*, she thought. Time none of them could get back.

Told in advance, Erik wasn't fazed by Marie's appearance at their home with a toddler that looked like his brother. "This is Gracie? Hi Grace, how are you?" Grace stared at him before her eyes darted to Santi. Erik turned to his brother. "She looks like you, 'mano. Wow."

Irma had done some shopping of her own. There were new toys in the living room, age-appropriate learning games, a few stuffed animals, and her famous version of Tex-Mex *carne guisada* simmering on the stove.

The scent of stewed meat and spices caused Marie's stomach to growl, reminding her that she hadn't eaten all day. "Mrs. Rivera, thank you for all of this. You didn't have to," Marie said, referring to the cache of toys. Grace wanted down from her mother's arms, already eying the goodies. Marie set her daughter on her feet.

"Want to play, Grace?" Susana asked, leading her niece away. "Come on."

Grace squealed with delight, "I wan play!"

"I had nothing in the house to entertain her. Besides, we'll need to distract her while you two leave. Let me spoil my granddaughter a little bit."

"Thank you, *mami*. We won't be late," Santi said.

"Take as much time as you need. You two need to get reacquainted. The baby can stay the night, if... well... you know," she intoned. "Come for her in the morning. I'll fix breakfast."

Santi and Marie exchanged surprised, awkward glances at his mother's implication.

Erik chuckled. "I have a date tonight too, can I come home tomorrow morning?"

"*Cállate*," Irma tapped his behind, playfully. "Go check my *guisada*, please *mijo*." Erik went to the stove to peek at the stew. Amused at their embarrassment she continued, "Come now, we're adults. You two have lots to discuss, no?"

They left while Grace was distracted. Santi opened the pick-up passenger door, helping Marie climb inside. Her dress fluttered up, revealing the shapely legs he knew quite well, or did at one time.

When he started the truck, backing out of the driveway, his instinct was to reach for her hand. It was an old habit. Something he did whenever they drove together. But that was years ago. He caught himself, refraining from touching her again.

"Thought we'd go to the Riverwalk," he said, putting the truck in gear. "Haven't been there in a while. Heard they've built and added on to it."

"That sounds nice, I've never been there."

"I think you'll like it. It's a public park along the river, you can walk, there's boat rides, shops, restaurants. Kind of like Navy Pier in Chicago, I guess."

She smiled at him. If she kept doing that, and looking the way she did tonight, he didn't think the barriers he'd erected would hold.

He parked the truck in one of the lots and hopped out. Marie was already opening her door. He reached for her, placing his hands around her waist, helping her down. Once on her feet they stood close together for a moment. "Still *la chaparrita*," he murmured.

Marie didn't miss the sensuous glint in his eyes, or the intimate feel of his voice. She smiled up at him. "I stopped growing in high school."

Ignoring the way his heart flipped, he said, "Come on, let's get a bite. I'm starving."

They walked on South Alamo Street, passing bars, a seafood restaurant, and a hotel. They crossed Market Street, veering onto the lush riverside path, lined with cypress trees, greenery, the various dining establishments all with outdoor umbrellas of every color.

Spanish architecture along with native influences were on display. A mariachi band played.

"It's beautiful here."

"Italian or Mexican?" he asked.

"Either is fine. We can choose something else."

"Steak it is." He found a steakhouse with a view of the river. Fortunately, as it was a weeknight, they were able to secure outdoor seats. Though they engaged in small talk, Santi couldn't help but think how easy it was to be with her. It was always easy. Like two friends who haven't seen each other for years but can somehow pick up where they left off. The pain of missing her hit him at once. An ache he'd hidden away, suddenly rose to fore, rendering him speechless. Santi was grateful for the outdoor seats. He didn't think he could handle being inside at this moment.

When their food arrived, they ate in companionable silence. Neither of them seemed willing to initiate the pressing topic at hand. *What would they do now?*

Santi studied her as he sipped his beer. Liquid courage. "Grace is a pretty name, any reason why you chose it?" He asked what he thought was a benign question as an easy way to begin a difficult conversation.

Marie set her fork on the plate. She studied her hands folded on her lap, silent. "At first, I didn't know I was pregnant. My mother suspected and took me to a clinic. I was afraid. I tried contacting you, but my mother insisted that you wanted nothing to do with me. You were… gone. My mother… she called me a slut, a whore. A disgrace."

Santi remained silent, the expression on his face shadowed with anguish. It sickened him to think of what she must have gone through.

She lifted her eyes to his. "I… my daughter is not a disgrace. She is Grace. It means, goodness and generosity, and every time I say her name, I'm reminded of goodness. It's why I never call her Gracie."

All the walls he'd built crumbled to dust. Santi extended his arm across the white tablecloth, palm up, beckoning her. Marie placed her hand in his. "I'm sorry, Marie. I'm sorry I wasn't there for you, I'm sorry I hurt you, I'm sorry for all of it."

"You did what you thought you had to do, Santi." She paused, taking a breath before continuing. "After Grace was born, I lived with my parents for a while. I returned to work as soon as I could to save money, so that I could move out. My mother was pissed. I found a little, one-bedroom apartment. The week I moved out, she sold Apollo without my knowledge, just to be spiteful. It was the last straw for me. I haven't spoken to her since. I have good relationships with my father and brother. They know I'm here and helped pay for this trip. But it's been me and Grace, pretty much. I work and take care of my daughter. That's my life."

He wanted to tell her about Apollo but held off. No sense adding to her heartache right now. There would be another time.

"When I received your letters, things started to make sense. I had to come see you. I didn't know what to expect. You could've been married or had other children. I know this might seem as though I'm trying to upset your life, but…"

"No. Never," he interrupted.

"You've been through so much. Beirut, your injuries, and recovery. It couldn't have been easy."

"No less easy for you, just a different kind of war." He motioned for the waiter. "Let's get out of here." When he saw her reach for her purse, he added, "I got this. Put your money away."

This time as they walked, he reached for her hand, because it felt natural and right. Their fingers interlaced as they always did. "After Beirut I was pretty fucked up," he said quietly. "Not just physically. Had nightmares, anxiety. I've been hiding out on the ranch. Training horses, working roundups, fixing machinery and fences. Did a little rodeoing with my Marine brother, Mike. Never did anything with my degree. No matter how much time I spend at the gym, I'll never walk without a limp. My hip pains me sometimes. I don't do well in crowded, enclosed spaces." He stopped as they neared the truck. "Stayed up most of last night thinking. Making plans, weighing options. Right now, I have nothing. Nothing but my pride, Marie. I need you to understand me, need you to let me be a man in this. I want to give my daughter a good life, but don't even know how to give myself one."

"What's a good life? Are you happy? Do you have everything you need?"

He looked away. It was growing dark, the lights of the Riverwalk shone in the distance. The night air grew chilly. "Haven't been happy, really happy since I was with you," he confessed. "And I don't have everything I need, not if I want to take care of my family." His eyes met hers. "You and Grace."

"Is that what you want? To take care of us?"

"Would like to try. Ashamed to admit, I'm a little scared."

"I understand about your male pride. I do. But no man - not even you, must do any of this alone. Don't let your pride stand in the way of partnership."

"I know you're more than capable. I know you value your independence. I need this. Can't explain it. Haven't felt worth a damn since…since all this mess. Leaving you was the worst thing I ever did." Santi shook his head. "I'm a father." He released his breath. "Just saying it is surreal. My father meant the world to me. The chance to be there for my own child means a chance to be something, do something good with my life. If you can forgive the hurtful things I said back then… None of it was true, Marie. None of it. Maybe I can make it right, make it up to you."

"Oh Santi, I forgave a long time ago."

"Time to cowboy up. Can't guarantee it'll always be easy. Still have my bad days, but I work on it every day. It's better," he said, then turned to her. "Where do we go from here, Marie?"

Marie stepped closer, reaching for his other hand. "If you'd like, that is - I mean, I know we've just seen each other after all this time, but – for tonight, we can go to the hotel."

His handsome face relaxed, lips turning up in a hint of provocative smile. He stared down at her. Marie could feel the heat sizzling in his dark eyes. His look still made her weak.

She wanted him, and there was no way in hell he'd turn away from her. "Not what I meant, but yes, I'd like that. More than you know."

Chapter Twenty

M arie entered the hotel room, flipping on the nearest lamp. Dim light suffused through the room. She placed the key on the cherrywood dresser along with her shoulder bag and slipped off her sandals. Santi entered the room behind her, set out the *Do Not Disturb* tag, and made sure the door was locked. She faced him.

His eyes flitted beyond her to the large four poster bed, replete with luxurious linens and pillows. He ran a hand through his hair. "Shit. Feel like a nervous kid."

Marie drew closer, taking his hands. "We're not kids anymore."

Santi closed his eyes, touching his forehead to hers. He recalled the last time he'd touched her, kissed her, made love to her. It was the same night he broke her heart. Her nearness both soothed and overwhelmed him. "Got scars from Beirut. They're not pretty."

"I've got stretch marks from carrying a baby for nine months. My body is not the same as you remember. You don't need to be perfect, Santi. You just need to be you. That's more than enough. You're more than enough." She lifted her head, meeting his eyes without apology. "I love you," she whispered. "I want you."

Gripping a fistful of her long curls, he tipped her head back, slanting his mouth over hers. Marie waited as their breaths mingled, her entire being on the edge of anticipation. Santi took her bottom lip into his mouth, nipped it gently, then crushed his lips to hers. Marie opened for him, eager for the taste and feel of his tongue.

The first touch of her lips against his, and the sound of his name on a sigh coursed through him, a bolt of electricity, filling him at once with need and hunger. Familiarity and newness coexisted in the same moment. Comfort and excitement lived side by side. He felt her hands, forcing the pearl snaps of his shirt open. She eased his shirt off, running her hands over the hard muscles of his chest and shoulders. Fingers blindly searched for and undid his belt, then the button of his jeans.

Santi shucked his arms out of the shirt. Groaning beneath his breath, he dragged his mouth away, blazing a trail of hot kisses over her throat, the curve of her neck, her shoulder. He nipped her there. His brain told him to slow down. His body disobeyed. This was Marie. His Marie. She'd always been a part of him. She was real and here in his arms, and nothing, no one would stop him from loving her. Hands sliding down the curve of her spine, he nudged her toward the bed. Lifting the flare skirt hem of her dress, he found the waistband of her panties.

"Rip it," she demanded, breathless.

Bunching enough lacy fabric in his fist, he pulled, once, twice, the thin material ripping from her body. Marie gasped softly, clinging to him as he dipped a finger inside her silken warmth, finding her slick and ready for him. He eased her onto the bed, the urgent need to taste her, as necessary as the air he breathed. Spreading her knees apart, he licked and nipped, swirling his tongue around her clit, until cries of pleasure escaped her. Until she bucked and trembled, surrendering to him completely. Santi toed off his boots, removing his jeans and boxers. He was fully aroused, desire pulsing through his swollen and rigid flesh.

Marie pulled the dress over her head, tossing it aside. She reached for him, wanting him, needing him now. She'd waited years, been apart from him for too long. He slid up her body, his skin brushing against hers sensuously as he cupped a hand beneath her bottom, tilting her hips. Marie guided him home. A deep moan on a breath left him as he sheathed himself inside her. Stretching, filling, complete.

He didn't move. The hot clasp of her body spasmed, twitching around his length. Trembling with desire for her, he pressed soft kisses to her lips, her eyes, her cheeks. "I never stopped, Marie. I never stopped loving you," he whispered. He ground his hips, filling her deep, deeper, then withdrew, plunging again. Again. Again. Again.

Marie thrilled to the sensation of having him inside her, at last. She countered his movement, her hips gyrating rhythmically. The motion building through her like a tidal wave and pushing her into rapture. "Santi.... Oh god." Marie spiraled, as currents jolted in her womb. She sensed his climax joining her own, tumbling over the edge, unable to stop her moans and cries of mindless bliss.

Years of dreaming of her, aching for her, loving her, all felt bound up, brimming full in this moment. His pleasure was pure, his release explosive, his seed pumping inside her, he emptied himself until there was nothing left. He fell beside Marie on the bed, panting. "Fuck," he rasped. His erection still pulsed, jerking involuntarily; his blood raced. "God, Marie," he breathed, astounded by the intensity of his climax. Complete and utter ecstasy. Santi pulled her to him, so that she lay against his side.

Marie was no less shaken by the magnitude of passion unleashed. Emotion flooded her. "I love you, Santi," she whispered, an edge of sadness colored her voice. "Too much has been taken from us."

He shifted, breathing a kiss to her forehead, smoothing soft curls away from her face. "We'll find a way, Marie. I didn't fight for us before. That's my regret. Won't happen again."

"You weren't given a choice."

He was quiet for a moment, as they settled back to earth. He ran gentle fingers down her arm. "Didn't use protection."

"I know."

"Didn't take my time."

"I didn't want you to."

"I need you more than once tonight."

Marie stroked and soothed his heated skin. Her fingers traced his scars. She rose up on an elbow, touching him, running her hand over the muscles of his chest and abdomen. *Too much pain,* she thought. Despite any scarring, his body was beautiful. "I'm grateful you're alive, and here with me now," she whispered.

He stilled her hand, holding it, then pressed a kiss to her palm. "For a long time, I wondered why I was alive, when others didn't make it. Guys like Dugan. Still wonder sometimes. It's not fair."

"It's a question you'll never be able to answer. You can't torture yourself."

"I'm learning. It's not easy."

They held each other as they dozed. When they awoke, Marie pulled him into the bathroom to shower together. They washed each other, laughing and splashing. Dried and refreshed, they hopped back into bed. He combed her hair, then watched as she plaited it into a single, damp braid.

They made love again. Santi went slow, relearning her body, taking his time to touch and kiss and caress every part of her. Her breasts and hips were fuller than he remembered, utterly feminine, and more beautiful because she embraced the changes. No longer the self-conscious girl who felt inadequate because she thought she had to be perfect, she was all woman. His woman.

He teased and coaxed, bringing her to exquisite heights of passion. They gave one another pleasure until they were both spent. The morning came too soon.

She held him to her breast. "Is there a chance for us, Santi?" she whispered as dawning light filtered through the gauzy draperies. "We're not the same people we fell in love with."

He scooted upward, nuzzling her neck, nipping her earlobe. "We're not. But we're not so different either. We've been through our own kind of hell." Dark eyes searched her beautiful, sleep-deprived face. "Been thinking about this. I'll move to Chicago, find work there. Don't want to live without you if I don't have to."

"I don't either," she said, brushing black strands of hair from his face. Gentle fingertips traced the thin scar over his cheek, then brushed his lips. "Now that I've found you, I don't want to leave. But I do have to use the bathroom." Marie grinned, sliding from under him and the bed. Pulling out her suitcase, she opened it, searching for a clean shirt and jeans. She went to the bathroom to wash and relieve herself.

He rolled to his back. "When are you leaving?" he asked when she returned.

"In a few days, to finalize some things. If we plan to make a go of this, I'll need to resign from my school position in Chicago and find a place to stay. I'll need to make moving arrangements. I'd like to find a job here, so I'll need to get a Texas state teaching license."

He sat up, swinging his legs over the side of the bed. "Don't need to do all that. Easier for me to move there and find work. Need a place for Rebelde. Not leaving him behind."

"You're right. It would be easier. I thought the farther away from my mother, the better. I didn't want you to give up ranch life if you didn't have to. I know how much you love it."

"Carla Rossi doesn't scare me. I'll have to try to sacrifice open spaces and wear a suit and tie for a spell." He was honest about the first part. He could give two hoots about Carla. Working in an enclosed area with other people in an office-type setting was something he wasn't sure about. He stepped up from behind, slipping his arms around her, pressing kisses to the curve of her neck. Santi didn't want to get ahead of himself but if he and Marie could make this work, it wasn't too late to have their own spread, like they'd dreamed about.

Marie tipped her head, offering him better access, his hard body at her back sending delightful shivers down her spine. She turned in his arms. "But you're forgetting something vital. The question of the loan my mother made. She can still ruin your family." Marie stepped back. "I think I have a way out of it."

His brows knit. "How?"

"I've got some ideas. I didn't want to involve my father or brother, but they'd be a last resort. I have a friend; his name is Wade Bennet. He's expressed a keen interest in commercial land development here."

Santi scanned the floor, finding his discarded shirt, boxers, and pants. Intrigued, he asked, "What are you thinking?"

"If he believes the land has potential, sell him the restaurant and the land. Pay off the loan to my mother. There'd be money left for your family to live comfortably, or to reinvest in another restaurant. My mother's hold on the Rivera family would end." Marie fastened her bra, zipped her jeans, and pulled a loose-fitting, purple tie-dyed t-shirt over her head.

It was his turn to head for the bathroom. "We tried selling the restaurant, would have made enough money to get out of the debt, but not much left over. It's a lot of money."

"Wade Bennet has it," she answered, at volume enough for him to hear through the open bathroom door. "He'd overpay for the land if he thought he could turn a profit." She heard the water running and waited for him to complete his grooming. "You've said they're building up the Riverwalk area. Your family's restaurant isn't far from there, and real estate values are rising."

"How'd you meet him?" Santi exited the bathroom, fully dressed. He slipped on his boots.

Marie found her discarded dress, folded it, and tossed the ripped panties in the trash receptacle. "Our mothers tried setting us up on a failed date."

"Hmm."

Marie walked up to him, stood on tip toe, and planted a kiss on his lips. "We were both in love with other people at the time. He's happily married now, with another baby on the way."

Santi slipped an arm around her waist, pulling her against him. He didn't care about the date. It was that her mother tried setting her up with someone she deemed more appropriate. Someone wealthy, no doubt with lighter skin, who could give Marie an extravagant life. "We'll need to talk to my mother."

"I know the restaurant means a lot to your family. She may want to think about it, but this could be a way out."

Chapter Twenty-One

Irma knew. They might as well have written it on a neon sign. Neither of them appeared to have slept much. Her son's posture and demeanor was more relaxed and at ease than she'd seen in a long time. Irma, still wearing her pink flowered robe and slippers, rose early to prepare a *huevos rancheros* type breakfast casserole, kept warm in the oven. It was a recipe she experimented with, created, and served as a specialty of the restaurant. Mexican chorizo, tortillas, cheeses, a bit of salsa, with fresh pico de gallo, topped with eggs. The patrons loved it.

Irma assured Marie that the baby was fine and well-adjusted while her mama was gone. Everyone in the house still slept, including Grace, who fell asleep in Susana's room. "Did you sort yourselves out?" Irma asked innocently, as she poured steaming, dark coffee into flowered cups.

Marie accepted the proffered beverage, thanking her. "Not all the details. Tossing around ideas about what we'll do next."

"Thinking about moving to Chicago for a while to spend more time with Marie and Grace. I'll need to find work." Santi added a spoon of sugar to his coffee. "I think I still have a resumé somewhere. Need to update it."

"I want you two to be happy, but you're sure about this? It would be a big change for you, Santi. Could you adjust? What about Carla? She'll find out."

"Won't know till I try," Santi answered.

"I have a friend. He's a commercial land developer. He's looking to expand, and the San Antonio area is one of the locations he's interested in. *La Frontera* is close enough to the Riverwalk and to the La Villita Arts Village to be viable."

"I tried selling to get out of the debt a few years ago. It's no use."

"If Wade thinks the location is what he's looking for, he'll pay more than it's worth, then turn it over at a profit."

Irma was silent for a moment, staring into her coffee. "What do you think, *mijo*?"

"Worth looking in to, if it means Carla is out of our lives."

"My other option is to speak to my father, and brother. Neither of them knew of my mother's coercion scheme at first, but they know now. My parents have become estranged these past years. Dad wants to retire, and my brother has been slowly taking away my mother's power and influence in the family business. Let's just say they've found some inconsistencies on the books. They no longer trust her. When I spoke to them about coming here, they were both supportive." Marie sipped her coffee, setting the cup gently onto the saucer. "I want you to know that my dad and brother hold your family in high regard. This was all my mother's plot."

Irma smiled. "Thank you. It does my heart good to know."

Marie continued, "There might be legal action we could take against her, but it would be difficult to prove, very costly and time consuming. After all that, we probably wouldn't win in court."

"No. Waste of time and money." Irma said. She breathed deeply, then blew out slowly. "Talk to your Mr. Wade friend. His offer would have to exceed my expectations. I still have a family to care for." Irma pushed herself up from the table, rising. She opened the oven to check the breakfast casserole. "Your father and I started *La Frontera*. It will break my heart to see it go." She slipped her hands into oven mitts, removing the glass baking pan, setting in on the stove top. "But I got myself into this whole mess with Carla. I need to find a way to get out."

Marie decided to extend her stay in Texas. Wade was interested in her proposal but was unable to travel with his team until the following week. Santi thought he figured out a way to get little Grace to feel more comfortable around him. He spent the morning on the living room floor playing with her and the new toys. She warmed up to him, but he had another ace up his sleeve.

"Got to get back to work at Ferguson's tomorrow," he said from the floor. Somehow, he became the keeper of pink bunny, the stuffed animal flopped on his lap. Grace offered him her new doll to feed. "Can you and Grace come to the ranch around 5:00 in the evening? I should be done by then."

"Of course," Marie answered, hoping she remembered how to get there.

"Trailer is unlocked if you're early, just go on in. Make yourselves at home."

They spent the day at Irma's. Marie had forgotten how welcoming Santi's family was, and how at ease she felt around them. They laughed often, and the love they had for one another could be felt in every interaction. Marie's estrangement from her mother struck a painful chord.

After dinner Santi walked Marie to her car. Grace was sleepy, snuggling in Marie's arms.

"Did you have fun today, Grace?" he asked,

She nodded. "I ha fun, play my toys. I play toys momomow."

Santi wasn't sure what she said. "Tomorrow?"

"Uh-huh."

"I'm getting better at this," Santi quipped. He leaned in, kissing Marie sweetly on the lips. "Spend tomorrow night with me?" he whispered in her ear.

"No, no, no, no!" Grace's little hand pushed at his shoulder. "My momma."

Santi stepped back; his lips quirked in a smile. "Someone's jealous."

It's okay Grace. *Papá* is saying good-bye." Marie soothed.

Grace went on an unintelligible toddler rant. "No *pa-apá*. My momma."

"She's tired, and this is all new to her. We'll stay the night with you."

"Understandable. Kind of new to all of us." Santi swooped in to kiss Marie once more before Grace could protest. "See you tomorrow."

The following day, Marie arrived at the ranch early. She brought the groceries inside, then went to gather up Grace, their bags, and toys. She wanted to surprise Santi with dinner.

The trailer was immaculate. Marie smiled when she saw that Santi had cleaned up and left a few horse magazines on the coffee table, knowing Grace would go through them. It wasn't a bad space. The kitchen was large, with lots of storage. A counter and cabinet peninsula separated the kitchen and living room areas. Beyond the living room was a narrow hallway that led to the full bath, where a washer and dryer were located in an attached room. Beyond that were two good-sized bedrooms. "This is nicer than our apartment, right Grace?"

Marie turned on the television, flipping through the channels. After some adjusting of the antenna, she found an episode of *Sesame Street*, much to Grace and her pink bunny's delight.

Marie unpacked groceries, then scoured the cabinets for pots and pans. He didn't have much. She found a suitably sized pot and started the tomato sauce, then began peeling and slicing the eggplant, dipping them in an egg mixture, then seasoned breadcrumbs, frying them in oil. Santi loved her eggplant parmesan. Once the layers were assembled and placed in the oven, she cleaned up, checking the clock. He'd be here soon.

Santi entered the trailer twenty minutes later, a delicious aroma wafted on the air. "Smells good in here. You didn't have to."

She offered him a smile. "I wanted to."

"Thank you," he kissed her soundly and well, bringing with him the scent of horse, and man, and the outdoors. "Got something for Grace outside."

Marie called to her. "Grace, come outside with *Papá*, he wants to show you something."

Grace tore her eyes away from the TV, scooted off the couch and ran to Marie.

"Come on, Grace. Let's see." Marie took her daughter's hand, leading her to the door.

Santi exited first. A stocky, buttermilk buckskin gelding with black legs, mane and tail was saddled, and ground tied in front of the trailer. His head lifted; black-tipped ears perked as Santi approached him.

"Horsey!" Grace hollered.

"Easy, Grace. We don't want to scare the horse," Marie instructed, picking up her child. "Let's go see him." Marie turned to Santi. "He's absolutely stunning."

Santi replaced his hat atop his head. "I gentled and trained him. One of Ferguson's horses, top breeding. He's a nice horse, got a kind eye, calm, young. Barn name's Biscuit."

"Hiii Bicket! I wan Bicket, mama! I wan pet him."

Marie stepped closer, allowing her daughter to pet the horse's shoulder. "Easy, nice and soft, don't scare him, be quiet, be gentle."

"Aww, Bicket pitty," she whispered, little hand stroking the horse's black, silky mane.

"He's used to it. Did lots of desensitizing with him. Kids, dogs, tractors, traffic, you name it. Chose him because I saw he had a good demeanor, and Ferguson wanted something kid-friendly, so his grandkids could ride when they visit." Santi picked up and adjusted the reins mounting the animal, saddle leather creaking with the movement. He looked down at them. "Want to ride him, Grace?"

Her face lit up; eyes wide. She extended little arms up to her father. "*Apá*, I wan ride?"

Santi smiled as he reached for her. "Come on." Marie hoisted her up. Grace squealed happily, wiggling with excitement on his lap. He situated her so that both little legs rested on one side over his thigh, out of the way of the saddle horn. "Be still, now. We're gonna move, okay? He's gonna walk. Remember what momma said, easy and quiet." His velvet drawl was soothing.

Grace understood, trying to calm herself. She shook her head, dark curls bobbing. "No s-care Bicket."

"Don't scare Biscuit." Santi took up the reins in his left hand, using his legs to pivot Biscuit around to a standstill. His other arm anchored his daughter. He looked back to see Marie, brushing away tears. His tender gaze warmed her like a caress. "Figured I got one girl to fall in love with me this way, might work for another."

A combination laugh-cry erupted from Marie.

Santi held her gaze, his eyes, sending a private message. Marie caught a flicker of a wink and a glimpse of his affectionate smile before he turned, reminding her of the man she fell in love with years before. "Ready Grace? I got you."

Marie watched the buckskin carry them away at a leisurely walk. She smiled through her tears, recalling their Sunday morning trail rides together. Marie wept for the beauty of Grace's burgeoning acceptance of Santi, a man she didn't know well, too young to comprehend that he was her father. One day they would explain it all to her, but for today, it was a beginning.

Santi showered before dinner. After eating and clean-up, they wound down, watching a bit of television. Father and daughter played together with the toys Marie brought. He was a big kid, talking into the red, plastic receiver of a toy telephone, or sipping pretend hot tea from a tiny pink cup, burning his lips. He made Grace laugh.

Marie took Grace to the bathroom to get her to use the potty, then changed and dressed her in short pajamas. They fixed a makeshift bed for her out of extra blankets and the folded comforter from Santi's bed. He sat on the floor with her as he read her favorite story, *If You Give a Mouse a Cookie.* His heart swelled when Grace fell asleep, nestled beneath his arm.

"Does she sleep through the night?" He whispered as they tucked her in.

"Yes, usually. Sometimes she'll wake up from her toddler bed and climb into bed with me. We have one bedroom at home."

He took Marie's hand in his, leading her to his room. Opening the side table drawer, he pulled out a newly purchased box of condoms, opening it. He flashed her a boyish grin. "Prepared this time."

They undressed one another in the dimness, eager hands and lips seeking and finding warm skin. Her body melted against his, and the world was filled with the hot tide of passion, sweeping through them like a restless ocean pounding the shore.

Marie pushed him back on the bed and climbed astride him. Her hand closed around his erection, stroking him carefully from base to wet tip. He watched as she licked and nipped her way down his body to the apex of his thighs, then inch by sweet inch took him into her mouth. Sucking, licking, swirling her tongue around the tip, his gut clenched tight, his reserve of willpower quickly dwindling.

"Wait," he rasped on a ragged breath. She moved over him, toyed with him, pleasuring herself, slick against his thick ridge. Marie stifled a laugh as Santi tore open the condom packet with his teeth, then unrolled it down his length.

"Come here," he whispered, gripping her hips, his hands slid to her bottom. His smile faded, his eyelids closed over, and his breath left him as she lowered herself, taking him into her body. Marie rode him, watching the pleasure on his face as she moved and ground herself against him. They were quiet, aware of their child sleeping in the next room. She arched her back, breasts thrust forward, inviting his touch.

Spiraling up and over, his hips coming up off the bed, her body milked him as she took him with her over the edge of ecstasy.

Marie floated down, languid against him. Santi held her close, as their breathing slowed, and their heartbeats returned to normal. They remained together, arms and legs entwined, feeling warm and more content than he could ever remember.

"Thank you for today," he whispered.

"You're good with her."

"Trying to make up for lost time."

"Patience, my dear."

He kissed her. "Couldn't ask for a better woman to be her momma."

"I try. It's not always easy."

He slipped from the bed, making a quick trip to the bathroom to dispose of the condom. When he returned, he scooped her up in his arms. They fell into contented sleep.

Santi felt the rumble of the building shake. He turned to the others. "It's go time!" A split second of silence, then concussion, and massive explosion. Concrete and steel weighed on his body atop the rubble. Smoke and ash filled the air. He struggled to breathe. Marie's voice filtered through, cottony in his ears, soothing him. "It's okay, Santi. I'm here. You're okay." Through a fog, he watched helplessly, as she picked up and tossed away building debris to free him. "I've got you," she vowed.

"Papi!" A little girl's hand took his, it was Grace, but somehow, she was a few years older. Her smaller fingers gripped his larger ones, tugging him from the rubble, pulling him. Pulling him, pulling him...

He blinked, sucking in an audible breath; a glimmer of dawning sunlight peeked through the window blinds. Little Grace stood at his side of the bed, her dark curls in disarray, the floppy pink bunny under her arm, her hand in his, tugging him. *"Pa-apá,"* she said, then other toddler words his muddled brain didn't quite understand.

A gentle touch caressed his bare chest. "Are you alright? You were dreaming."

He turned his head to find Marie next to him. Instinctively, he reached for her.

Marie held him. "Grace, be easy, gentle. Let *Papá* wake up, okay? We'll get you changed and dressed soon. Come here by mama."

Santi sat up, his back against the headboard, arranging the sheet to make certain his lower half was covered. He scrubbed a hand over his face as though it would clear the cobwebs from his brain. "They come and go. Not had one in a while."

"I'm sorry. There's been a lot happening this past week. Surprises and changes you didn't expect could have triggered something," she said, concern creasing her brow. Marie motioned for Grace to come to her side of the bed, helping her up. Grace snuggled against her mother, talking to her stuffed bunny.

"This one was different. Don't remember all of it, the explosion, the debris. You and Grace were there at the end. That was a good part."

Marie kissed his shoulder, worried. "We should slow things down," she suggested. "It's too much, too soon. We're moving too fast."

"Some might say that. I'll be alright," he assured her. "I want this to work for us. Want you and Grace in my life. Believe that." He turned his head, his lips against her forehead, he pressed a kiss there. "Loved you for too long to go any slower, Marie. There'll be plenty of time to slow down once we're caught up."

Grace stood up, bouncing on the bed. "*Papá*, I wan ride Bicket?"

Marie and Santi shared a knowing glance. Grace said it correctly. *Papá*.

"I wan ride Bicket!" Grace bounced, laughing. She then said something that sounded like Biscuit being a good horse, but the jumping and giggling made it difficult to understand.

"You know you've created a little monster, right?" Marie reached for her daughter so she wouldn't fall. "You've got way too much energy in the morning, Grace."

He smiled, watching his daughter bounce and land on her bottom, then falling sideways on top of their legs, chortling. "That's my girl." He checked the bedside clock. "I've gotta work. You're welcome to stay, or we can meet up later?"

"I want to return to the hotel, to see if I've gotten any messages, and grab a change of clothes for us. We can come back later."

Upon return to the hotel Marie stopped at the front desk to ask whether there were any messages. The clerk handed her three slips of paper. Marie sifted through them. One from Wade, one from her brother, one from her mother. Marie crumpled her mother's message, tossed it into the trash, and took her daughter to their room.

Chapter Twenty-Two

"I received a call from Carla," Irma said the following evening. "She knows Marie is here."

Marie's face clouded with confusion. How was this possible? "She left a message for me at the hotel. I never told her, haven't spoken to her."

"She has her ways."

"What did she say?" Santi asked.

"To be prepared. She's calling on the loan. I told her to do her worst and to stick it. She hid my granddaughter from me. Hurt so many people. Karma is coming for her."

Marie expressed surprise. "You said that?"

Irma shrugged. "More or less. Let's hope I'm right."

Wade Bennet arrived as promised with a team. Irma, Santi, and Marie gave them a tour of the property, as well as nearby areas including the Riverwalk, and La Villita Historic Arts Village. He seemed impressed and promised that his team would perform a detailed survey of the area and get back to them within the month. Irma seemed defeated at the length of time it would take. She wanted out of her deal with Carla as soon as possible. She still had to make payments until then.

Santi wasn't too keen on Bennet, thinking the man arrogant, but if he could get the Rivera family out of a bad deal, he'd take it.

Marie returned to Chicago. Wade Bennet's proposal and purchase of the property could take weeks, possibly months. She had to continue her work and life. She promised to return during the summer break.

Santi hated to see her go, but now there was a path forward and renewed purpose. He stood with his mother in the gravel driveway of their home, watching as Marie drove away.

"Are you sure about all of this?" his mother asked.

"Can't be sure about anything, but maybe this is a start."

"She's different. Changed."

"Suppose I'm different too."

"You don't think you're rushing it? Talk of moving and jobs in Chicago?"

"Hasn't enough time been wasted? Got a little girl who doesn't know her father."

Irma hoped her son could handle working a nine-to-five job in a high-pressure, white-collar setting. He'd improved greatly since he first returned from Beirut. He loved the engineering field, but he was meant for open spaces. She hoped for the best for her son and his new family.

Weeks later, Irma signed the final sales documents. She made sure she had a lawyer present. Payouts were made to all debtors, including Carla Rossi, who also received a cease-and-desist notice. Hopefully, she'd leave them alone. There was plenty of money left to start a new life.

*　　　*　　　*

The months they were apart were not wasted. They spoke on the phone as often as possible, short or long conversations, it didn't matter. They were rebuilding a relationship they each thought they'd lost. Grace loved to talk on the phone and give *papá* a rundown of her day. Santi savored every phone call.

Summer couldn't come fast enough. Santi picked up Marie and Grace from the airport. They visited with the Rivera family for a day before heading to the Ferguson Ranch. Santi loaded Rebelde into the trailer. It would be a long drive to Chicago. They'd need to make stops along the way to allow everyone to stretch their legs, including the horse.

Marie helped him pack his meager belongings. She helped him stack hay. They both kept an eye on Grace, who's curiosity could take her to wandering.

Santi had already spoken to Mr. Ferguson, told him about Marie and Grace, and that he'd be moving to Chicago. He expressed his desire to own land. It was still his dream.

A rider on a gray mount leading a buckskin behind trotted up to them. Grace recognized the horse being ponied. She pointed excitedly. "Bicket!"

Ferguson chuckled as he dismounted the gray, and watched the little one run toward him, her features aglow with delight. He removed his hat. "Hello there, little lady."

"I want ride?"

Ferguson glanced at Santi and Marie as they approached, acknowledging them with a nod. "Spittin' image of you both." He turned his attention to the dark-haired girl. "You gonna ride barrels like your momma?"

"I ride too!" she said, as she skipped her way to her mother's side.

Santi wiped the sweat from his brow with a kerchief, then stuffed it in his back pocket. "Morning, sir."

"Just wanted to see you two off and give you a going away present. Doubles as a wedding gift if you make an honest woman of your lady."

Marie blushed. She wanted to say she was already honest, but she understood Ferguson's intent behind the statement and took no offense.

"Oh, I will. Once things get settled," Santi said. "Much appreciated, but you don't have to gift us, sir."

Ferguson dropped the gray's reins, ground tying him. He tugged gently on Biscuit's lead rope, moving the horse forward. Offering the rope to Santi he said, "He's yours."

Marie's mouth opened in surprise. Obviously, Ferguson thought highly of Santi. This was a valuable animal.

"Sir?"

"You trained him. Besides, I don't think Ms. Grace would let you leave without him."

After a brief hesitation, Santi accepted the lead rope. "Thank you. Don't know what to say, this is too much."

Marie found her voice. "Thank you, Mr. Ferguson. He will be well-loved and cared for."

"Let me know when you get your place. We'll do business. You know my stock. Quality animals."

"Yes, sir."

"You do right by them, son. Family is everything." The two men shook hands.

"Yes sir, I will."

Ferguson mounted his horse. "Y'all take care. Keep in touch. If you need anything, you know how to find me." He tipped his hat before turning his horse away.

"We will," they said in unison.

They watched Ferguson ride away. "Can you believe it?" Santi said, as he loaded Biscuit into the trailer. Rebelde pinned his ears and squealed at the presence of another horse before settling into his hay. They'd have to learn to get along, or it would be a longer ride than expected. One or the other horse could be injured if they tried to kick or bite each other. If that didn't work, he'd have to create a better divider between them. Santi secured Biscuit, setting out more hay and water. He exited the trailer, watching their behavior for a time before pulling Marie in for a hug. "I can't believe it. That's one expensive horse he just gave us."

"I know. Did you mean what you said? Are you going to make an honest woman of me?"

"Damn right."

"Is this a proposal?"

"Only if you say yes."

She didn't think. "Yes," she said, for it was the only answer in her head.

Santi dipped his head, capturing her lips in a passionate kiss.

"No, no, no kiss, *papi*!"

He looked down at his daughter, extending his hands to her. Grace lifted her arms accepting his offer. His heart filled with joy, as he picked her up. "Ready to go home, Grace?"

"*Papá* come home my house?" Grace asked, reaffirming what she had been told prior.

"Yes, *papá* is coming home with you and mommy."

"Okay."

Santi grinned. "Okay. I'll take what I can get."

Chapter Twenty-Three

Chicago, Illinois
1986/1987

After applying for a Cook County marriage license, they were married at the First Municipal District court in a civil union.

They exchanged simple gold bands. There was no fancy ceremony. No reception at a lavish banquet hall. No Marine dress blues. No extravagant wedding gown, or matching bridesmaids or tuxedoed groomsmen. Grace was their little flower girl, Mr. Rossi, and Tony were witnesses.

They celebrated, enjoying dinner together at one of her father's favorite Italian restaurants. Mr. Rossi, ever generous, stuffed an envelope into Santi suit jacket breast pocket before they parted. Santi protested politely. "You don't have to, sir."

"It's a little something, a wedding present. You're family now, son. We stick together, eh?" Vincent Rossi insisted, patting Santi's chest pocket, then going in for a hug.

Santi returned the hug, feeling like he was in one of *The Godfather* movies, as a combination of apprehension and belonging swept over him. "Yes sir, thank you."

Marie laughed at her new husband's wide-eyed expression. "Thank you for the wedding gift, daddy."

Carla was aware of her daughter's marriage but refused to attend. Her daughter should have a church wedding, she'd said. Marie wasn't sure she wanted to see her mother and was grateful for her absence. Still, a tiny seed of guilt over their broken relationship sat like a stone in her stomach.

Santi found an entry-level engineering job with a major electronics company. He was placed on a design team. Mobile phones were big and bulky brick-like objects. The company wanted to use new technologies to streamline phone designs, make them durable and convenient, portable, and mostly smaller. And they wanted it yesterday. Competition was fierce in the tech design industry. Development of designs and prototypes produced quickly and efficiently was paramount.

He performed well, kept cordial but distant relationships with his team members. He felt numb, robotic, going through the motions. The only time he felt remotely like himself was when he was with Marie, Grace, and the horses.

Santi got Marie to ride again. She hadn't ridden since her loss of Apollo. When she told him that her mother sold Apollo, he couldn't bring himself to tell her that when he last saw the horse, Charlene owned him. He would never tell her of the meaningless one-night stand with their former rodeo teammate. To what end? Marie might be hurt by it, even though they were apart at the time, and he thought he'd never see her again. She'd been hurt enough because of him. He couldn't do that to her.

Their horses were boarded at a facility that stood adjacent to the Cook County riding trails. Riding the trails with Marie brought back the fondest memories of riding together back at Liberty Creek on a lazy Sunday morning. He put Grace on Biscuit leading her around in the large indoor arena. Even at a young age, she took to it like a duckling to water. In her child's mind, Biscuit was her horse. Santi humored her.

When other boarders and horse people saw him working his horses, they'd often stop and ask for advice or tips and tricks they could use with their own horses. Two of the boarders asked if he'd refresh their horses and offered payment. As word of mouth grew about his reputation, he'd received a few referrals from people outside the boarder barn. Santi was good, but he didn't have the time required to train or refresh every horse that came his way and coach the owners as well. Not with a demanding day job, plus a wife and child he needed to reacquaint himself with. There seemed less time to do anything. The days grew shorter, colder.

As the Chicago winter set in, he had to admit, he'd been struggling at work. It wasn't the work; in that he excelled. All the pointless meetings, stiff deadlines, and enclosed office spaces caused his anxiety to resurface. Horses required empathy, patience, and time. Slow and steady. The high-pressured nature and constant, unrealistic demands from higher-up executives was exhausting. He was burning out, quick.

Santi hid being triggered by the stresses of his job, and feeling stretched thin by all that required his attention. He didn't want to scare Marie or Grace, and so he began to keep himself apart, withdrawing emotionally.

As the months wore on, Marie noticed his gradual change in demeanor. His diminished interest in activities with his family, his detachment. He'd become withdrawn one moment or agitated the next. He'd pace as though his body were too big for their small apartment, as though he'd burst if he didn't get out. He'd go for jogs by himself or leave the apartment to spend time with the horses. She knew he did this so as not to create tensions in their home, but it worried her. His behavior reminded her of the day he left her. Cold. Detached.

The phone rang as Marie slipped her arms though her jacket. It was a Friday; the weekend could start now. She'd invited Santi to join them at the park, as it was one of the first nicest days of spring. She wanted them to spend time as a family and needed to tell him something important. She made it to the phone on the fourth ring. "Hello?"

"Marie, please don't hang up."

Marie froze at the sound of the familiar voice on the line. "How did you get this number?"

"I would like to see you."

"Why?"

"I need to talk to you."

"About?"

"I haven't seen my grandchild in a very long time."

"There's a reason for that."

"I haven't been feeling well."

Marie assumed her mother was attempting to garner sympathy in one of her twisted ploys. "I'm sorry to hear that. I hope you feel better soon."

"No. I don't think so."

Grace was tugging at Marie's sleeve. The park was waiting. "Mom, I don't have time for this. Say what you need to say, or don't, but I have to go."

"All right. I'm sorry. Goodbye, Marie."

Marie hung up. Her stomach balled up in knots. Grace asking her about the park. Marie inhaled deeply, releasing her breath slowly. "Okay, Grace, let's tell *Papá* we're ready."

Marie took her daughter to the living room, where Santi sat slouched, remote in hand. His shirt and tie partially opened, shirt tails hanging out over black dress slacks. She zipped up Grace's jacket. "Come with Grace and me to the park. It's not so bad out."

Santi remained on the couch, not paying much attention to the program on the TV. "I'm tired. You go on," he said, his voice hollow, empty.

"You said that last time."

"Worked all day, Marie. I'm tired." Anger narrowed his eyes, stiffened his jaw.

"I worked today too. My mother just called; I can't deal with this. I need to get out of the house, please come with us."

Grace tapped his leg. "*Papi*, let's go to park, I go on the swing?"

His words left him much harsher than he intended, his voice erupted cold, flat, furious. "I said no."

Grace's bottom lip protruded. Her eyes widened in surprise and fear. She sought comfort from her mother.

His angry outburst stopped her cold. Marie sent him a look that would melt ice. She reached for her daughter's hand. "What's going on, Santi? That wasn't necessary."

Annoyance laced his words. He gritted his teeth, his voice rising. "Nothing's going on, just take her to the park. I'm fine here."

Marie didn't believe him. He wasn't fine. She watched him, but he would not meet her eyes. He stared at the television, unseeing. "Come on, baby. Let's go."

When she and Grace returned an hour later, Santi was gone. His absence filled Marie with uneasy worry. This wasn't the man she knew, the calm, self-assured, charismatic cowboy was fading away. She felt helpless. Grace asked questions, Marie lied, making up a story about where *papi* had gone. She prepared a light dinner for herself and Grace. Santi didn't come home. She held it together as she put Grace to bed.

One of the ways Santi coped was taking long drives. He drove down Lake Shore Drive. Marie had taken him to the lakefront a few times. Oak Street Beach. He enjoyed playing with Grace and spending time with his family. That was a good day.

This time of year, in early spring, the Chicago lakefront was cold. Santi didn't care. He parked the truck, then walked across a street. He removed his shoes and socks. The sensation of soft, cool sand beneath his feet, he stared out against the immense vastness of the blue-green water of Lake Michigan. The waves were choppy, the lake restless. Wind tossed his dark hair about his face. Chicago hotels, condos, high-rises, and the John Hancock building stood like sentinels against a gray-cloaked sky. This was Marie's world. And while he could appreciate its beauty and grandeur, it wasn't his.

He loved Marie. He loved Grace. Before they married, he told his wife he wanted the chance to build a life. She trusted him. He'd been here almost a year. He felt like a failure. In college he was on top of the world. The popular Liberty Creek rodeo hero, a charmer. Now, he was just an asshole.

If he couldn't get his stresses under control, he'd spiral. He'd continue to distance himself, isolate himself from the most important people in his life. Anxiety and anger would build. He couldn't do that to Marie. She'd lived with enough volatility and antagonism. He didn't want his daughter to grow up with it either. He thought he was doing the noble thing by sucking up his pain and keeping it to himself. He was wrong.

He'd been talking to Mike more frequently. He reminded Santi of the Marine Corps values, Honor, Courage, Commitment. MJ talked him down from a proverbial ledge a time or two. He shared what he'd experienced as one who was an able-bodied witness to the horrific aftermath of that day in October of 1983 in Beirut. Mike's voice was full of grief and emotion as he told Santi about the worst part. Hearing the screams for help, unable to get them out. And then there were no more screams, just silence. Santi was lucky. He hadn't seen the horrors MJ did, but he felt them in his heart just the same.

His work pager vibrated. He resisted the urge to peek, and for a second, thought about tossing the object into the water. Santi inhaled a lungful of cold Lake Michigan air. He watched as several people and families also braved the chilly spring evening. Their laughter drifted on the wind. He made his way back to the truck. He couldn't go home yet. He sat in the vehicle for some time before turning on the engine. He drove. Stopped at a twenty-four-hour pancake house not far from the apartment. A waitress flirted with him despite the wedding ring on his finger. Santi remained detached but polite. He missed his wife and daughter, though he'd seen them hours before. He had to find a way to fight for them because the alternative was no life at all. Family was everything.

He didn't arrive home until just before the sun came up.

Marie couldn't sleep. She heard him enter their room and undress. She felt the weight of the mattress shift as he slid into bed. Without turning, she asked, "Where have you been?" Marie kept her voice low so as not to wake Grace in the makeshift, sectioned off bedroom they'd made for her in what was once a dining area.

"Out."

"I know that. Where have you been?"

"Nowhere. Needed to clear my head."

Marie rolled over to face him. "You're taking on too much. You need to slow down."

Santi made light of it. "Trying to hustle as the kids say."

"Trying to kill yourself. You don't need to."

Again, he avoided the issue. "Making a better life for us. Would you rather have a no-good lazy dog for a husband?"

"I'd rather have a physically and mentally healthy husband."

He made a joke of it, flexing a bicep. "That's not healthy? Check these guns."

"You know what I mean."

"Aren't we trying to get our spread?"

"I'm scared, Santi. Afraid I'm losing you. You think I don't notice a change in you? You're replaceable at work. You're not replaceable to me or to Grace." Marie paused. This isn't how she wanted to tell him. "Or to the new little one."

He turned to his side, facing her, surprised. Ashamed. "Mrs. Rivera, you've got another bun in the oven?"

"Yes."

The news sobered him. "Shit." Santi lowered himself, lifting the hem of her oversized t-shirt, he bent his head and kissed her belly, then pressed his cheek against her warm skin, caressing her with a gentle hand. A father for the second time. This time he'd be there for his child's birth. He'd get to experience it all. His heart brimmed with a combination of joy and regret. "I know I've been acting out of sorts," he whispered against her. "Hell, I've been a jackass. Sometimes it just comes up out of nowhere for no reason. Had a panic attack at work thinking about all the things that could go wrong. Had to go outside. Made up some excuse to my coworkers about forgetting something in the truck. Sat in the parking lot for a good bit. I'm scared too, Marie. I'm afraid I'll hurt you. I saw my daughter's face yesterday. Saw the fear in my little girl's eyes. Fear of me. It about killed me. Made me feel worthless. What kind of father does that? Mine never did. He could lay down the law, be head of the family, but we knew he loved us. Never scared the shit out of us."

Marie threaded her fingers through silky strands of his shoulder-length hair, stroking, soothing him.

"I didn't go anywhere. Just drove around. Went to the lakefront, parked the truck, and watched the people on the beach, wondering how they could walk around and be so normal, happy."

"Are you unhappy with me?" Her voice broke.

"No. Never."

It was this place. The small apartment, the stressful workplace environment. This move to Chicago was a huge change for him, yet he sacrificed all he knew to be with her, to make a go of being a husband and father. He said he hadn't felt worth a damn since leaving her. Since Beirut. He wasn't meant for this. He didn't want to talk to her about it. He locked it away until it festered and turned into anxiety and anger. She didn't know how to help him. He wouldn't allow her to. He sucked it up, internalized it.

She was silent for a moment. "Daddy would lend us the money to buy land if I asked," she whispered.

Santi rose up on an elbow. "No. We have to do this on our own. No loans or handouts from family members. Learned that the hard way." He slid up her body, kissing her deeply. "Forgive me, Marie. I'm trying. I keep it to myself because I don't want to let you down. I'm trying not to close myself off, but don't want you to know or see what's in my head sometimes. I'm trying to be the man you need, but...."

"I don't need a man," she interrupted. "You're the man I want. There's a difference."

He chewed on that for a minute, nodding his understanding. "Listen, remember I told you about MJ?"

"Your Marine friend?"

"Marine brother, yup. We keep in touch. He and his wife are looking to sell some land. How would you feel about moving south?"

"How far south?"

"Central Illinois."

"Hm."

"With what we've saved and a V.A. loan it could work. I know you're a city girl at heart, but, something to consider."

Marie hesitated. She'd have to give up her job. After she left her parent's high-rise, becoming a single mother on her own taught her self-reliance. She'd been sheltered, spoiled. Paying for rent, childcare, utility bills, groceries, the balance between the stresses of her own job and caring for a child taught Marie some hard lessons. There were difficult days, but nothing compared to what Santi went through, what he was going through now.

"I don't mind. Talk to MJ." Marie traced the edges of his mouth with lazy fingertips. "And if you're having panic attacks and anxiety, please talk to me, talk to someone. Promise me. I want my Santi back, healthy, and whole."

He pressed a soft kiss to her palm. "I know someone I can call. Not sure that college rodeo champ guy will ever come back. Not completely anyhow. Will you still have me?"

"I'll take you anyway I can. Please don't leave without saying anything. I understand if you need your space or time to clear your mind, I do too sometimes, but please remember that we love you."

Santi lifted the shirt over her head, baring her completely. He began a sensuous trail along her jawline with his tongue and nibbling teeth. Every kiss, every touch was an apology. Marie arched her body, accepting him, forgiving him. As he roused her passion, his own grew stronger. When they were spent, Santi held her close, reveling in the feel of her as he cradled her with his body. He wouldn't lose her. Not again, not after all they'd gone through. They'd find a way to be a family.

What seemed a short time later, Grace ambled into their bedroom, sleepy-eyed, her brown curls tousled, her stuffed pink bunny dragging on the floor.

Marie was out cold. Santi sat up, silently beckoning his daughter to come to him, arms extended. Grace reached for him, wrapping her arms around his neck, resting her head on his shoulder. He held her, stroking his sleepy girl's hair as she snuggled into her father's embrace. Relief flooded him. He never wanted his child to fear him.

Santi rose from the bed, set Grace down and held a finger to his lips. "Shh. Don't wake mama," he whispered. Grace turned to see her mother sleeping on her side. She covered her mouth to stifle a giggle as though this was all a conspiratorial plot. Santi pulled on a pair of shorts and grabbed a T-shirt from the edge of the bed. After dressing, he picked up his daughter, gathered clothes for her, had her use the potty, washed her, dressed her, and brushed her hair. He took her to the kitchen.

Marie awoke, startled. What time was it? The apartment was quiet. Where was Grace? Why did Santi not wake her? Marie threw the covers aside. Glancing at the clock on the side table, she saw that it was nearing noon. She found her discarded t-shirt, slipping it on.

Padding into the kitchen, she saw evidence of breakfast dishes in the sink. Moving to the living room, she found father and daughter napping together on the couch, Grace curled up on Santi's chest. She wished she had a camera.

The three of them spent the rest of the day together with their horses.

That evening, Santi called Ferguson. Told him about what he'd been experiencing and how he'd begun to isolate himself and feel emotionally numb.

"You know what I hated most?" Ferguson asked.

"No sir."

"The sound of helicopters. In person, on TV, didn't matter. Still don't like the sound of 'em." Helicopters were used in almost every aspect of the Vietnam War. Choppers were employed by all branches of the military, from troop transport, moving equipment and supplies, medical evacuations, scouting and rescue missions. Nearly 12,000 helicopters were used in the Vietnam conflict. Ferguson took a moment to reminisce. "When you worked for me, I had you gentling and training young horses, mostly. Know why?"

"You said I had a way with them."

"You always did, but after Beirut, I thought the best thing for you was to put you to training. It helped me after 'Nam. Thought it might help you too."

It made sense. Horses are prey animals. Hypervigilant. You can't fool them because they sense everything. You can't be amped up or agitated. You have to learn to drop your guard and build trust or they won't allow you to get close. You must be present and in the moment. It was what he'd taught Marie during their rodeo years.

"Horses don't lie," Santi responded. He realized that training horses had been a type of therapy. Mr. Ferguson knew this and purposely put him to work. The greatest improvement to his mental state after Beirut occurred when he had the opportunity to work with horses. His life now didn't allow for spending as much time with them as he'd like.

"No, they don't. Sounds crazy, but I swear they helped save my life," Ferguson paused. "And possibly my marriage," he added. "Horses need their herd. If they're isolated, eventually they'll die without the herd's protection. Maybe we're not so different."

His wife, his child, his mother and siblings, even MJ and Bev. They were Santi's herd, his support system, they gave him connection and a sense of belonging. He'd die without them. "Thank you, Mr. Ferguson. Guess I didn't think of it that way before."

"Don't push your loved ones away if you can help it. Call me anytime, son."

Chapter Twenty-Four

They left before dawn. They drove four hours outside of Chicago, through mostly flat green prairies, dotted with misted farmland, the occasional hill, and a variety of trees sprouting new growth. They passed through small towns and villages. Santi examined his notes to confirm directions. He pulled onto a gravel road. A white clapboard farmhouse with hunter green roof came into view. Cows were grazing and lolling about contentedly in nearby pastures. A thin spring drizzle fell. As they drove up to the home, two fluffy mixed-breed brown and white dogs barked, tails wagging chasing the truck until it came to a stop.

"Doggies!" Grace loved dogs, but apartment living didn't allow for one. "Mommy, I want a puppy dog!"

"If we get this land, she can have two," Santiago said to his wife. He'd grown up with dogs and missed having one.

The barking alerted the property owner. Mike exited the home, his grin wide. "Welcome, welcome."

As Santi stepped down from the truck, he was engulfed in a warm bear hug.

Mike hushed the dogs. "So good to see you, man. Where'd the Mrs. go?"

Marie released the buckles of Grace's car seat, pulling the four-year-old out from the back seat and setting her on her feet, taking her child's hand. "That would be me," she smiled as she rounded the rear of the vehicle.

Mike offered a gentlemanly hug. "Happy to finally meet you. Congratulations. I'm glad everything worked out for you all." He turned his attention to little Grace. "Hello Grace, how are you?"

Grace was oddly outgoing after her car nap. "I want a puppy dog. Look! Chickens!" She laughed with delight watching the hens.

Mike chuckled. "She looks like you, Riv. Hey, come inside, Bev's wrangling up breakfast for us."

They entered through an outer door into a bright mudroom, walls covered in softly striped wallpaper. One wall was lined with work boots, and shoes: men's, women's, and a child's. Coats and jackets hung neatly from hooks above the assortment of footwear.

Mike opened the main entrance that led into a kitchen and dining area. "Bev, our guests have arrived," he announced.

Beverly smoothed her dark, tight curls from her forehead. A dimpled smile lit her face. "So happy to see you." So, this was Marie. The young woman Santi had written letters to during his stint in the Marines, his time in Beirut. When MJ told her that Santi had reunited with his ladylove, Bev knew the letters reached the right hands. She couldn't imagine Santi's reaction to discovering he had a child. Bev hugged Santi and Marie in turn. "I have a friend for you, Ms. Grace."

Grace clapped her hands, but when three-year-old Angela scampered into the room, neat, long braids bobbing with every step, Grace grew shy. Angela reached for her mother's hand. "Angela, this is Grace. Say hello," Bev encouraged.

Uncertain, Angela made a little nervous wave of hello. "Hi."

"Hi."

"Wan see my toys?"

Grace looked at her parents. Marie had already prepared her daughter with information about where they were going, and who she'd meet. "Go on, it's okay," Santi said.

Grace turned back to Angela. "Okay."

Angela grasped her new friend's hand and the two ran out of the kitchen, giggling.

"Well, that was easy," Mike joked.

"I'll check on them in a bit," Beverly said. "They need to eat, too. In the meantime, please sit, everything's ready." She brought out mugs, steaming coffee, cream and sugar. A home-baked Bundt poundcake smothered, dripping in thick caramel icing sat on a decorative plate. Farm fresh scrambled eggs, country sausage and gravy, biscuits, strawberry jam, and cheesy grits rounded out the meal. Bev had cooked for an army.

"She loves to cook and bake. Making me fat," Mike groused playfully, the wooden chair scraped the floor lightly as he pulled it out for Marie, inviting her to sit.

Bev laughed. "You are not," she protested.

Santi gestured toward his own wife. "This one too. I'm spoiled. Have to work out twice as hard."

"Know what you call a Marine?" Mike queried good-naturedly as he grabbed a warm biscuit, passing the cloth-covered basket to Marie.

"Anything but late for chow!" Santi and Mike rejoined together, their laughter filling the room.

They talked and laughed, the mood jovial, spirits high. Marie felt comfortable and at ease, as though she'd known Mike and Bev for years.

Beverly rounded up the girls to join them. During the breakfast feast, she started the business conversation. "We've got eighty acres of land. Looking to downsize."

"We'd like to offer to sell you half. I'd never use all of it. Like to keep my operations manageable," Mike said, before taking a bite of scrambled eggs. He set his fork down. "We're looking to upgrade and modernize with the money we make from the sale. We figured you could use the land to raise horses or do like us and raise cattle, or heck why not both? You could grow corn, or plant hay fields for your animals, anything. We're one of the few Black families in the area. Bev's family has been here for years. Still makes some folks nervous, but they know I raise quality beef, and I've earned a reputation as a good neighbor. Out here, people rely on each other, help each other. With your knowledge of ranch work and horsemanship, your family would be a welcome addition to the area."

Marie and Santi exchanged a glance.

Mike continued. "I know you've got to talk it over. It's a big move from Chicago. I'll take you both out and show you the land. Already set for utility hook up. You'd need to dig a well and septic at the homesite."

After the girls had eaten, they ran outside to join their fathers, dogs trotting happily alongside them. Mike gave Santi a tour of the barn and nearby pastures. Marie stayed behind, helping Beverly clear the table and put away leftovers.

"Thank you, Beverly. Everything was delicious."

"It's my pleasure. You know, if you decide to move down here, it'll be nice having someone my age living close by. Most of the women around here are older. Nothing wrong with that, but…"

"I understand. It would be a huge change for me. Growing up in the city. My teaching career," Marie's voice trailed off.

Bev smiled. "We've got schools here, too."

Marie laughed. "I know."

"I worked for a major accounting firm in Chicago. Made good money. Always thought having a corporate job was where it was at. All the hustle and bustle, the city life, music, night clubs, cultural events. Then I met MJ. He showed me a different way of living. Thought I'd be bored out of my mind. The only time I visited this place was to see my grandparents. When they passed, they left this land to their only grandchild. Me. What was I going to do with it? But MJ had ideas, dreams, plans. It's not so bad. There's never a dull moment. And – I still make money working the books for other people. Tax season is especially busy for me."

"I can imagine."

"Santi and Mike, they've been through hell. They have a bond some real brothers don't share."

"This could be good for us," Marie conceded. "Santi tries to hide it, but I know he's not happy living in a cramped apartment, working in a high-stress job. It's always been my dream to be my own woman. Independent, never having to rely on anyone's income to survive, except my own."

"Your husband's your partner, right?"

"Of course."

"You can still work, have your independence. MJ's never stopped me from doing anything I wanted." Beverly smiled. "He could try, but he knows better."

*   *   *

They stood together in the kitchen of their Chicago apartment, staring down at the surveyor's plat, spread out on the table for the land they now owned. Marie seemed pensive.

"You alright?"

"Yes."

"Don't worry, *mi amor.*"

"I'm not," she assured him. It was a phrase he used often throughout their relationship, she realized. He'd always been her rock, her anchor. *Don't worry.* Everything would be okay when he was by her side. She had to be his rock too.

He nudged her. "I know you."

Marie managed a smile for him. "It's a big step, that's all."

He reached for her, turning her to face him. His eyes searched hers. "Marrying me was a big step."

"True."

"You know I'd never keep you from doing anything you wanted, right?"

She nodded.

"Never try to keep you from being your own woman, with your own mind."

"I know."

"I understand what it's like to feel suffocated, trapped, in more ways than one. You know what it's like to feel controlled, manipulated. I'd never do that to you. You'd never do it to me."

He'd been working on trust and vulnerability. He was confident in her love for him. He was asking her to trust him too, to trust in his love. They deserved this. This is what they'd dreamed about in college. They'd been saving for it, working for it. "Can we build our home close to Mike and Bev?"

"We can build the house anywhere you'd like. Just want you to be sure about this. About us."

Marie wrapped her arms around his waist. He held her for a time. "I'm sure."

He pressed a kiss to the top of her head, while keeping an arm around her as he resumed his focus on the surveyor's plat. "Look here," he drew her attention, pointing to various spots on the diagram. "Barn can go here. Fenced-in pastures here. Even a space for a chicken coop and a dog run. Thinking we'd build a sign at the entrance leading up to the place. Call it Double R Ranch."

"Double R?"

"Rossi-Rivera. Thought about calling it S & M Ranch for Santi and Marie, but folks might think it's a sex club."

Marie burst out laughing. "Well, we do have some of the equipment for it. Spurs, ropes, whips, leather…"

Santi's lips curved into a seductive smile. "Don't give me ideas, woman."

It would take anywhere from six to nine months from breaking ground to finished build. Knowing they'd be moving out of the city, made it easier for Santi to deal with the demands of his job. That, and revisiting the coping strategies he'd learned in the past, as well as opening himself up to Marie, helped. Marie and Santi made frequent trips to visit Mike and Bev. They checked the progress of the homesite and barn construction. Grace loved visiting too, since she and Angela could play, run, and wreak havoc together. Like their daughters, Marie and Beverly became fast friends. They traded recipes and enjoyed choosing final touches to the new house such as kitchen cabinets, counter tops, room furnishings and décor. Santi wanted her to have whatever she desired. Marie wanted a basement added to the four-bedroom, two-bath ranch style home. Tornado season in Illinois could be brutal. They needed a storm shelter. And a long, covered wrap around porch with a swing. She had to have that.

It was during one of these visits, as they perused stacks of home and garden magazines and catalogues, that Beverly confessed to sending Santi's letters. She wasn't sure how Marie would respond but couldn't keep it to herself any longer.

"Neither MJ nor Santi know I sent them to you. I hope to keep it that way."

Marie was quiet. She placed a hand over her growing belly, unconsciously caressing her unborn child. "What if you hadn't found them? What if Mike didn't keep them safe thinking to give them back to Santi? What if they'd been destroyed in the bombing? What if I never received them?" She rose from the kitchen chair. Tears welled in her eyes. She covered her face.

Bev stood up, concerned. She embraced her friend. "I'm sorry, I didn't mean to upset you."

"No, no. I don't know why I'm crying. Pregnancy hormones, maybe." Marie lifted her head. "If it weren't for you, I wouldn't be here right now, with my husband, planning a home and a life." A wistful smile curved her lips through her tears. "It's crazy, isn't it? How one act can change the trajectory of a person's life? My mother's act separated us. Yours brought us back together. Thank you, Beverly. I'll be forever grateful that you sent those letters."

"I did what I thought was right."

"What you did… was beautiful and perfect."

"Well, don't know if I'd go that far, but…" They both laughed. Beverly handed Marie a tissue, inviting her to sit. She refreshed their tea. "Come on, we've got a house to make beautiful and perfect."

Just before moving day arrived, Marie went into labor. Santi was with her the entire way. He held his newborn son in the delivery room. As tears welled in his eyes, he stared down at the newborn he'd helped bring into the world. They named him Luca Rossi-Rivera, bringer of light.

*   *   *

Once the main barn and small indoor arena were built, and pastures were fenced in, they needed to fill them. Santi and MJ traveled to Oklahoma for a horse auction. Santi hoped to find a nice stud. They'd been to Missouri and Tennessee with no luck. He'd purchased three well-bred quarter mares from Mr. Ferguson, to expand his breeding line. He decided that if he couldn't find a stallion to his liking, he'd negotiate a fee for one of Ferguson's standing studs.

Before the auction began, potential buyers had the opportunity to walk around the various pens to peruse the upcoming sale horses. The stock ranged from older trail horses nearing retirement, to younger green horses, trained working horses, along with ponies, mules, donkeys, and everything in-between. Santi saw a paint with familiar bay and white markings in a pen with other, older, last chance geldings. He climbed through the metal rails of the pen. Mike followed.

The horse was still. His head hung low, he was thin, hip bones protruding, ribs visible enough to count. When Santi approached, the animal lifted its head, acknowledging the human presence. "Hey boy, easy now," he crooned as he stroked the horse's neck, moving his hands over the animal's body, continuing to examine his feet and legs. Gentle hands touched and probed, checking for any sore spots or injuries. Santi moved to the horse's hind end, looking for the familiar. Black tail, black and white mane. Bay and white, all the body markings were there as he remembered them.

"This one's seen better days," MJ remarked sadly, wondering why Santi would be interested.

Santi checked the horse's teeth. "He's about to see them again. I'm buying him."

"This boy's at least twenty years old. Maybe more."

"Sixteen or seventeen by now. I know this horse. Liberty Creek University Rodeo barrel champion, 1982. He needs groceries, a vet visit, and good care. Teeth need floating, and feet need trimming, too." He looked at Mike, unable to suppress the anger in his expression over the poor condition of the horse. "Bet my last dollar. I'm damn sure this is Apollo. If we get his papers, I'll know one hundred percent. This boy gave his all to Marie. We owe him. She loved him. She needs him." Santi knew that if he didn't bring Apollo home to Marie, the horse would end up shipped to slaughter sooner rather than later. No way that would happen.

Santiago was relieved to find the horse had papers. He was right. He had no idea how Apollo ended up here. There was no way of knowing what happened. He'd apparently changed owners a few times after Charlene. Santi didn't find a stallion to his liking in his price range, and instead purchased Apollo for next to nothing, and two other working geldings in great condition.

He decided to prepare Marie instead of surprising her. To find her beloved horse had been neglected and possibly abused would break her heart. It was early morning when he stepped into their darkened home. He found Marie already dressed and awake, nursing baby Luke in their bedroom recliner, while Grace slept. When he entered, she smiled at him in greeting, lifting her head to meet his kiss. He pressed a long, quiet kiss to her lips, then brushed gentle fingers over a tuft of his son's dark hair. "Got a surprise for you," he whispered.

Luke had fallen asleep, milk drunk. Marie set him down carefully in his crib. "What is it?" she asked as they exited the room. She closed the door quietly behind them. "Did you find a nice stallion?"

"Nope. Mike's unloading some geldings, letting them settle in. Listen, Marie. I found Apollo."

Her fingers fumbled with the buttons of her blouse. "You found him? Where? Is he here? Did you buy him?"

He grasped her hands gently to stay her. "Hold on. I found him. He's in the trailer. But he's been neglected. Needs food and caring for. We'll get him right again, I promise."

"I want to see him," she said, whirling away, bounding for the back door.

Mike led Apollo out of the trailer and walked him to the barn where the other newly purchased horses were settling in their stalls, munching hay. Marie ran, slowing her steps as she approached. She gasped at the sight of him. "Oh my God. Oh no." Tears formed, slipping down her cheeks. Her beautiful horse. "Apollo," she called to him. At the sound of Marie's voice, the horse's ears perked up, a soft nicker followed. He took a step toward her. She stroked his head and neck. She hugged him. "Oh, my baby. My baby. Thank you, Santi. Thank you."

"Of course, *mi amor*. Would never leave him there. He belongs with us. Let's get him in a stall to rest. We'll call Doc Johnson, see if he can't come by today."

Marie led Apollo to a clean, empty stall. Santi and Mike set out fresh hay and filled a water bucket as she examined her horse, tears streaming down her face. Apollo nosed her hand, then snuffled her hair. "I think he remembers you," Mike said.

Marie continued to weep and pet Apollo as he ate. "I'm never losing you again." Her vision blurred, she looked up at the two men watching her, wiping the tears from her face. "I don't care if he can never be ridden, or if he's just a hay burning, lawn ornament. He's not going anywhere."

Chapter Twenty-Five

Illinois, 1988

M
r. Rossi and Tony visited as often as possible. Tony was accompanied by a different female guest every time. Marie wondered if he'd ever settle down with just one. Irma Rivera traveled to Illinois with Erik and Susana. There was discussion of possibly moving from Texas to Illinois to be closer together. For several days, the house was pleasantly full. Irma doted on her grandchildren.

Marie's parents had been estranged for some time. Her dad took to sleeping in Marie's old room. Vincent Rossi tried to convince his daughter to call her mother, but Marie couldn't bring herself to dial the number.

Carla appeared to have given up her quest to contact Marie. She'd heard nothing for some time.

The evening grew cool as the sun set. Most everyone was seated around the bonfire on the back patio. Mike and Bev had joined them. "Mom would like to see you," Vincent Rossi said on the last night together. His statement caused the others to pause in their various conversations.

Marie took a sip of her wine. It tasted bitter. "I don't know if I'm ready for that, dad."

"There may not be time for you to be ready. There's no easy way to say it. She's dying. She didn't want me to tell you. Stage four lung cancer from all those years she smoked."

Marie looked to her brother, who simply nodded, his expression solemn. She remained silent, processing this news. Marie didn't know how to feel. A part of her would always have some love for her mother. There were good times. She recalled the care and goodness her mother gifted her with as a young child. Something changed once Marie hit puberty. She could love her mother, love her from a distance, but she didn't like her very much.

Her father's voice broke into her thoughts. "Might be a nice gesture to visit her, bring the babies for her to see. She hasn't seen Grace in a long while. She'd love to meet Luca."

All the insecurities and anxiety Marie had not felt in years rushed in, flooding her entire being. She pushed up from her lawn chair, wrapping her sweater around herself against the cool night air. "I'll think about it."

"We'll have to move her to a full care facility soon. Please don't take too long."

"I won't."

Later that evening she asked Beverly's opinion.

"I would go," she said. "Not for her. For myself. To know that as a human being, I did the right thing, or tried to. If it all goes sideways, and the meeting is a disaster I'd have no regrets about the visit. I could reason it away, and say well, at least I tried to come to some kind of resolution. I'd leave with some answers." Bev reached for her friend's hands. "But, if you think seeing her again would be too traumatic, affecting your life with your husband and your children, then keep your personal peace. As long as you can completely rid yourself of any animosity you might have toward her. Because that won't harm her now. But it'll eat you from inside, and harm you. And she'd still be controlling you, even after she's gone. Don't give her your power."

*　　　*　　　*

Marie entered the quiet, dimly lit patient room, consisting of a hospital bed, various medical equipment, I.V., and an oxygen tank. A small wooden table with two chairs sat along the opposite wall. A separate door led to a bathroom to the left of the bed. The intermittent beep from a monitor and the soft whooshing of the oxygen machine were the only sounds. She carried baby Luke bundled, asleep in his carrier over her arm. Five-year-old Grace gripped her mother's hand.

Carla's eyes were closed, her head was tipped to one side, adorned in a colorful, flowered head wrap to cover the hair loss from chemotherapy treatments. Thin nasal tubes assisted her breathing, increasing her oxygen intake. Her lashes fluttered open. A look of surprise crossed her features. She was thin and wan.

"Oh, Marie!" Carla struggled to sit up. She covered her mouth with a trembling, bony hand. "Please come in. Bring that chair closer."

Marie set her son's carrier on the floor, moving the chair next to the bed.

"Oh, my goodness. Grace? Such a big girl. Come here. Do you remember your *Nonna*? Oh, she doesn't remember me. It's been so long."

Grace's expression was solemn, yet she stepped closer.

"Such a beautiful girl." Carla turned her attention to the sleeping baby. "Please let me see the baby. May I hold him?"

Marie lifted her six-month-old from his carrier and set him gently on Carla's lap.

"Oh my, so precious."

"That's my brother," Grace announced proudly. "His name is Luca, but we call him Luke too."

Carla's lips formed a genuine smile. Something Marie hadn't seen in years. "And I know you are a good big sister."

"Uh-huh."

"Marie, please sit. I can hold him. He won't fall. How are you?"

"I'm fine, mom," she lied. She wasn't fine. Seeing her once vibrant, fiery, beautiful, venomous mother, reduced to a frail, helpless shell of her former self shook Marie to her core.

"I heard you and Santiago have a nice place with lots of land."

"Yes, we do." Marie dug into her large, everything tote bag. She pulled out a book, some paper, and crayons, setting them on the little table for Grace to occupy herself. Marie invited her daughter to sit at the table. "*Nonna* and I are going to talk for a bit. Can you draw some pictures for her? She's not feeling well."

"Okay, mommy. The pictures would make her feel better?" Grace opened her box of crayons and began to draw doodles and flowers.

"I would love some pictures," Carla offered her granddaughter an encouraging smile, then turned to Marie. "Are you working? she asked.

Marie took the seat next to the bed. "Not yet. I plan to teach again once we're more settled."

"Santiago is doing well?'

"Yes." After a short silence, Marie added, "I'm sorry you're going through all of this," she said, with a vague gesture indicating the room and medical equipment. She meant it. No one should go through it.

"All the smoking I did in the past. Lots of things in the past I regret." She looked down at the sleeping infant on her lap, smoothing his dark brow with her fingertips. "He's the perfect combination of you both." She lifted her eyes to her daughter. "Do you know how I met your father?"

Confused by the odd question, Marie answered. "You were high school sweethearts."

Carla shook her head. She coughed lightly, wheezing as she inhaled. She motioned for Marie to take the baby as he stirred. When she could speak again, she continued, her voice gravelly. "No. We were friends. His family lived in the apartment building next door. We practically grew up together. I was what my father would call a wild child. My older brothers thought the same. I didn't finish high school. I wanted to work outside the home. I wanted to buy my own clothes, my own car, drive, and go out with friends. My father was from the old country. Young women didn't do those things. Not in the '40s and '50s. The more he tried to control me, the more rebellious I became."

Carla paused, growing visibly emotional. Marie waited for her to continue. It was the first time her mother ever spoke of her upbringing in depth. It seemed she needed to unburden herself.

"One evening, I went out with some girlfriends downtown. There was some drinking. We were a bit tipsy but could make our way home. I could've snuck back inside. My father would never have known. We met up with some boys from the neighborhood that we knew from around, acquaintances. Troublemakers mostly, but they knew us, so we didn't feel completely unsafe. Some of the other girls went home. I don't know how or why I ended up alone with these boys. Young men. I think they told me they'd see that I got home alright, and I trusted them. Honestly, I don't recall. I'm sure I've blocked so much…," Carla's voice trailed off.

Marie sensed where the story was headed. She reached for a tissue, passing it to her mother. "It's okay mom. You don't have to…"

"No. I want to. I need to. Please." Carla wiped her eyes and dabbed her nose, adjusting the oxygen tubes, her tears fell freely now. "They attacked me. In the back seat of a 1957 Oldsmobile. Beat me because I tried to fight them off. Beat me until I couldn't fight anymore. Took their turns, then dumped me in front of the building where I lived. My dress was torn in several places. I could barely walk. I had one shoe. My face was battered. I couldn't hide that from my father or my brothers." Carla took a needed, shuddering breath as she stared down at her hands. "I thought... I thought my brothers would find those guys and beat the hell out of them. I thought they would defend my honor, so to speak. No. They blamed me. It was my fault. They called me bad names, *puttana*. A whore. I asked for it. No decent girl goes out with her friends at night. Years later I called you the same terrible names. I'm so sorry."

Marie reached for her mother's hand. Her mother squeezed in return. "Mom... you don't need to relive this."

Carla waved the suggestion away, continuing. "After that, I was ostracized. The subject of everyone's gossip. And I was pregnant. I didn't know. My mother was long dead. I had no aunts. My friends couldn't associate with me anymore. I had no woman to talk to. You didn't talk about such intimate things back then; I didn't even know what my period was the first time I got it. I was twelve. I thought I was dying. But there was Vinnie, always. My childhood friend. He said he'd marry me. There'd be no shame. I could save face. After we got married, I'm sure some people counted the months after Anthony was born." She looked Marie in the eye, her face tired and worn.

Marie thought her mother looked old, frail. It pained her.

"Your father is a good man. He loved me. So kind and generous. He was of the gentle sort. Nothing bothered him. All he wanted was for everyone to be happy. Your dad promised to take care of me and the baby. No one would ever know Tony was not his son. Not even your brother knows this, and I hope to take that secret to the grave. Your father kept his word throughout our marriage, though I didn't always make it easy for him. I'm still a rebel inside. I poured myself into the Rossi Construction Company. I remade myself. Success, money, power. That was my revenge against those who scorned me, hurt me.

I didn't want you to go through the hell I went through. I wanted to protect you from everything. I know the need to keep you safe became twisted. I had to control everything, manipulate everything because I couldn't stop what happened to me, but I could keep anything like that from happening to you. I did and said terrible things to keep you in your place. I know I made you feel unworthy. I think now, it was me who wasn't worthy. Little did I know you had my rebellious spirit." The effort Carla put forth to speak had tired her. She was quiet for a moment. "I wonder if there were times, I was jealous of you. Your child was born out of love. Mine was born from violence. Don't misunderstand. I love my son. I could never blame him for how he was conceived, but at times, he was a reminder of that night."

"I'm so sorry that happened to you, mama. None of it was your fault."

Carla looked up at her daughter, her expression almost childlike. "I know I may not deserve your forgiveness, or Santiago's, but I'm asking. Before I leave this earth. I'm asking for your forgiveness. Please tell Santiago and his family – I am deeply sorry."

Marie was silent for a time. She didn't know what to think, how to feel. "I think I can work on forgiveness, but it might take longer to forget, so many things came between us. I can't speak for Santi. He'll do what's best for himself."

Carla sighed, lifting slight shoulders. "That's all I can hope for. And perhaps, no more than I deserve." Carla saw that Grace was becoming restless, sitting quietly with her book and crayons for so long. Luca began to fuss. The entire conversation had worn her out. She settled back into the pillows. "One last thing before you go. I know that Wade Bennet helped you and Santiago's family. Don't trust him, Marie. Please don't trust him."

"You tried to set me up with him years ago."

"That was before I learned about his shady business practices. Just, please. Don't trust Wade Bennet."

Before they left, Grace gave her *Nonna* the pictures she drew of a farmhouse and barn, with flowers and horses. Carla treasured them.

It was dark when Marie arrived home. They were tired from the long drive. Santi met her at the car, helping her with kids and bags. They changed and put the children to bed.

Once in their own room, they snuggled together under the sheets. "How did it go?" Santi asked.

Marie slid her leg up his thigh, moving closer. "My mother told me about what happened to her as a young woman. She was raped. Tony is the result of that. He doesn't know."

"I'm sorry," he said, his tone sincere.

"She said she was trying to protect me in some twisted way. She asks for forgiveness. Mine, yours, your family. I don't know if I fully understand, or if I can forget everything she's done, but the way she was today, the way she acted and spoke to us," Marie paused. "She was kind, caring. It could have been that way all this time. It wasn't. She chose not to be. It didn't have to be this way."

Santi was thoughtful for a moment. "Bad things happen to us. Doesn't give us an excuse to treat others badly. I'm learning that myself. What she did was evil."

"It was, but you're lucky. You're learning it before it's too late. She doesn't have much time left."

Santi pulled her closer, enfolding her in his arms. "How are you feeling?"

"I spent the last years trying to get away from her. She has so many regrets. I don't want that for myself at the end of my life." Marie pressed her cheek to the hard wall of his chest. "She also said not to trust Wade Bennet."

"Now there's something Carla and I can agree on. He'd break his own arm patting himself on the back. Slicker than a slop jar."

Marie lifted her head, her lips turned up in a small smile. She loved his occasional Texan turns of phrase. "I don't think we'll need to worry about him. Haven't heard from him since he bought and sold *La Frontera*."

Santi respectfully attended Carla's funeral service to support his wife. He wasn't as forgiving, but perhaps in time forgiveness would come, and if it didn't, he could live with that.

Epilogue

Marie groomed Apollo in the barn aisle after taking the children for a short ride. Restored to health, he was the perfect horse for them. Calm and gentle, his barrel racing days behind him, he enjoyed semi-retirement. Luca and Grace helped their mother, each with a brush, grooming any part of the horse they could reach. Apollo stood patiently, happy, and unbothered.

"Nice looking paint," Santi said as he entered the barn, Rebelde in tow.

"Thank you, your horse is beautiful too."

"This rascal here is Rebelde."

"Rebel!" Luke jumped up and down, raising his toddler arms so that his father could lift him onto the bay horse's back.

"Make him dance, *papi!*" Grace urged.

Santi smiled at his daughter. "He might be getting a little too old for that, *mija.*"

"He can do it," she insisted. "Mommy says that's when she knew she liked you. The first time she saw you riding Rebelde. He was dancing."

"There's an old vaquero song about a cowboy who attracts his lady love by showing off his horse. Guess it works." He turned his attention to the bay gelding, scratching him behind the ear. His mouth quirked with humor. "It's all your fault, Rebelde."

They turned the horses out together in the nearest pasture, where freshly groomed Apollo proceeded to roll in the dirt. He rose up on all fours, shook himself off, then bolted, bucking and kicking at the air. Rebelde and Biscuit joined him in the fun, snorting and whinnying as they ran circles.

"I think they're happy, mommy."

Marie smiled down at her daughter, placing an arm around her shoulder. "I think so too."

Business was exceptional this year. Santi and Mike raised cattle and horses. Santi earned a reputation as an honest horse trainer, breeder, and trader. People from several states away purchased horses from the Double R Ranch. Others sent their horses to be trained there. Marie found a part-time teaching position at the local high school. She also gave riding lessons on the weekends. She and Santi discussed building an additional barn to offer boarding facilities, as well as possibly hiring barn help. After finding Apollo, Marie decided to take in a few neglect cases, nursing horses back to health. If they were sound and rideable, once healthy, Santi worked with them, adding them to the list of finished sale horses. Horses that required maintenance could be adopted as pasture pets or companion animals. If they didn't already have names, Grace loved to give them new ones.

They all watched the horses settle down to graze. Luke wandered off to chase the chickens, laughing as they squawked and fluttered out of his way. Grace followed to guide him back to the house. She grasped her brother's hand. "Let's race to the porch, Luca!" Two black and tan shepherd-mixed dogs, Sol, and Luna, tails wagging, trotted after the children.

Santi put his arm around his wife. He drew her close. "How you feeling, Ms. Marie?"

"I'm so happy right now, if I felt any better, I'd think it was a setup. I love you."

Santi kissed her full on the lips, slow and sweet. "I'll never stop," he whispered.

*   *   *

There'd been rumblings for years about building an airport in central Illinois. Legislation, lack of funding, red tape, and protests from residents bottlenecked any movement. For now, Wade Bennet had other interests in land deals around the country.

He could buy land cheaply, then sell it to the state department of transportation at a profit. He had inside connections. Could bribe a few officials and make it happen. When nothing came of the Illinois airport, Wade put it on the back burner. If an airport deal ever came to fruition, he knew he'd be the first to scoop up privately owned land if he wanted it. And Wade always got what he wanted.

END OF
BOOK I

ABOUT THE AUTHOR

Jen Caruso works in the field of education. She's a mom to two children, a horse, and dogs.

Authors Note:

This is a novel of fiction. Any errors made with regard to actual events, or institutions are my own. I'd love to hear your opinions. Honest reviews help other readers find books for their needs and interests. Feedback also helps writers grow and improve. Let me know your thoughts!

Thank you,
Jen Caruso